THREE THIEVES
BOOK FOUR

The King's Dragon

Kids Can Press acknowledges the financial support of the Government of Ontario, through the Ontario Media Development Corporation's Ontario Book Initiative; the Ontario Arts Council; the Canada Council for the Arts; and the Government of Canada, through the CBF, for our publishing activity.

Published in Canada by
Kids Can Press Ltd.
25 Dockside Drive
Toronto, ON M5A 0B5

Published in the U.S. by
Kids Can Press Ltd.
2250 Military Road
Tonawanda, NY 14150

www.kidscanpress.com

Edited by Karen Li and Yasemin Uçar
Designed by Scott Chantler and Marie Bartholomew
Pages lettered with Blambot comic fonts

The hardcover edition of this book is smyth sewn casebound.
The paperback edition of this book is limp sewn with a drawn-on cover.
Manufactured in Buji, Shenzhen, China, in 11/2013 by WKT Company

CM 14 0 9 8 7 6 5 4 3 2 1
CM PA 14 0 9 8 7 6 5 4 3 2 1

Library and Archives Canada Cataloguing in Publication

Chantler, Scott, author, artist
    The king's dragon / Scott Chantler.

(Three thieves ; bk. 4)
ISBN 978-1-55453-778-5 (bound)   ISBN 978-1-55453-779-2 (pbk.)

    1. Graphic novels. I. Title. II. Series: Chantler, Scott.
Three thieves ; bk. 4.

PN6733.C53K56 2014   j741.5'971   C2013-905641-6

Kids Can Press is a /o**rʊs**™ Entertainment company

THREE THIEVES
BOOK FOUR

The King's Dragon

SCOTT CHANTLER

Kids Can Press

ACT ONE

Knighted

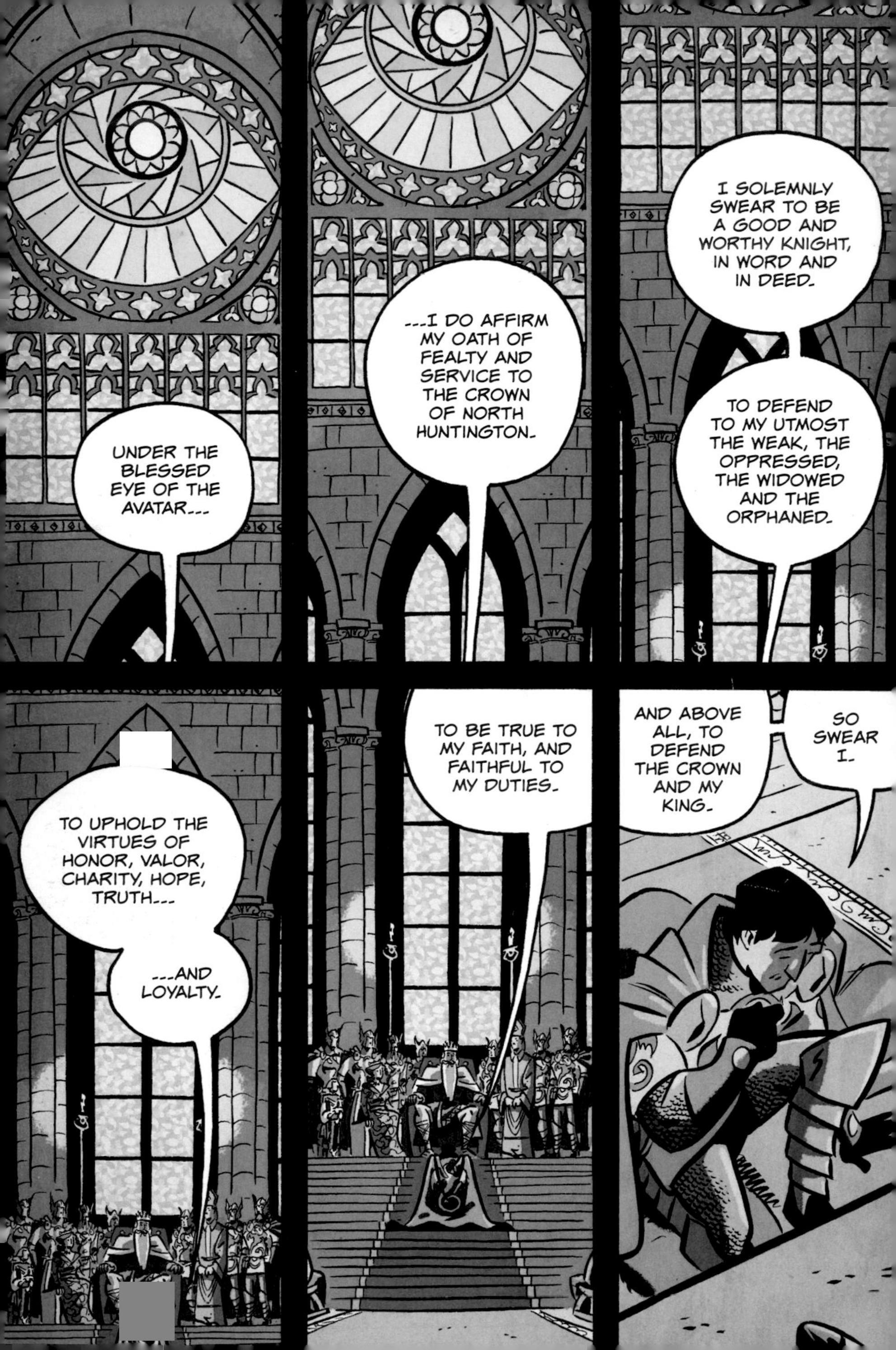
UNDER THE BLESSED EYE OF THE AVATAR...
...I DO AFFIRM MY OATH OF FEALTY AND SERVICE TO THE CROWN OF NORTH HUNTINGTON.
I SOLEMNLY SWEAR TO BE A GOOD AND WORTHY KNIGHT, IN WORD AND IN DEED.
TO DEFEND TO MY UTMOST THE WEAK, THE OPPRESSED, THE WIDOWED AND THE ORPHANED.
TO UPHOLD THE VIRTUES OF HONOR, VALOR, CHARITY, HOPE, TRUTH...
...AND LOYALTY.
TO BE TRUE TO MY FAITH, AND FAITHFUL TO MY DUTIES.
AND ABOVE ALL, TO DEFEND THE CROWN AND MY KING.
SO SWEAR I.

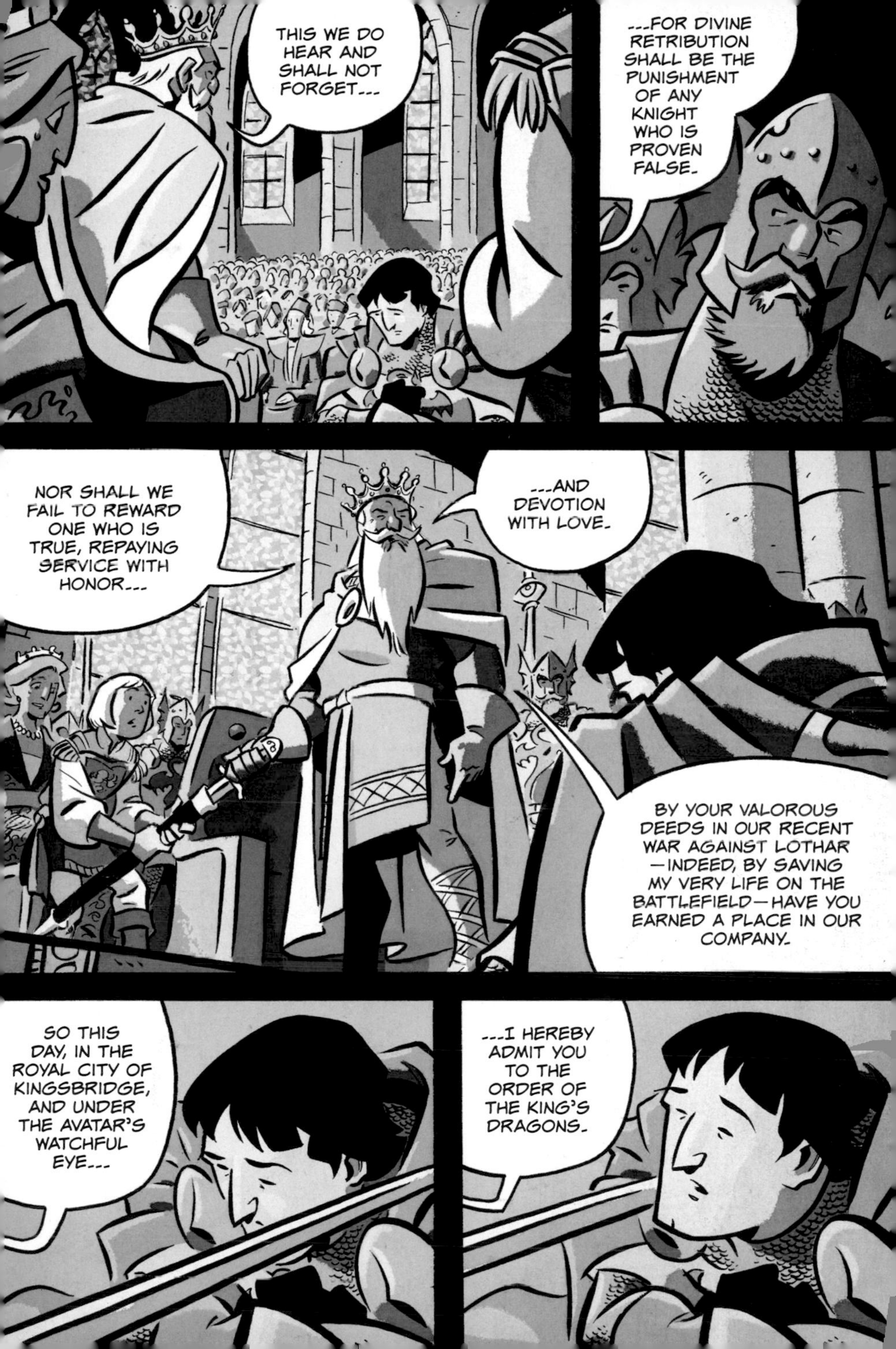
THIS WE DO HEAR AND SHALL NOT FORGET...
...FOR DIVINE RETRIBUTION SHALL BE THE PUNISHMENT OF ANY KNIGHT WHO IS PROVEN FALSE.
NOR SHALL WE FAIL TO REWARD ONE WHO IS TRUE, REPAYING SERVICE WITH HONOR...
...AND DEVOTION WITH LOVE.
BY YOUR VALOROUS DEEDS IN OUR RECENT WAR AGAINST LOTHAR—INDEED, BY SAVING MY VERY LIFE ON THE BATTLEFIELD—HAVE YOU EARNED A PLACE IN OUR COMPANY.
SO THIS DAY, IN THE ROYAL CITY OF KINGSBRIDGE, AND UNDER THE AVATAR'S WATCHFUL EYE...
...I HEREBY ADMIT YOU TO THE ORDER OF THE KING'S DRAGONS.

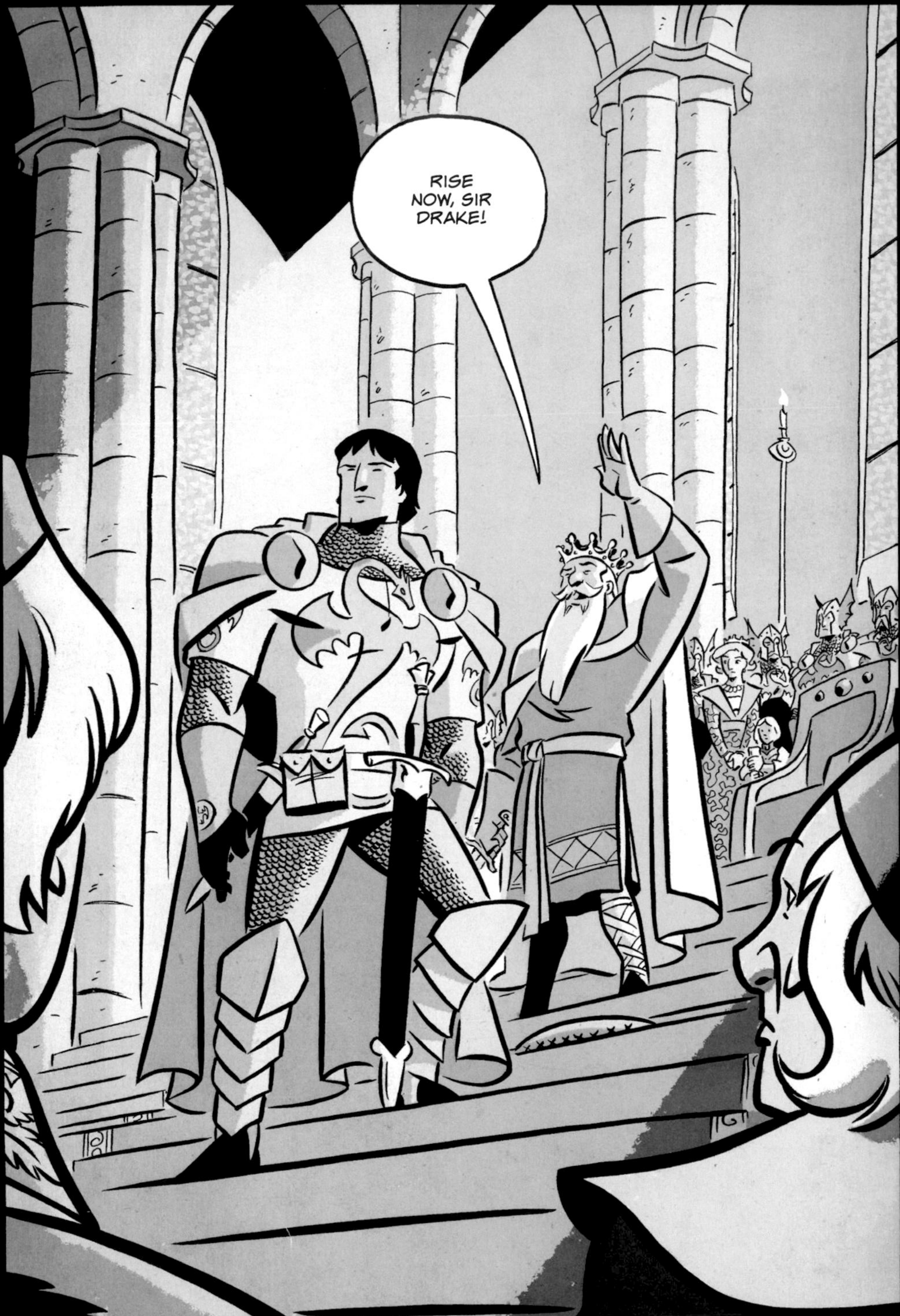
RISE NOW, SIR DRAKE!

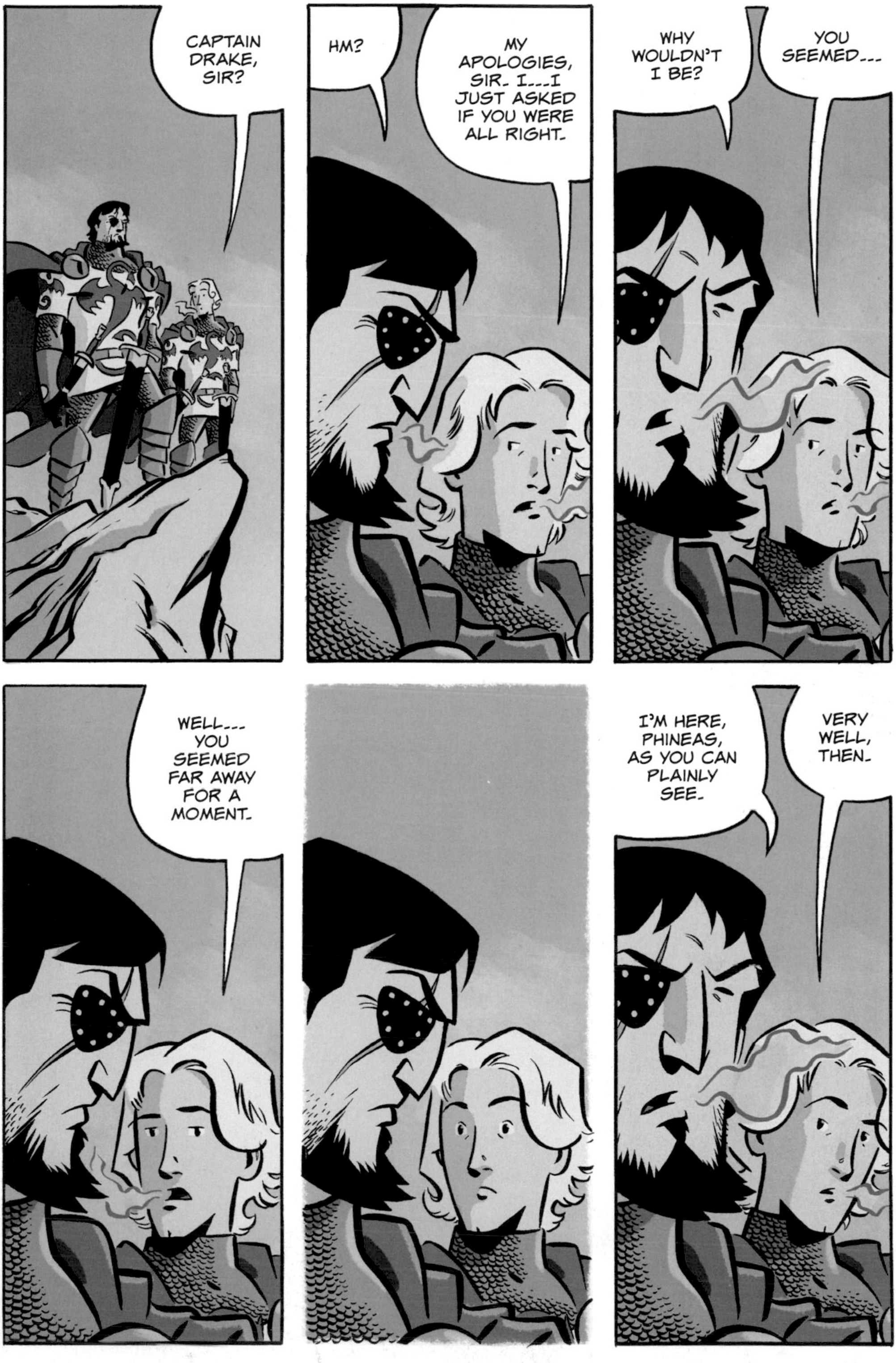
CAPTAIN DRAKE, SIR?
HM?
MY APOLOGIES, SIR. I...I JUST ASKED IF YOU WERE ALL RIGHT.
WHY WOULDN'T I BE?
YOU SEEMED...
WELL... YOU SEEMED FAR AWAY FOR A MOMENT.
I'M HERE, PHINEAS, AS YOU CAN PLAINLY SEE.
VERY WELL, THEN.

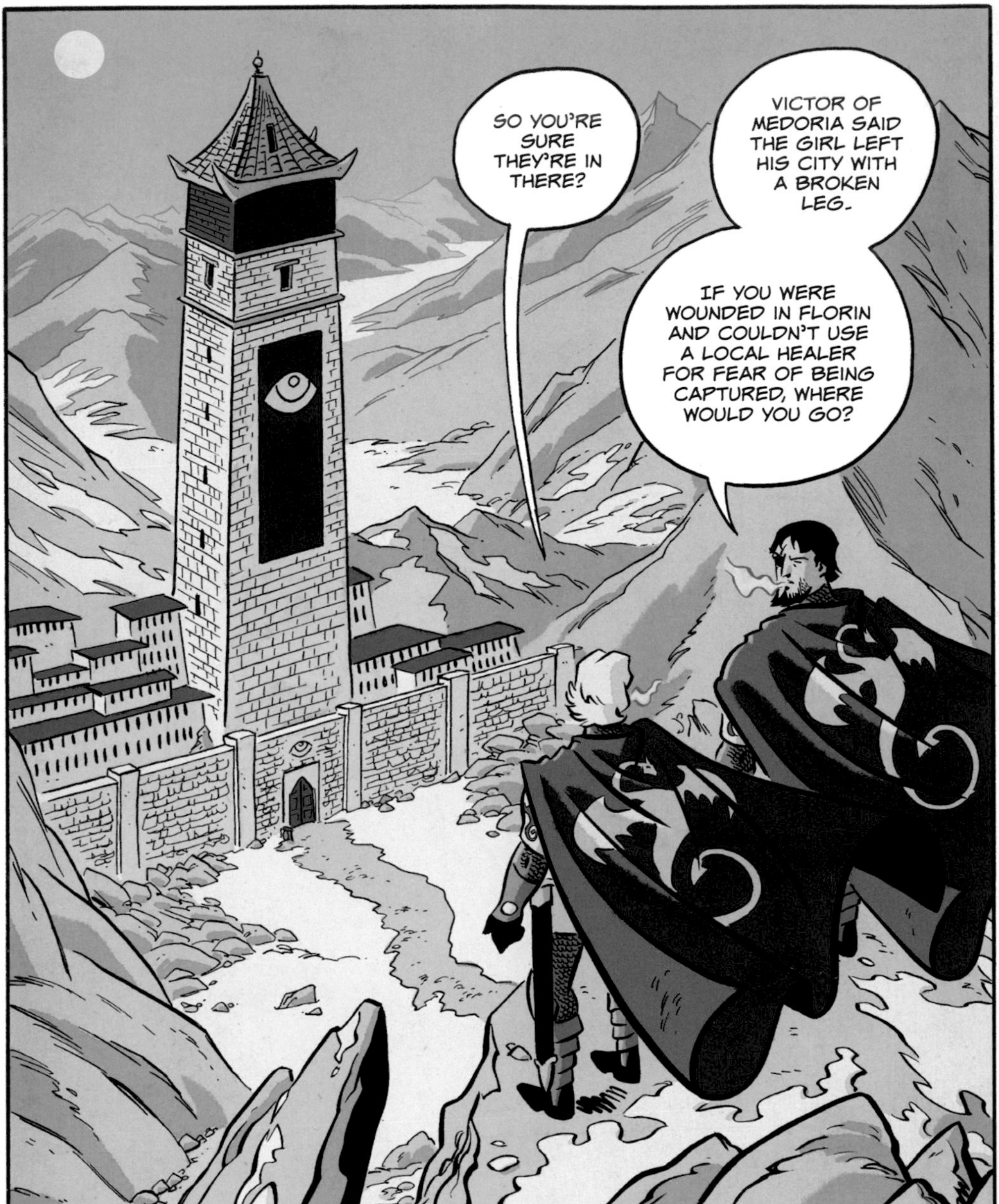
SO YOU'RE SURE THEY'RE IN THERE?
VICTOR OF MEDORIA SAID THE GIRL LEFT HIS CITY WITH A BROKEN LEG.
IF YOU WERE WOUNDED IN FLORIN AND COULDN'T USE A LOCAL HEALER FOR FEAR OF BEING CAPTURED, WHERE WOULD YOU GO?

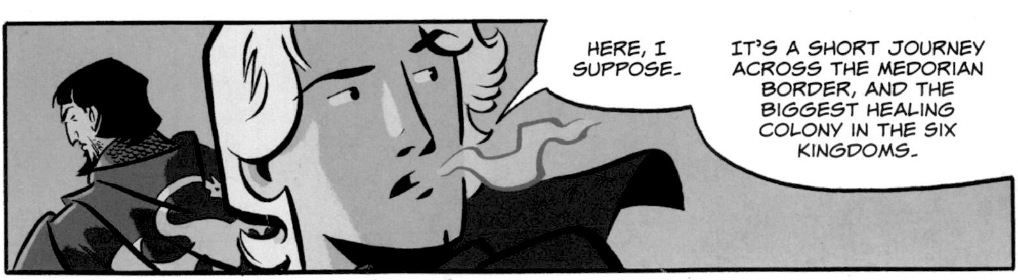
HERE, I SUPPOSE.
IT'S A SHORT JOURNEY ACROSS THE MEDORIAN BORDER, AND THE BIGGEST HEALING COLONY IN THE SIX KINGDOMS.

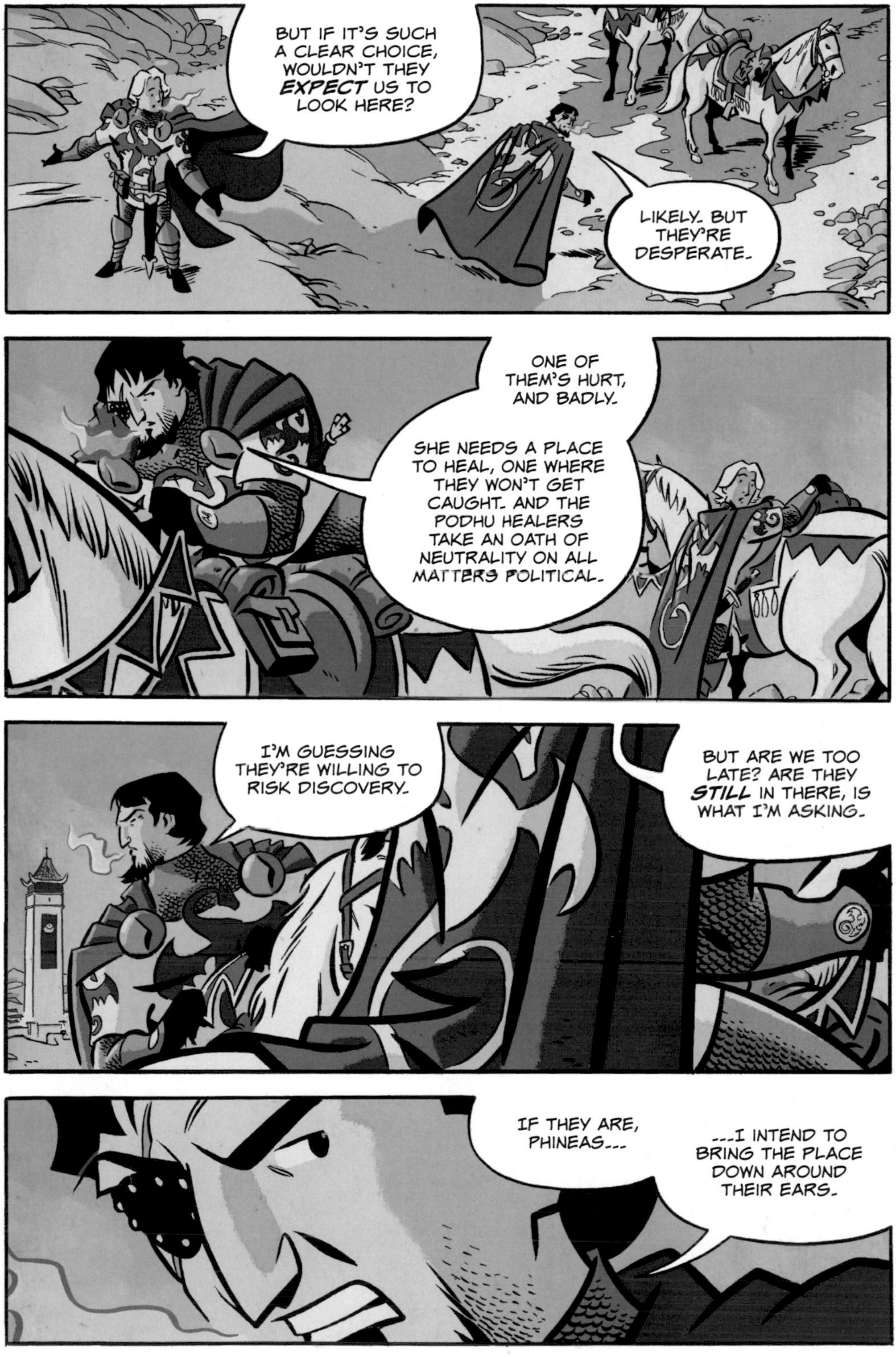
BUT IF IT'S SUCH A CLEAR CHOICE, WOULDN'T THEY *EXPECT* US TO LOOK HERE?
LIKELY. BUT THEY'RE DESPERATE.
ONE OF THEM'S HURT, AND BADLY.
SHE NEEDS A PLACE TO HEAL, ONE WHERE THEY WON'T GET CAUGHT. AND THE PODHU HEALERS TAKE AN OATH OF NEUTRALITY ON ALL MATTERS POLITICAL.
I'M GUESSING THEY'RE WILLING TO RISK DISCOVERY.
BUT ARE WE TOO LATE? ARE THEY *STILL* IN THERE, IS WHAT I'M ASKING.
IF THEY ARE, PHINEAS...
...I INTEND TO BRING THE PLACE DOWN AROUND THEIR EARS.

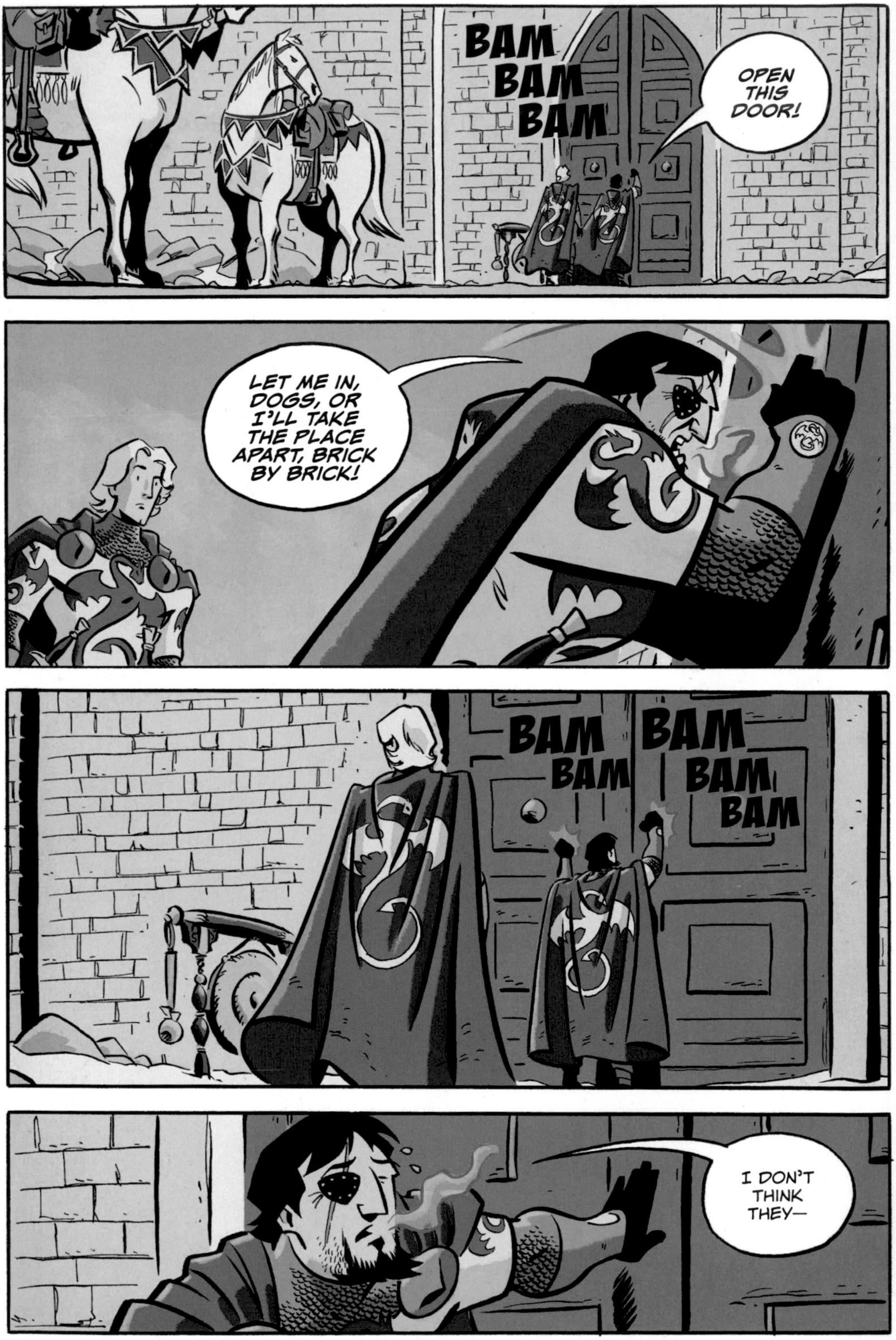
BAM
BAM
BAM
OPEN THIS DOOR!
LET ME IN, DOGS, OR I'LL TAKE THE PLACE APART, BRICK BY BRICK!
BAM BAM BAM BAM BAM BAM
I DON'T THINK THEY—

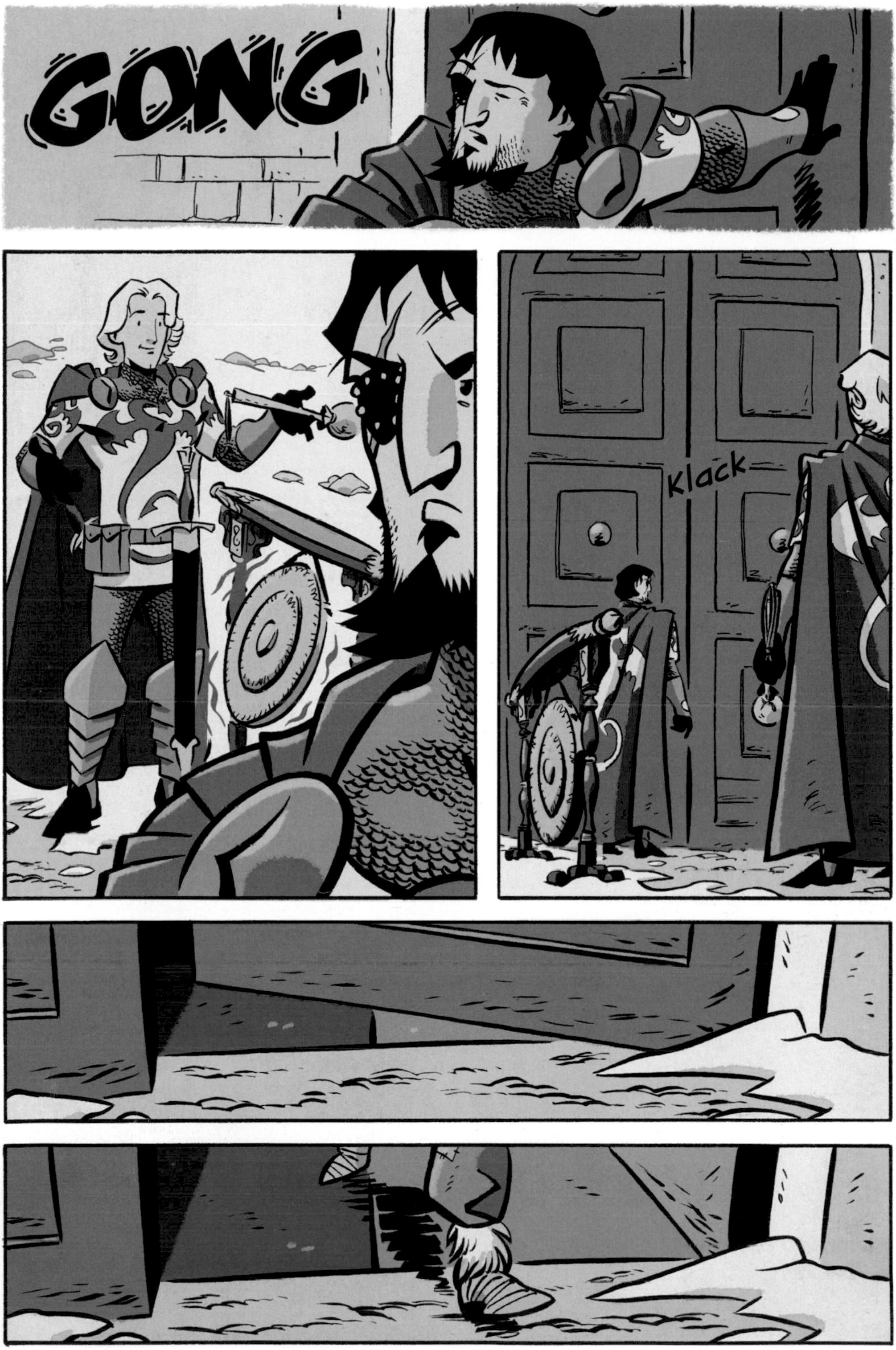
GONG
Klack

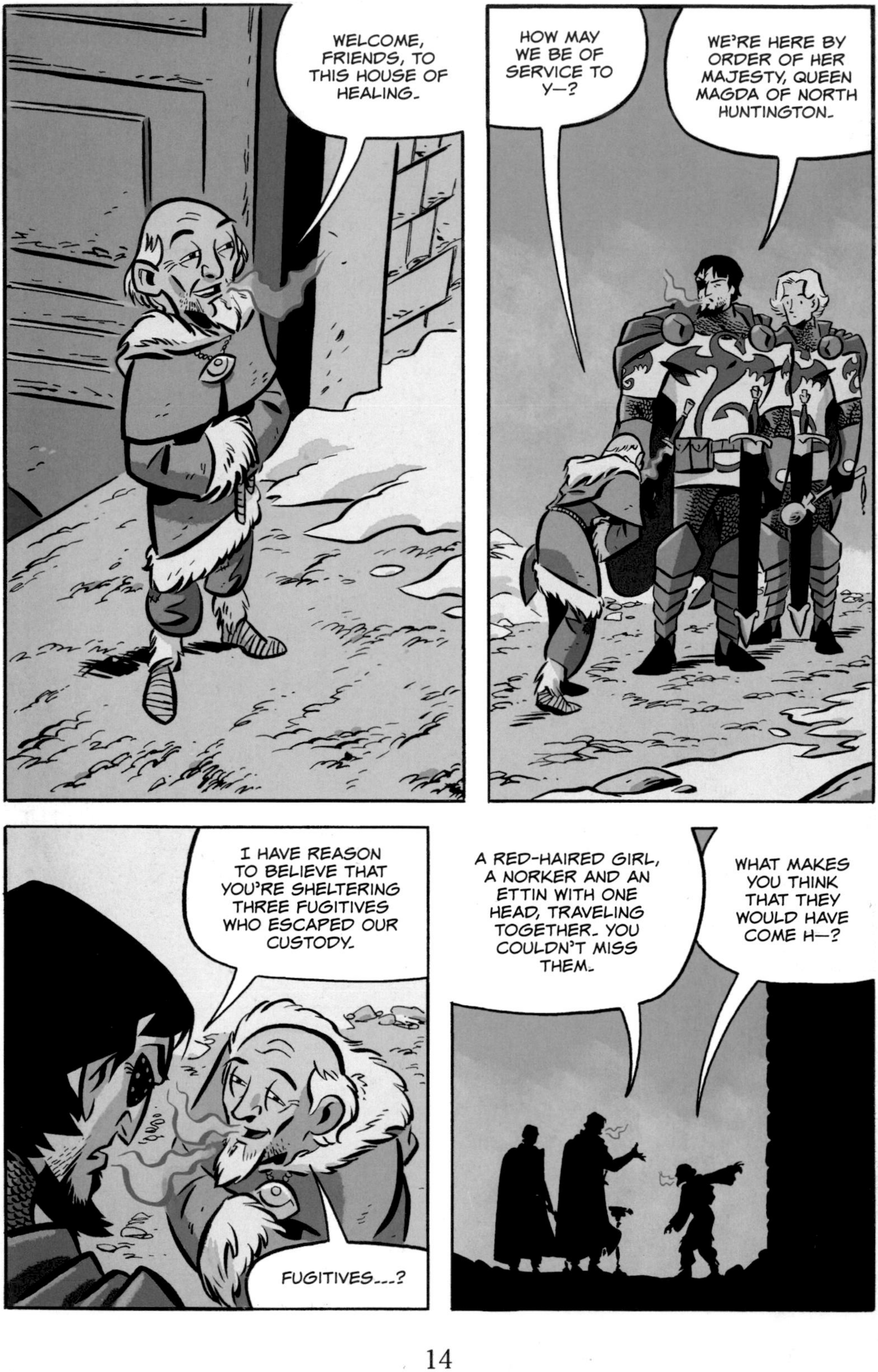
WELCOME, FRIENDS, TO THIS HOUSE OF HEALING.
HOW MAY WE BE OF SERVICE TO Y—?
WE'RE HERE BY ORDER OF HER MAJESTY, QUEEN MAGDA OF NORTH HUNTINGTON.
I HAVE REASON TO BELIEVE THAT YOU'RE SHELTERING THREE FUGITIVES WHO ESCAPED OUR CUSTODY.
FUGITIVES...?
A RED-HAIRED GIRL, A NORKER AND AN ETTIN WITH ONE HEAD, TRAVELING TOGETHER. YOU COULDN'T MISS THEM.
WHAT MAKES YOU THINK THAT THEY WOULD HAVE COME H—?

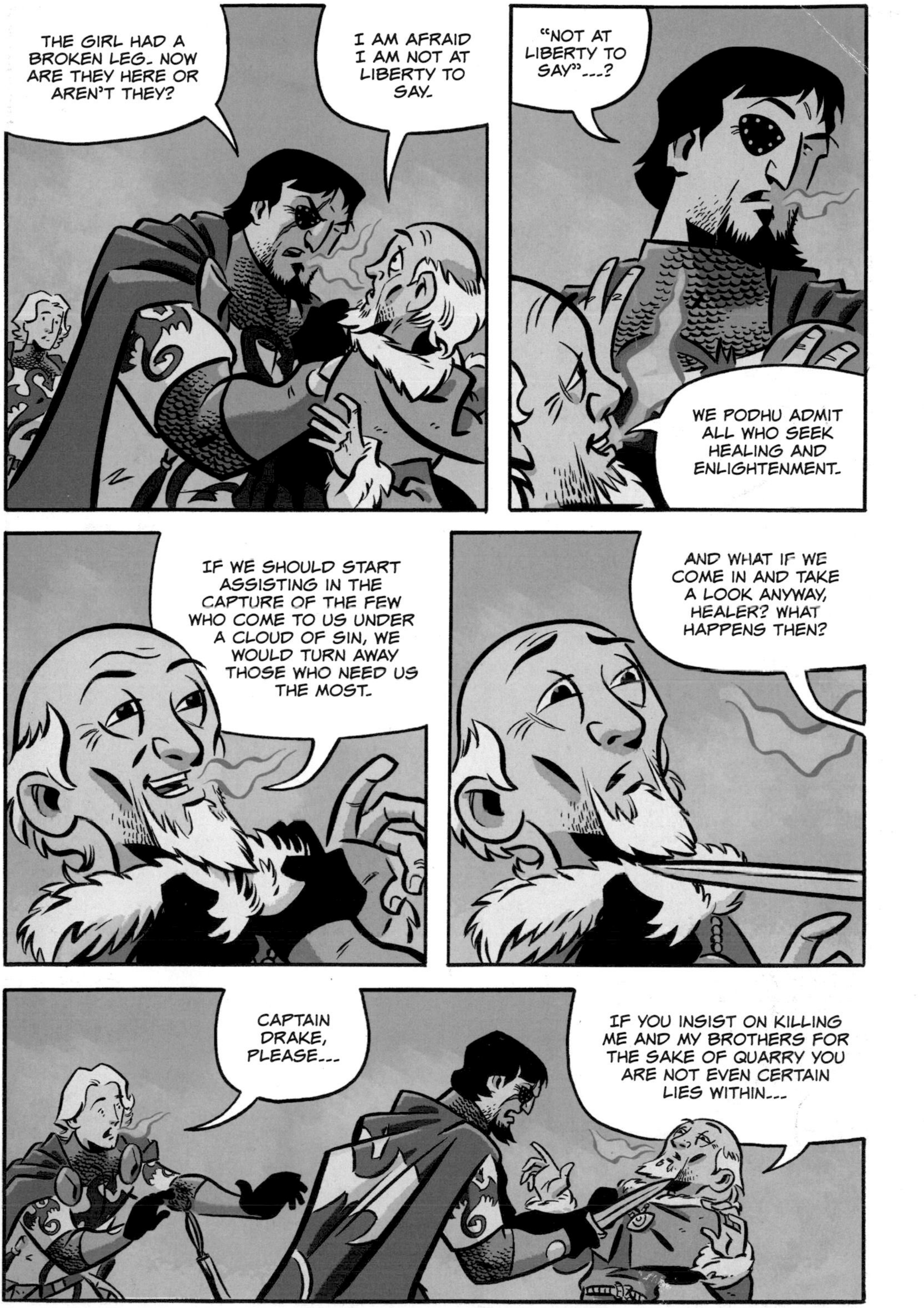
THE GIRL HAD A BROKEN LEG. NOW ARE THEY HERE OR AREN'T THEY?
I AM AFRAID I AM NOT AT LIBERTY TO SAY.
"NOT AT LIBERTY TO SAY"...?
WE PODHU ADMIT ALL WHO SEEK HEALING AND ENLIGHTENMENT.
IF WE SHOULD START ASSISTING IN THE CAPTURE OF THE FEW WHO COME TO US UNDER A CLOUD OF SIN, WE WOULD TURN AWAY THOSE WHO NEED US THE MOST.
AND WHAT IF WE COME IN AND TAKE A LOOK ANYWAY, HEALER? WHAT HAPPENS THEN?
CAPTAIN DRAKE, PLEASE...
IF YOU INSIST ON KILLING ME AND MY BROTHERS FOR THE SAKE OF QUARRY YOU ARE NOT EVEN CERTAIN LIES WITHIN...

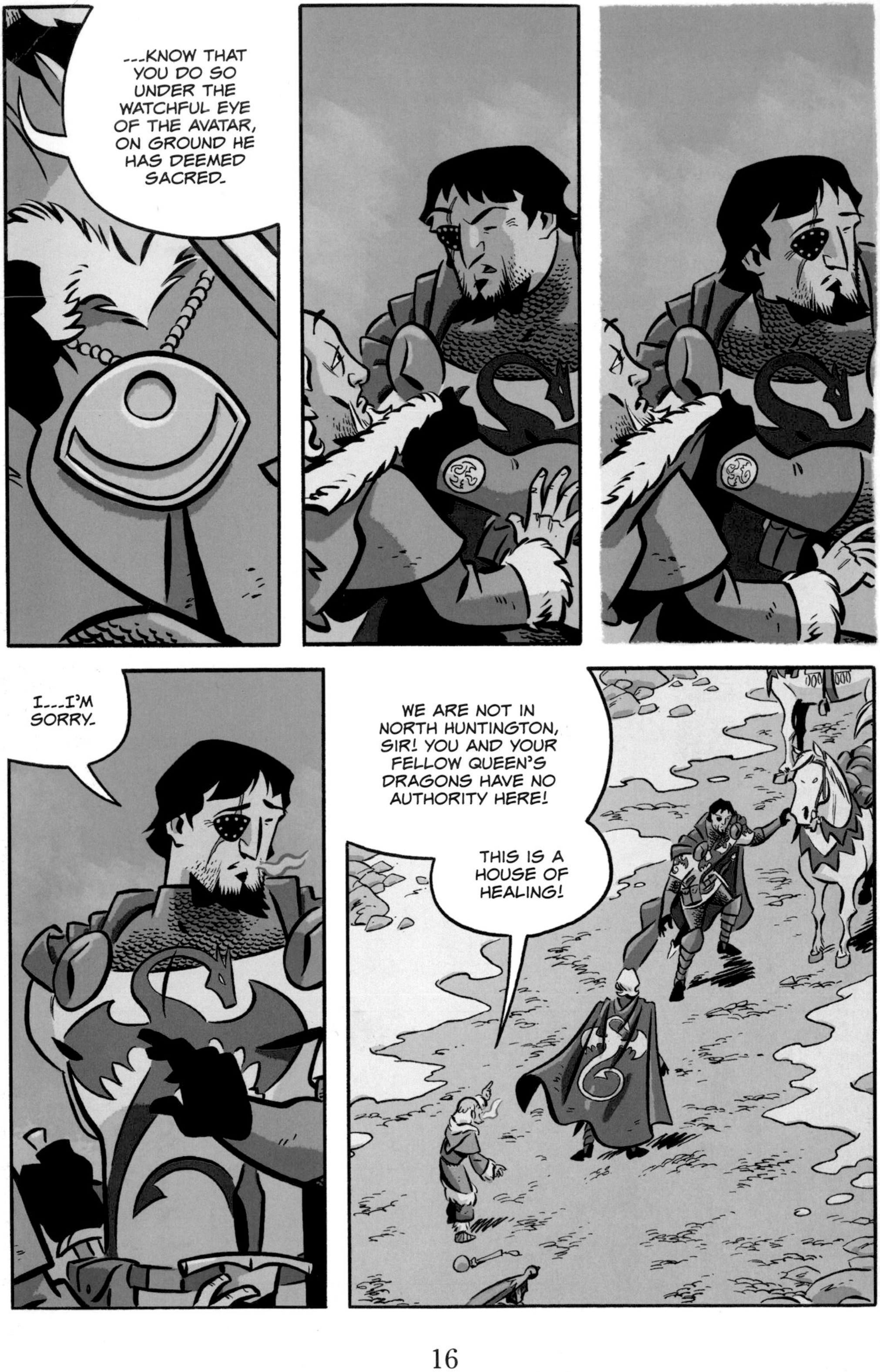
---KNOW THAT YOU DO SO UNDER THE WATCHFUL EYE OF THE AVATAR, ON GROUND HE HAS DEEMED SACRED.
I---I'M SORRY.
WE ARE NOT IN NORTH HUNTINGTON, SIR! YOU AND YOUR FELLOW QUEEN'S DRAGONS HAVE NO AUTHORITY HERE!
THIS IS A HOUSE OF HEALING!

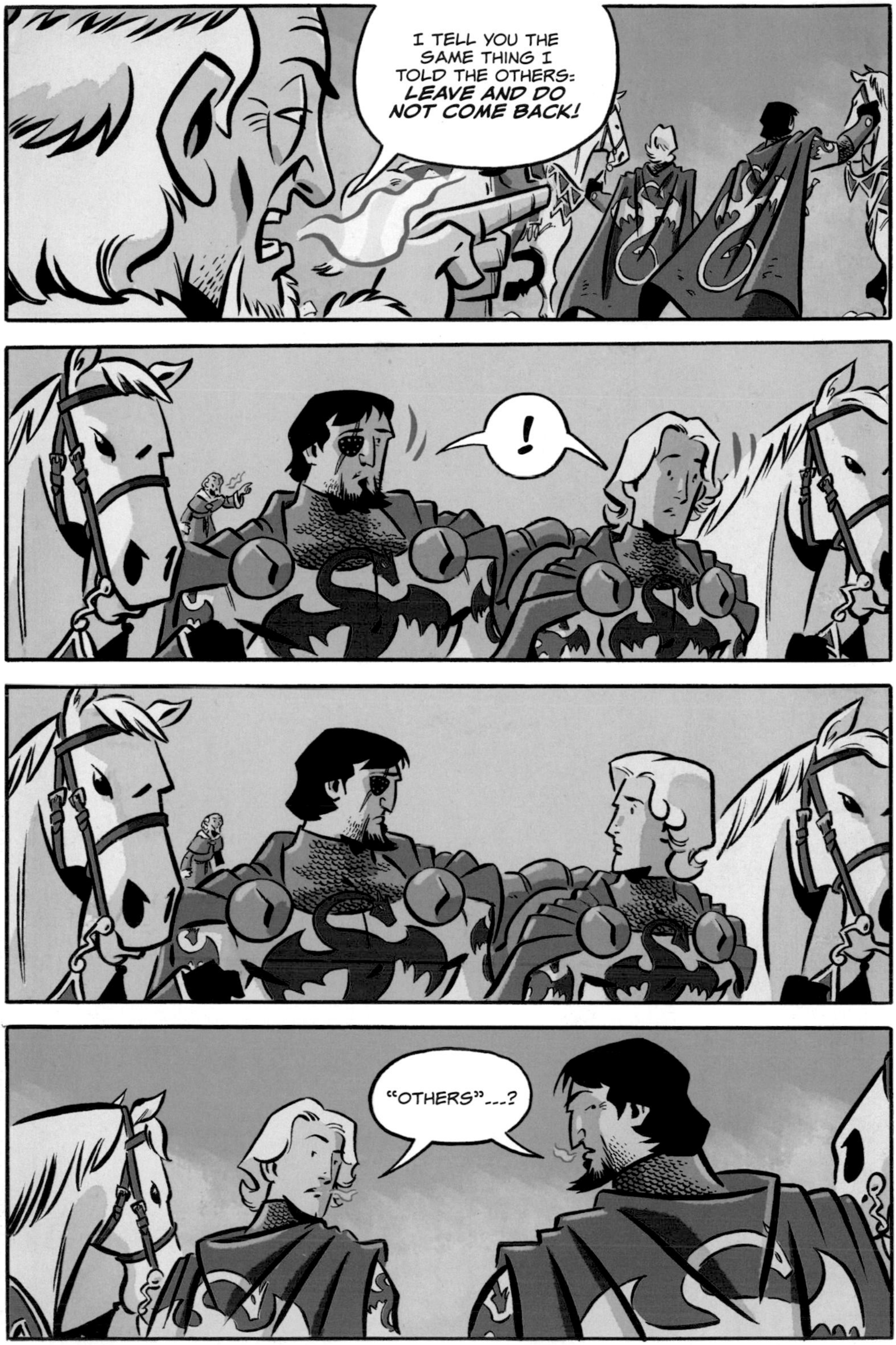
I TELL YOU THE SAME THING I TOLD THE OTHERS: *LEAVE AND DO NOT COME BACK!*
!
"OTHERS"...?

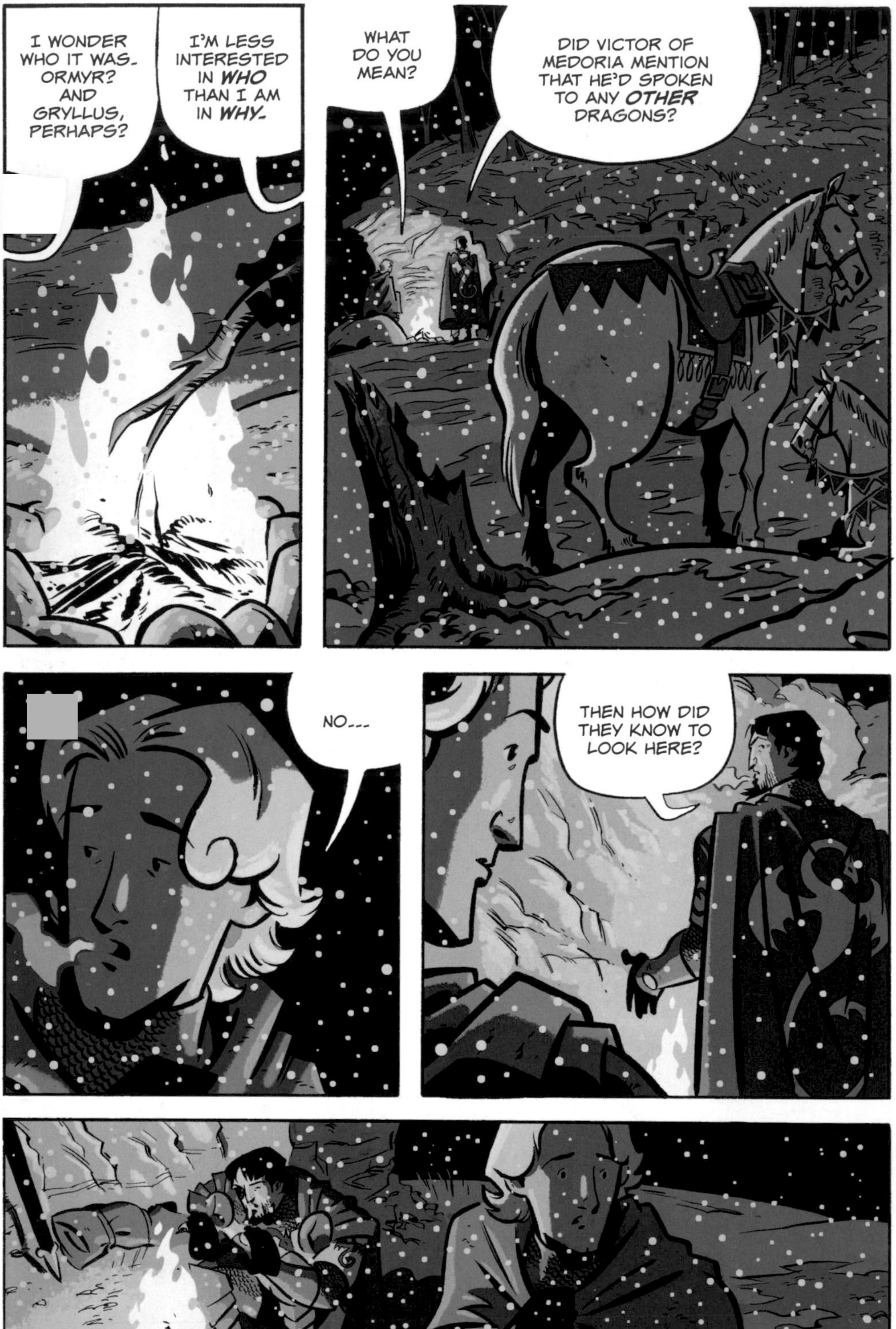
I WONDER WHO IT WAS. ORMYR? AND GRYLLUS, PERHAPS?
I'M LESS INTERESTED IN WHO THAN I AM IN WHY.
WHAT DO YOU MEAN?
DID VICTOR OF MEDORIA MENTION THAT HE'D SPOKEN TO ANY OTHER DRAGONS?
NO...
THEN HOW DID THEY KNOW TO LOOK HERE?

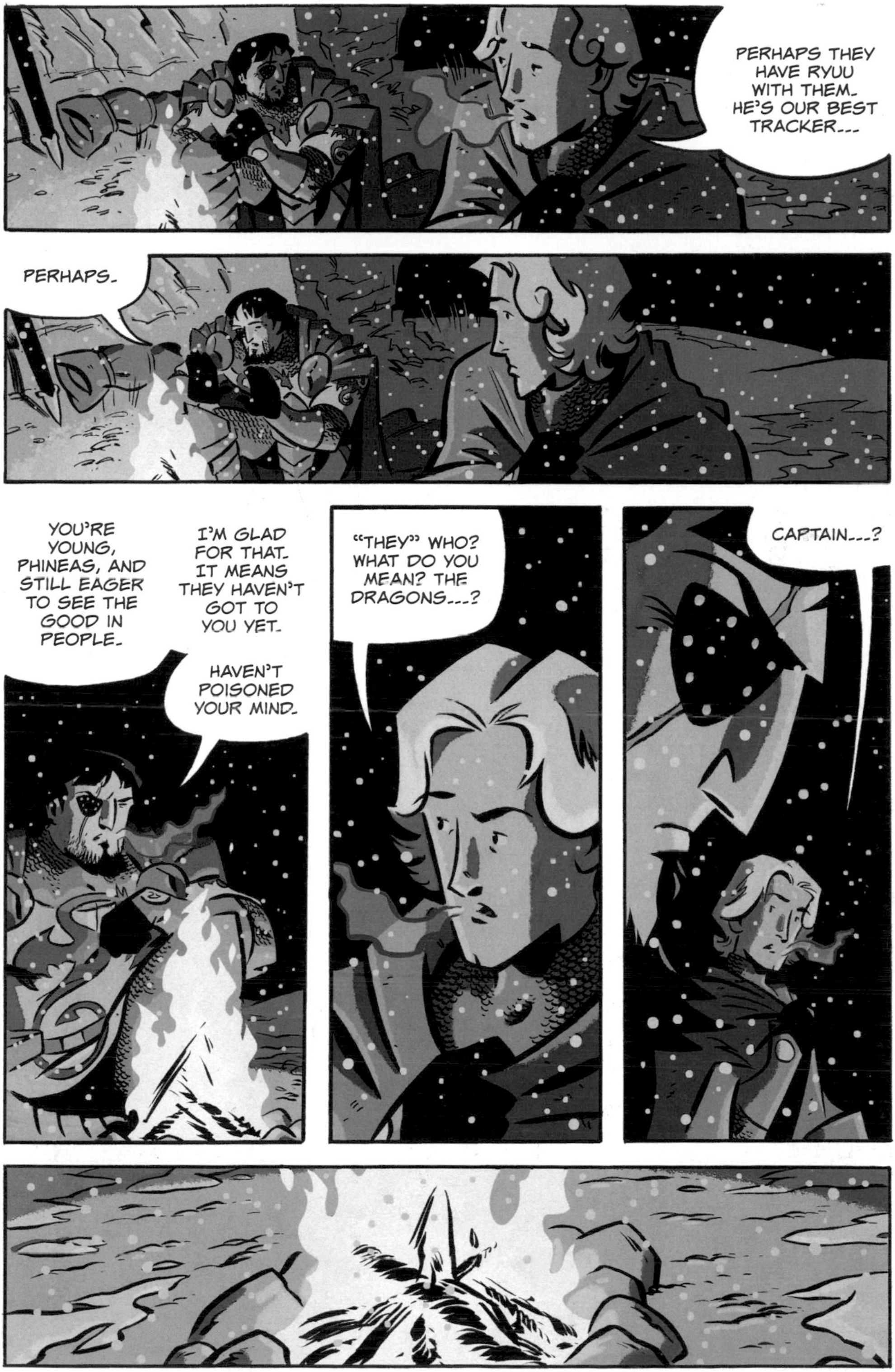
PERHAPS THEY HAVE RYUU WITH THEM. HE'S OUR BEST TRACKER...
PERHAPS.
YOU'RE YOUNG, PHINEAS, AND STILL EAGER TO SEE THE GOOD IN PEOPLE.
I'M GLAD FOR THAT. IT MEANS THEY HAVEN'T GOT TO YOU YET.
HAVEN'T POISONED YOUR MIND.
"THEY" WHO? WHAT DO YOU MEAN? THE DRAGONS...?
CAPTAIN...?

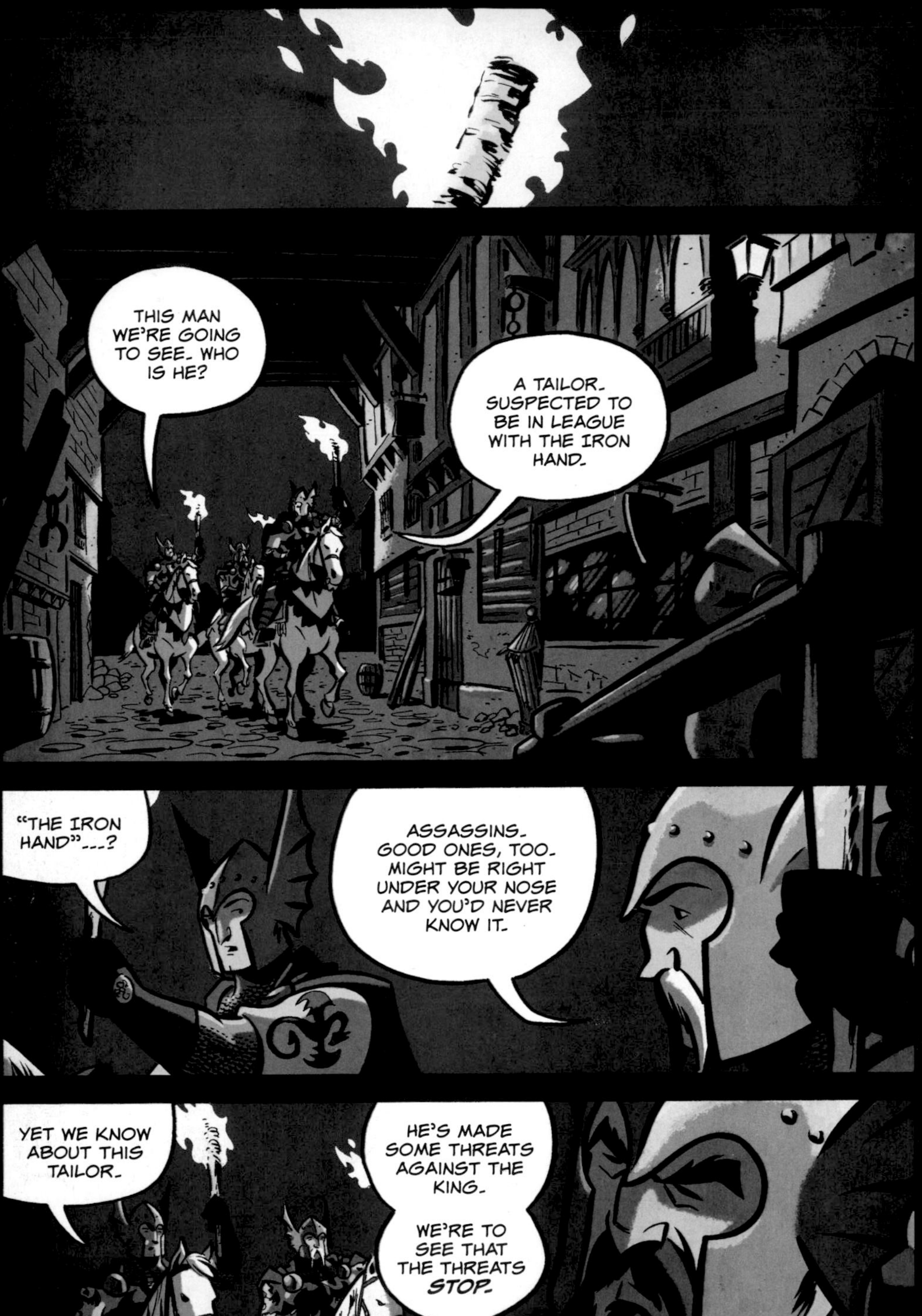
THIS MAN WE'RE GOING TO SEE. WHO IS HE?
A TAILOR. SUSPECTED TO BE IN LEAGUE WITH THE IRON HAND.
"THE IRON HAND"...?
ASSASSINS. GOOD ONES, TOO. MIGHT BE RIGHT UNDER YOUR NOSE AND YOU'D NEVER KNOW IT.
YET WE KNOW ABOUT THIS TAILOR.
HE'S MADE SOME THREATS AGAINST THE KING.
WE'RE TO SEE THAT THE THREATS *STOP*.

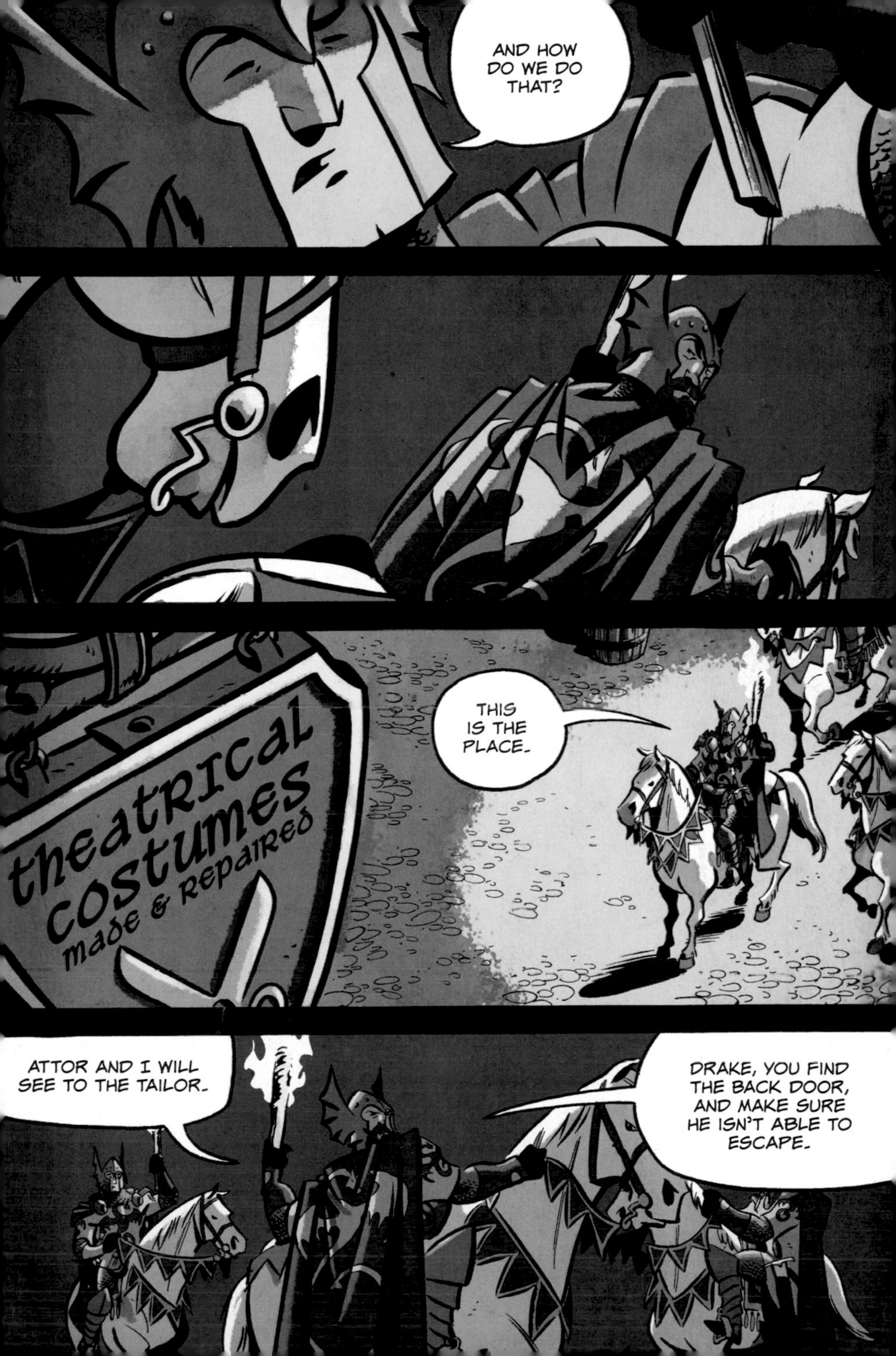
AND HOW DO WE DO THAT?
theatrical costumes made & repaired
THIS IS THE PLACE.
ATTOR AND I WILL SEE TO THE TAILOR.
DRAKE, YOU FIND THE BACK DOOR, AND MAKE SURE HE ISN'T ABLE TO ESCAPE.

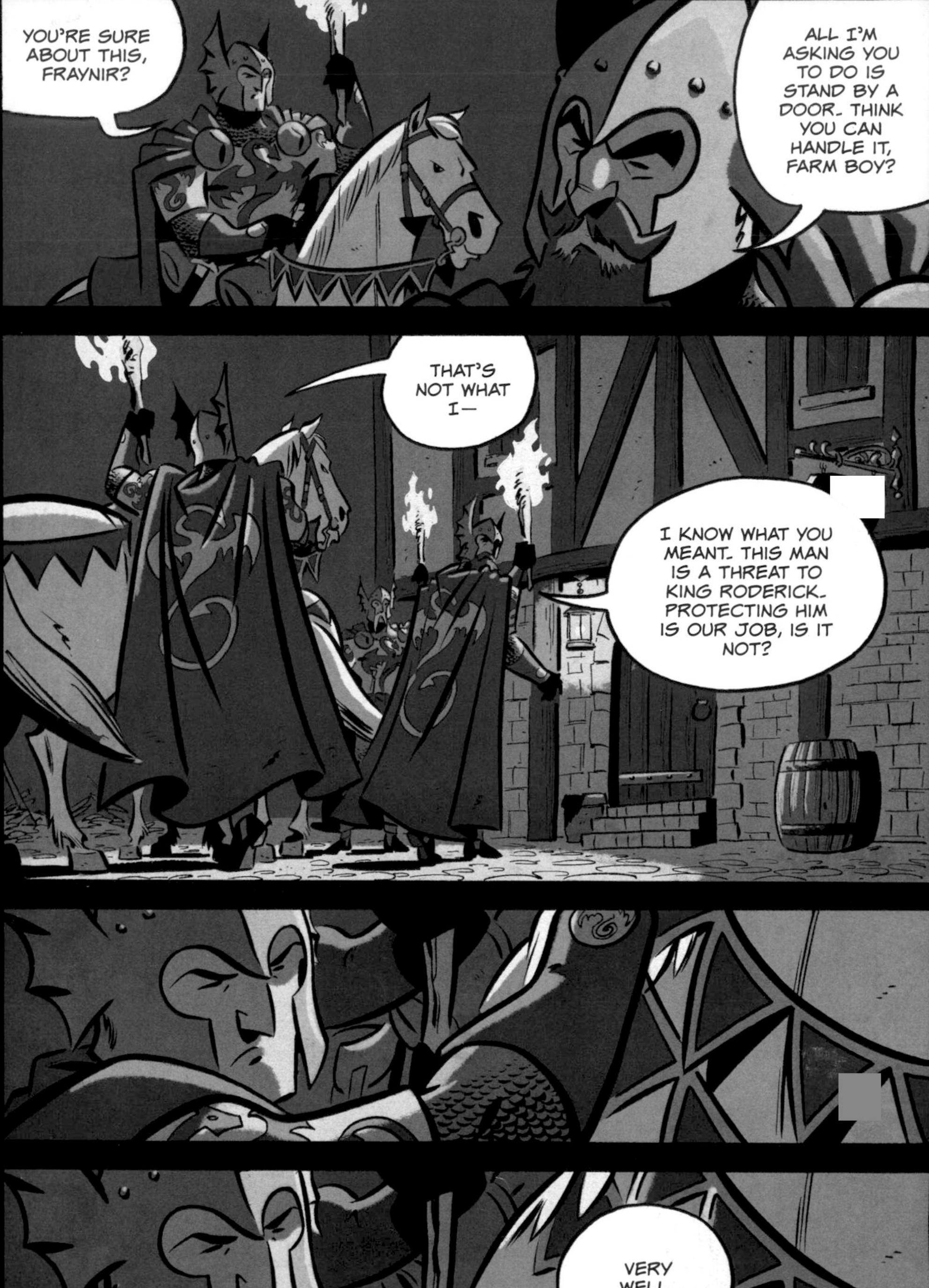
YOU'RE SURE ABOUT THIS, FRAYNIR?
ALL I'M ASKING YOU TO DO IS STAND BY A DOOR. THINK YOU CAN HANDLE IT, FARM BOY?
THAT'S NOT WHAT I—
I KNOW WHAT YOU MEANT. THIS MAN IS A THREAT TO KING RODERICK. PROTECTING HIM IS OUR JOB, IS IT NOT?
VERY WELL.

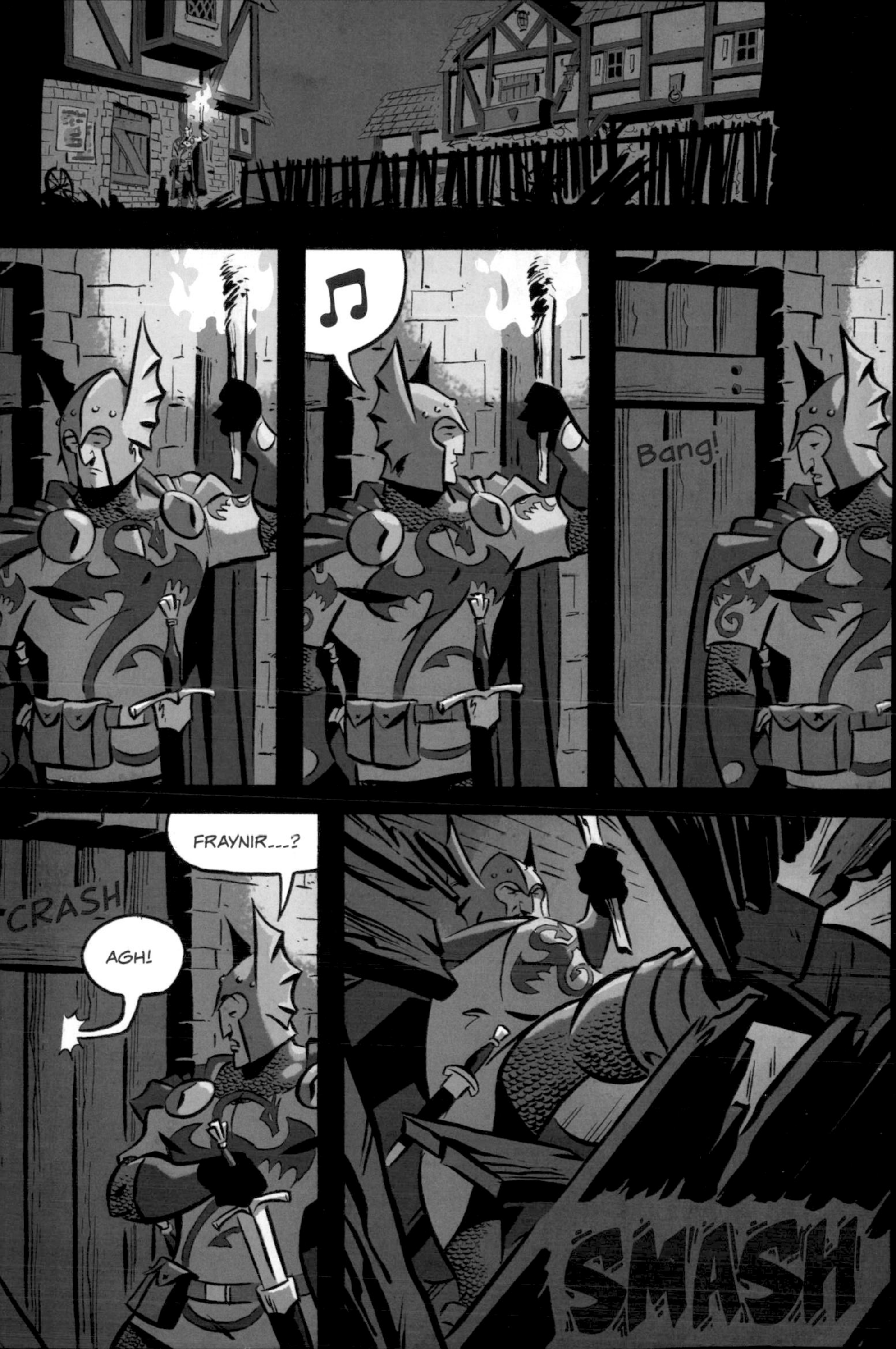

♫
Bang!
CRASH
FRAYNIR...?
AGH!
SMASH

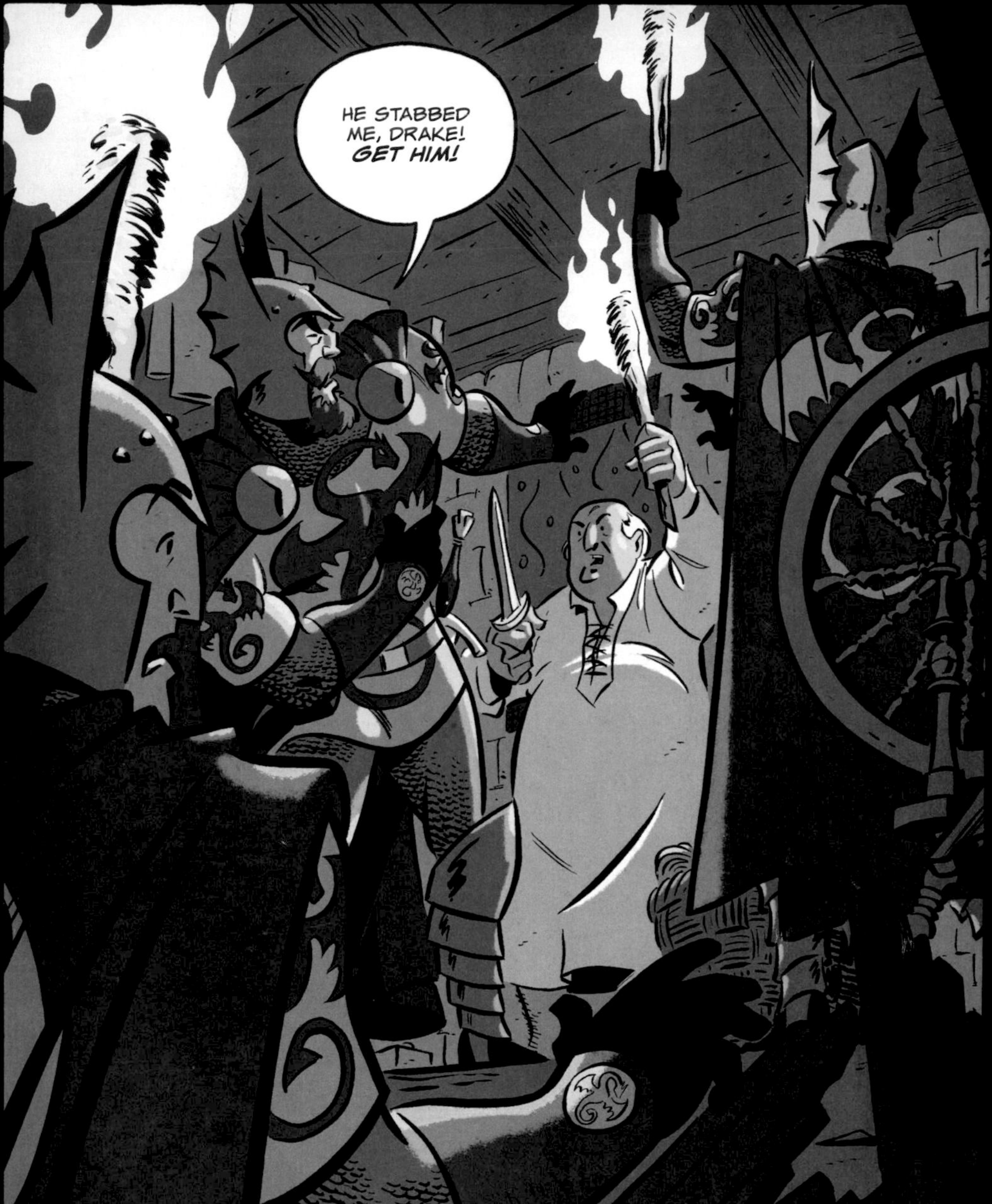
HE STABBED ME, DRAKE! GET HIM!

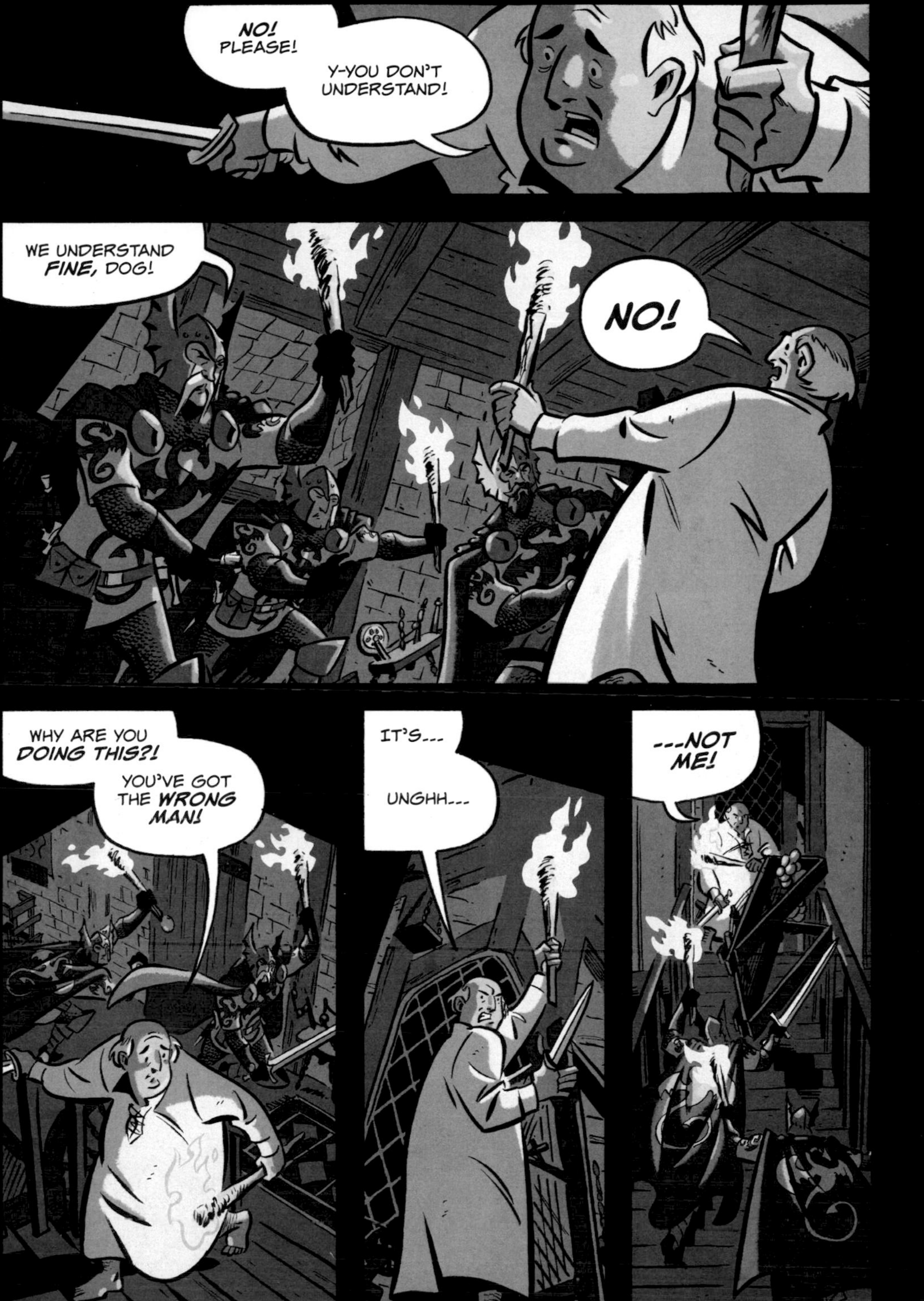
NO! PLEASE!
Y-YOU DON'T UNDERSTAND!
WE UNDERSTAND FINE, DOG!
NO!
WHY ARE YOU DOING THIS?!
YOU'VE GOT THE WRONG MAN!
IT'S...
UNGHH...
...NOT ME!

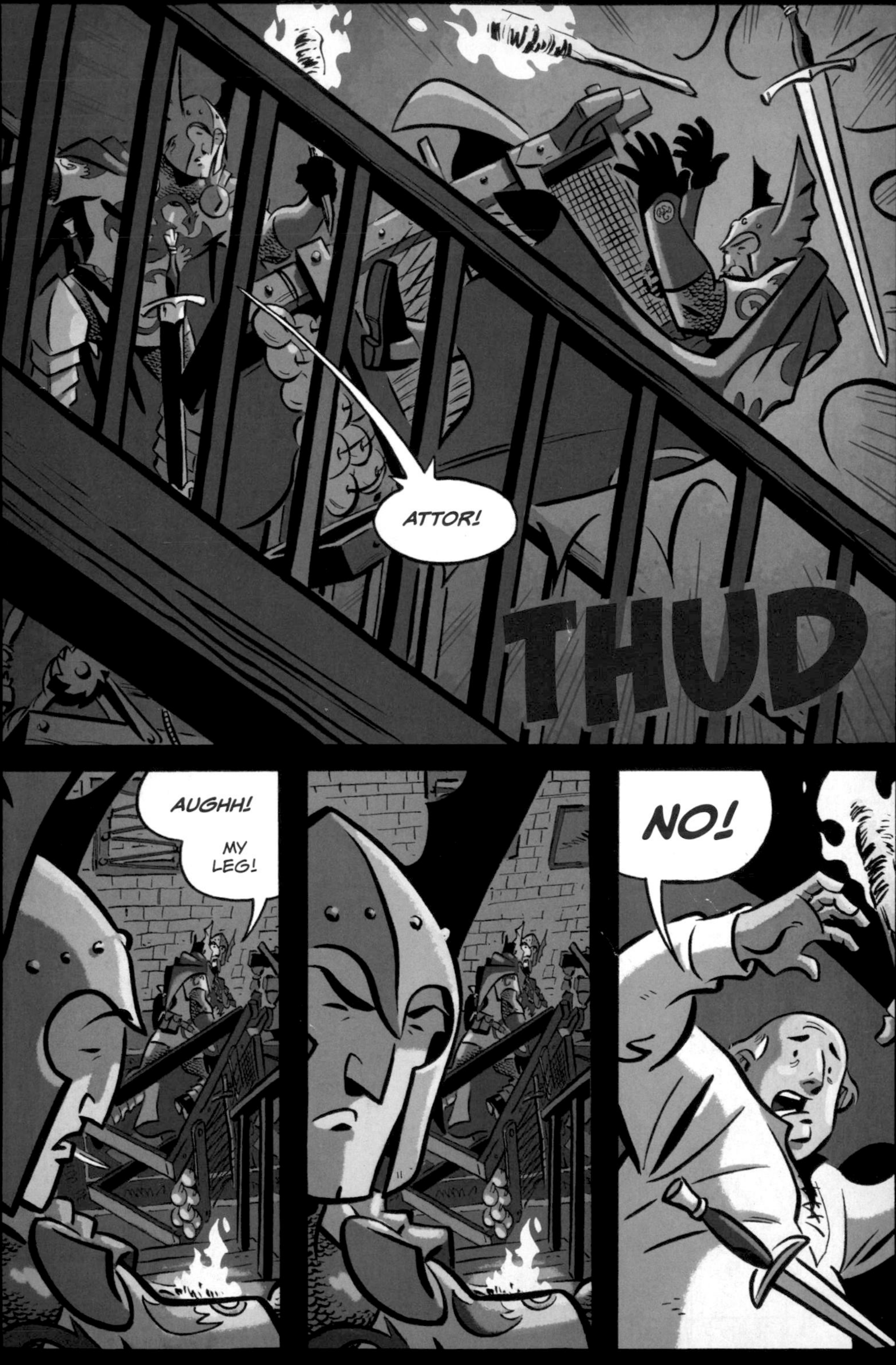
ATTOR!
THUD
AUGHH!
MY LEG!
NO!

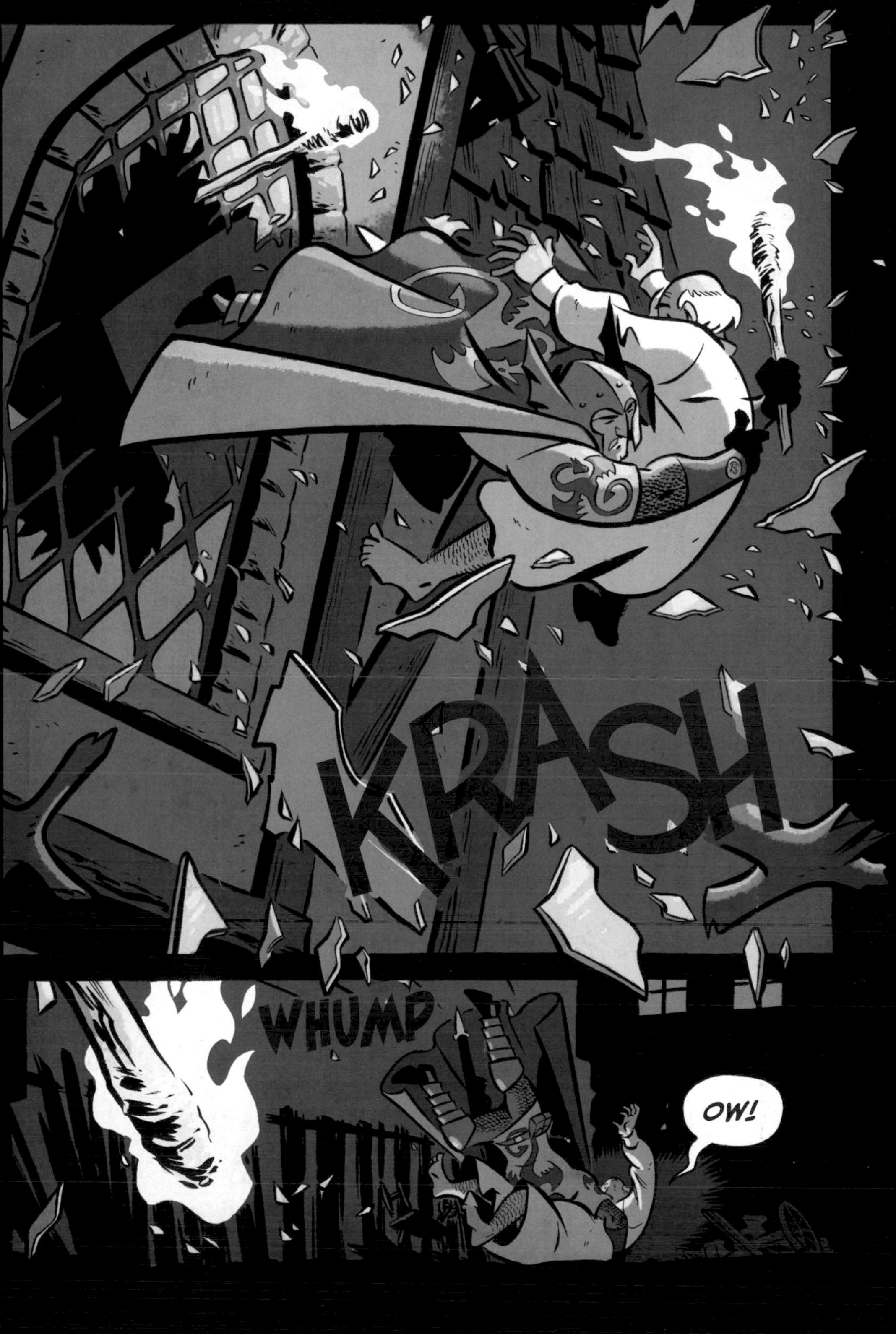
KRASH
WHUMP
OW!

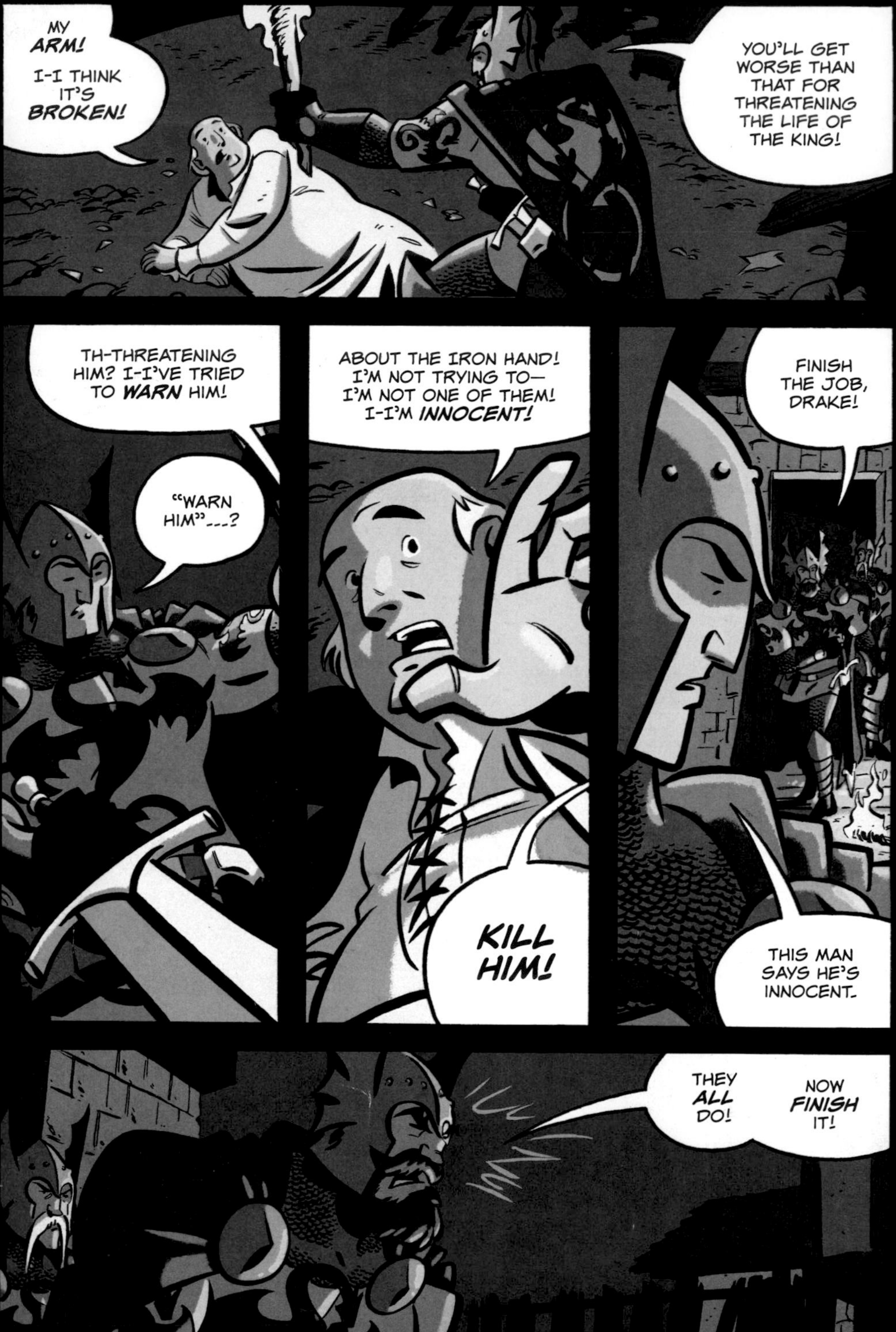

MY ARM! I-I THINK IT'S BROKEN!
YOU'LL GET WORSE THAN THAT FOR THREATENING THE LIFE OF THE KING!
TH-THREATENING HIM? I-I'VE TRIED TO WARN HIM!
"WARN HIM"---?
ABOUT THE IRON HAND! I'M NOT TRYING TO— I'M NOT ONE OF THEM! I-I'M INNOCENT!
FINISH THE JOB, DRAKE!
KILL HIM!
THIS MAN SAYS HE'S INNOCENT.
THEY ALL DO!
NOW FINISH IT!

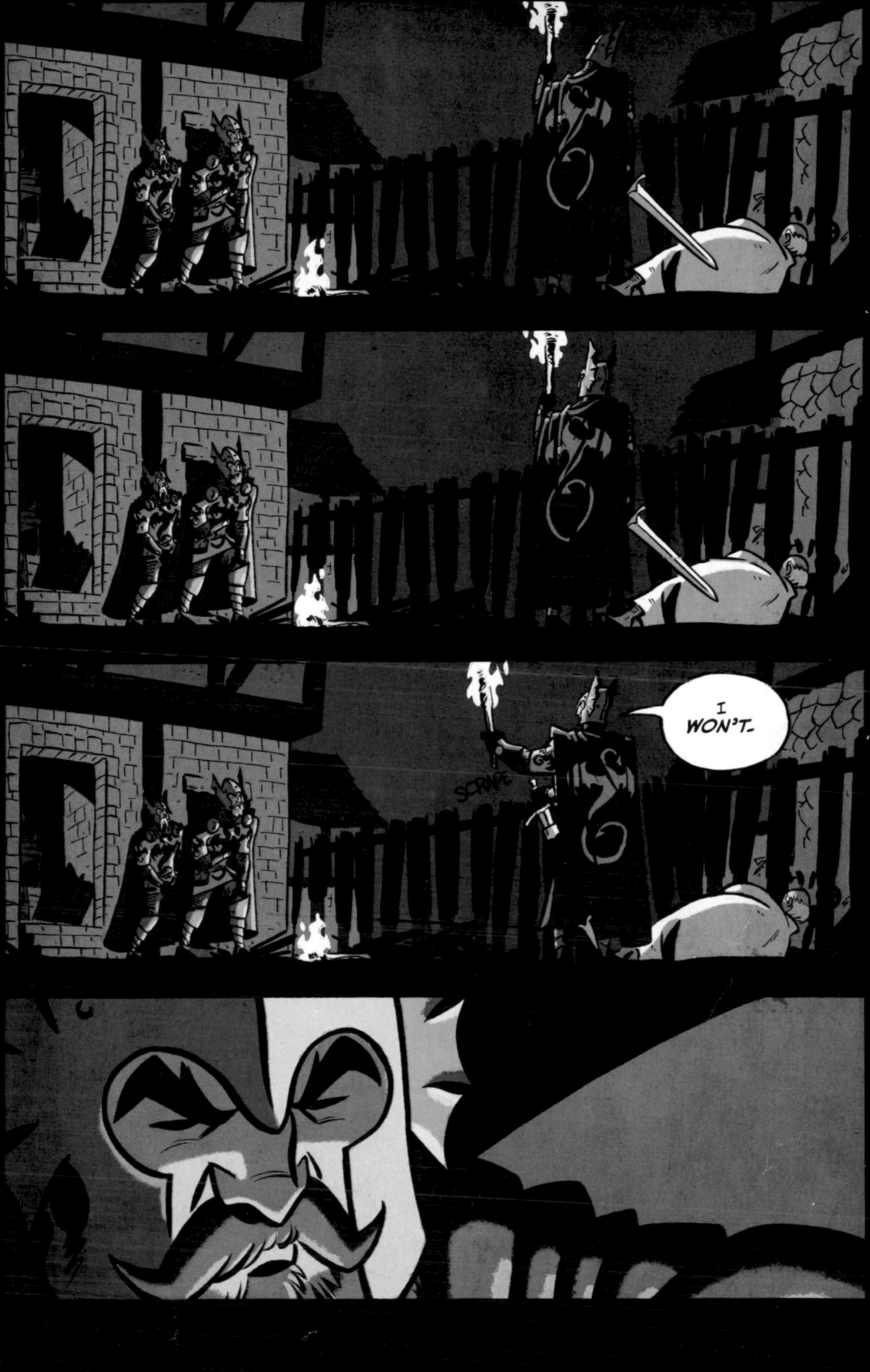
I WON'T–

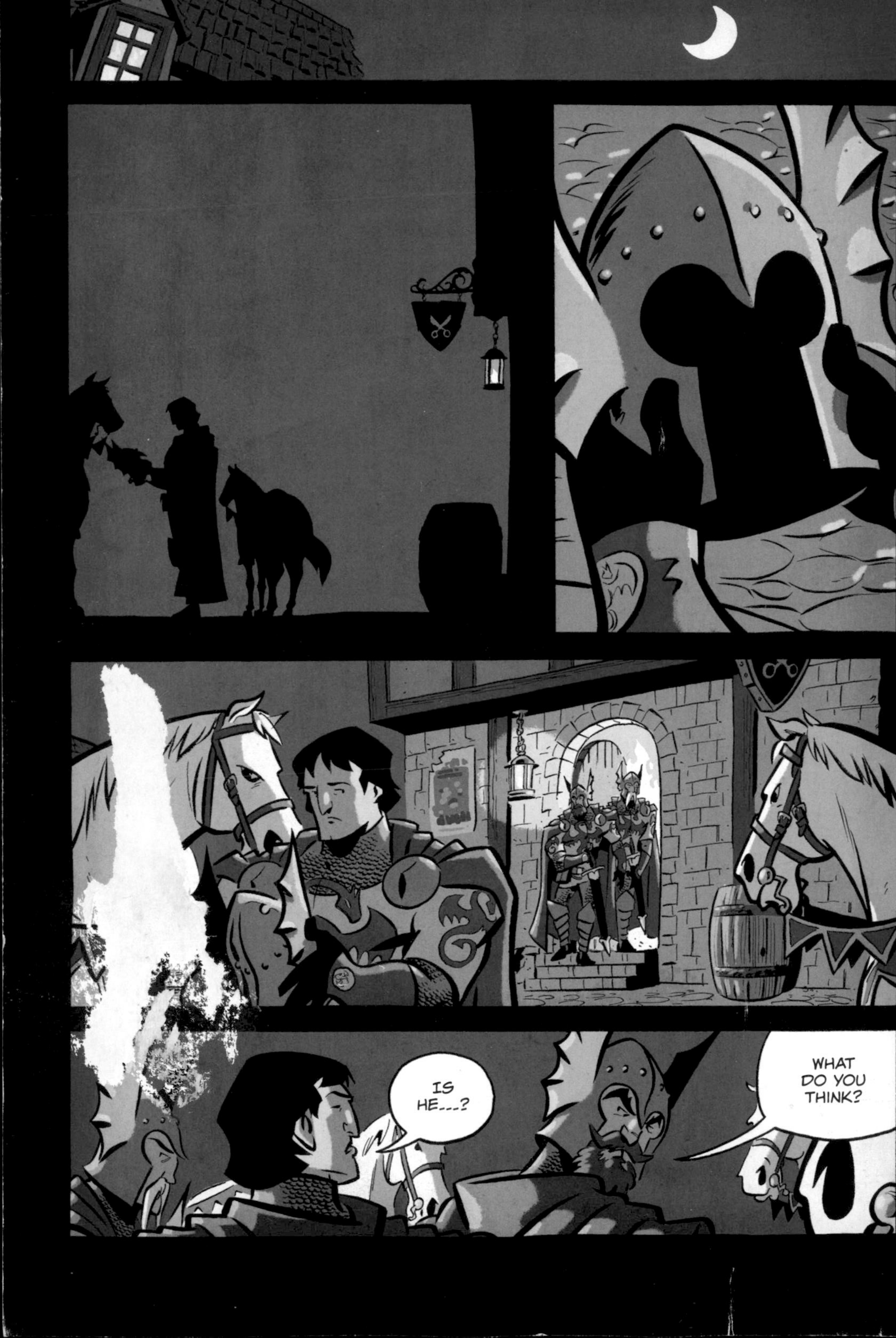
IS
HE---?
WHAT
DO YOU
THINK?

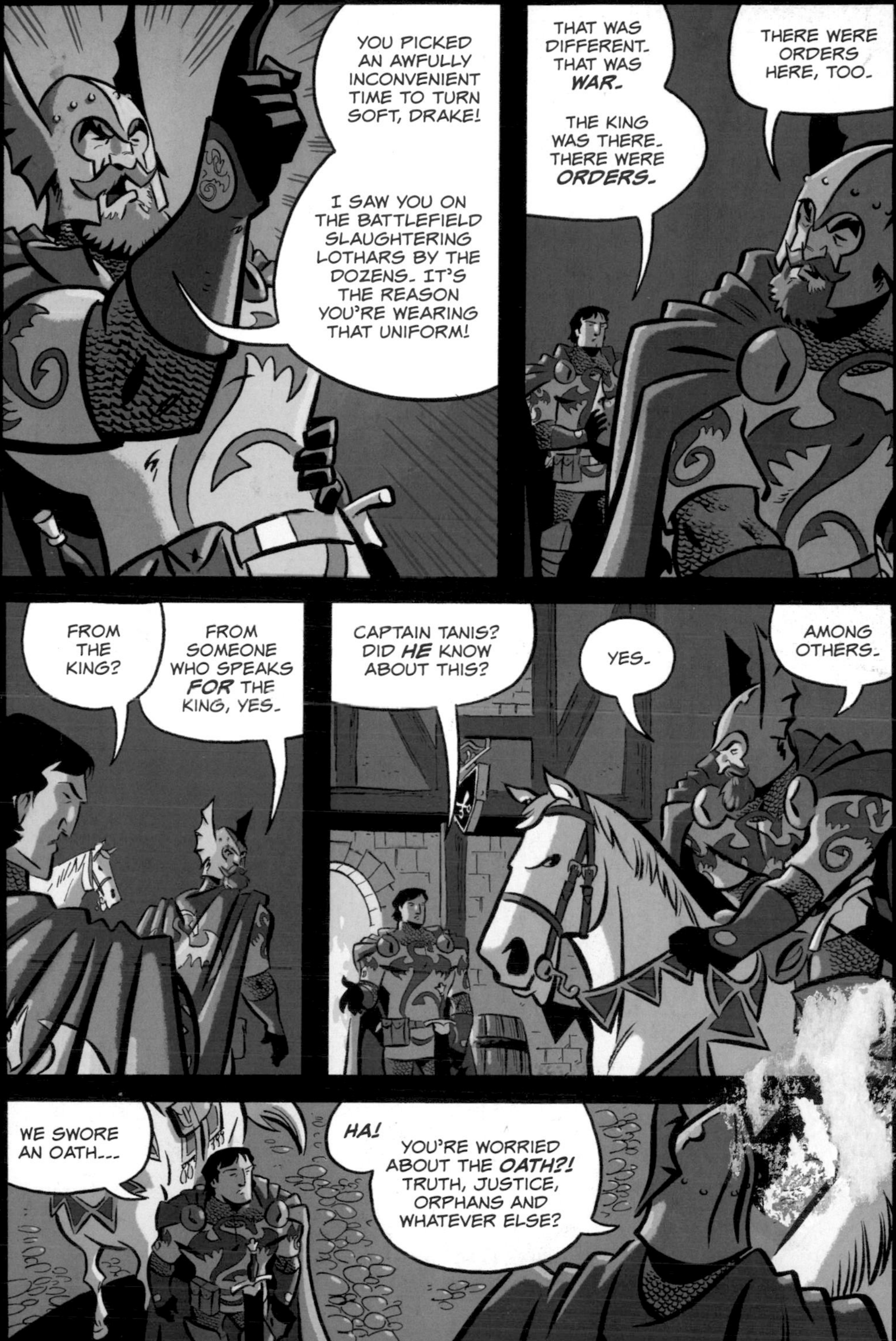
YOU PICKED AN AWFULLY INCONVENIENT TIME TO TURN SOFT, DRAKE!
I SAW YOU ON THE BATTLEFIELD SLAUGHTERING LOTHARS BY THE DOZENS. IT'S THE REASON YOU'RE WEARING THAT UNIFORM!
THAT WAS DIFFERENT. THAT WAS WAR.
THE KING WAS THERE. THERE WERE ORDERS.
THERE WERE ORDERS HERE, TOO.
FROM THE KING?
FROM SOMEONE WHO SPEAKS FOR THE KING, YES.
CAPTAIN TANIS? DID HE KNOW ABOUT THIS?
YES.
AMONG OTHERS.
WE SWORE AN OATH...
HA!
YOU'RE WORRIED ABOUT THE OATH?! TRUTH, JUSTICE, ORPHANS AND WHATEVER ELSE?

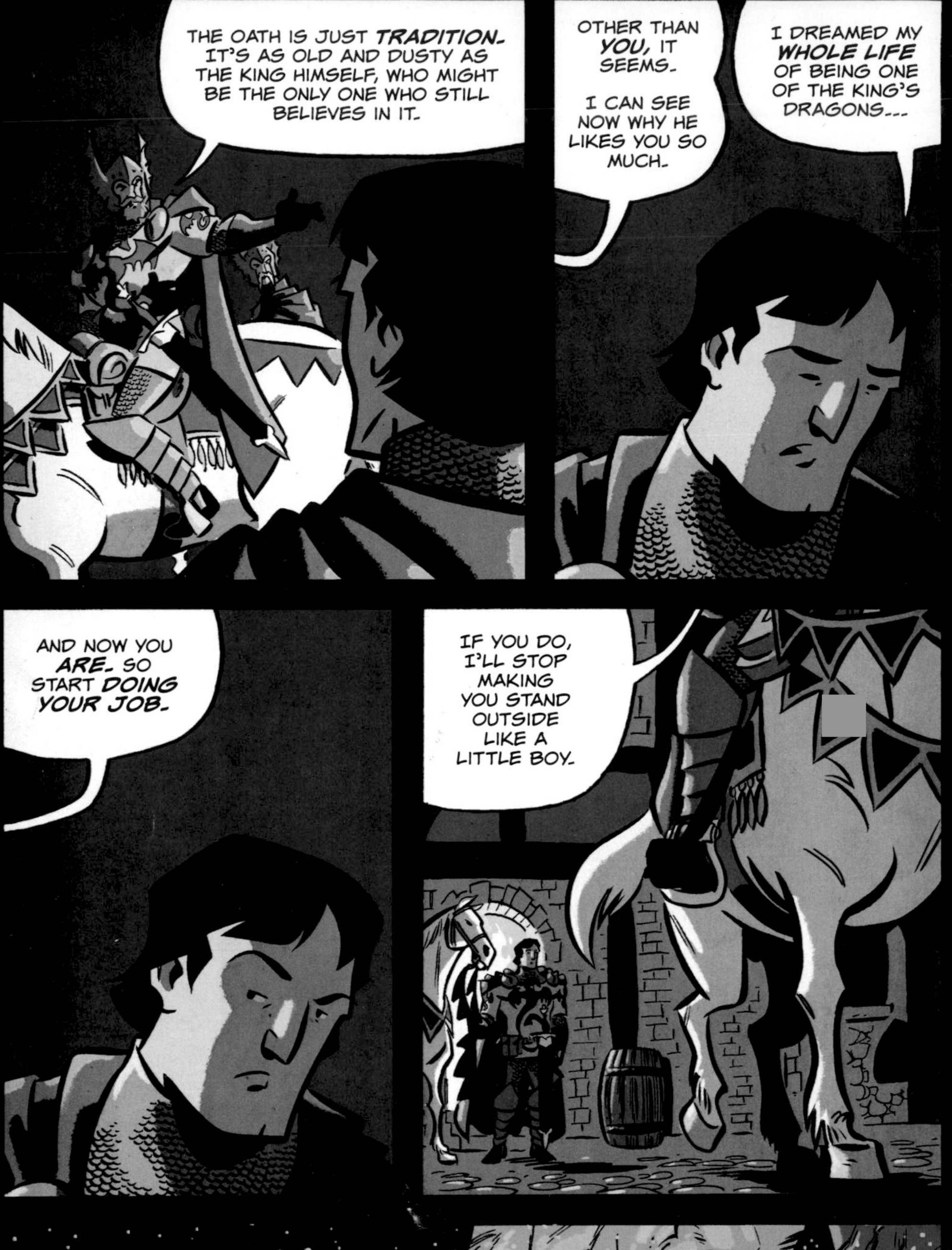
THE OATH IS JUST TRADITION. IT'S AS OLD AND DUSTY AS THE KING HIMSELF, WHO MIGHT BE THE ONLY ONE WHO STILL BELIEVES IN IT.
OTHER THAN YOU, IT SEEMS.
I CAN SEE NOW WHY HE LIKES YOU SO MUCH.
I DREAMED MY WHOLE LIFE OF BEING ONE OF THE KING'S DRAGONS...
AND NOW YOU ARE. SO START DOING YOUR JOB.
IF YOU DO, I'LL STOP MAKING YOU STAND OUTSIDE LIKE A LITTLE BOY.

ACT TWO

Tested

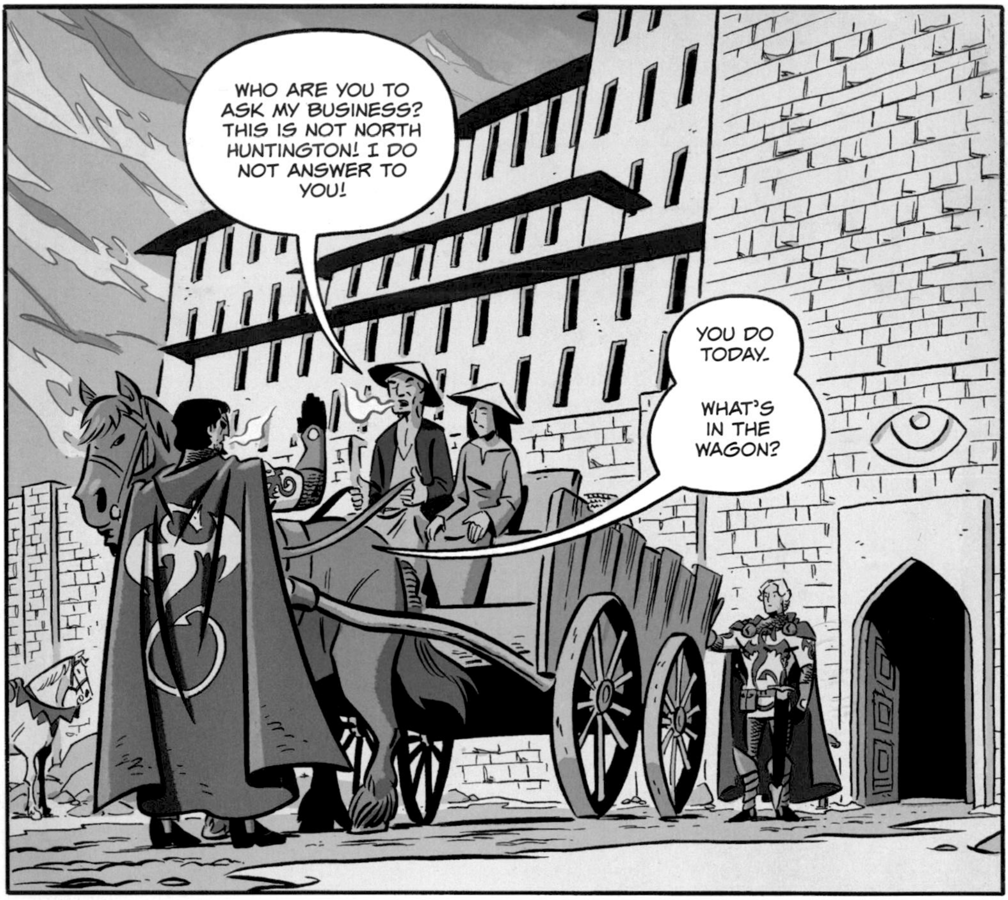
WHO ARE YOU TO ASK MY BUSINESS? THIS IS NOT NORTH HUNTINGTON! I DO NOT ANSWER TO YOU!
YOU DO TODAY.
WHAT'S IN THE WAGON?

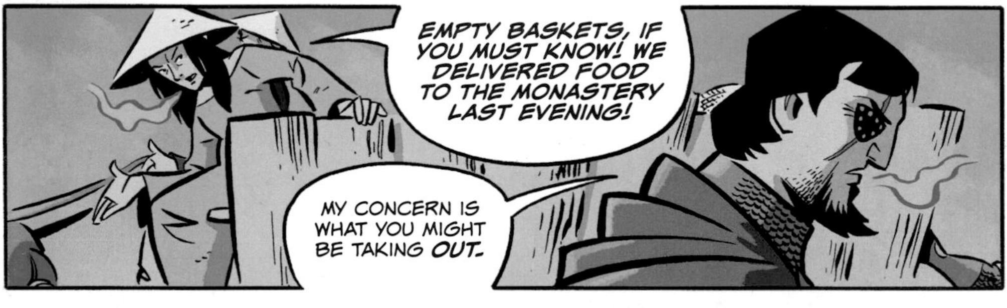
EMPTY BASKETS, IF YOU MUST KNOW! WE DELIVERED FOOD TO THE MONASTERY LAST EVENING!
MY CONCERN IS WHAT YOU MIGHT BE TAKING OUT.

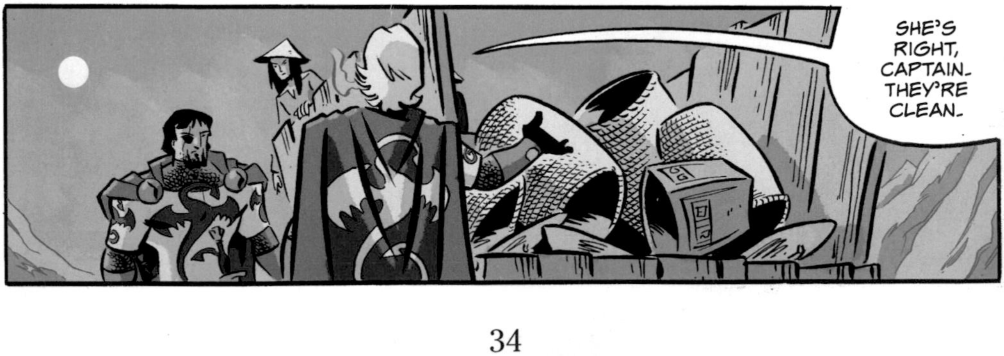
SHE'S RIGHT, CAPTAIN. THEY'RE CLEAN.

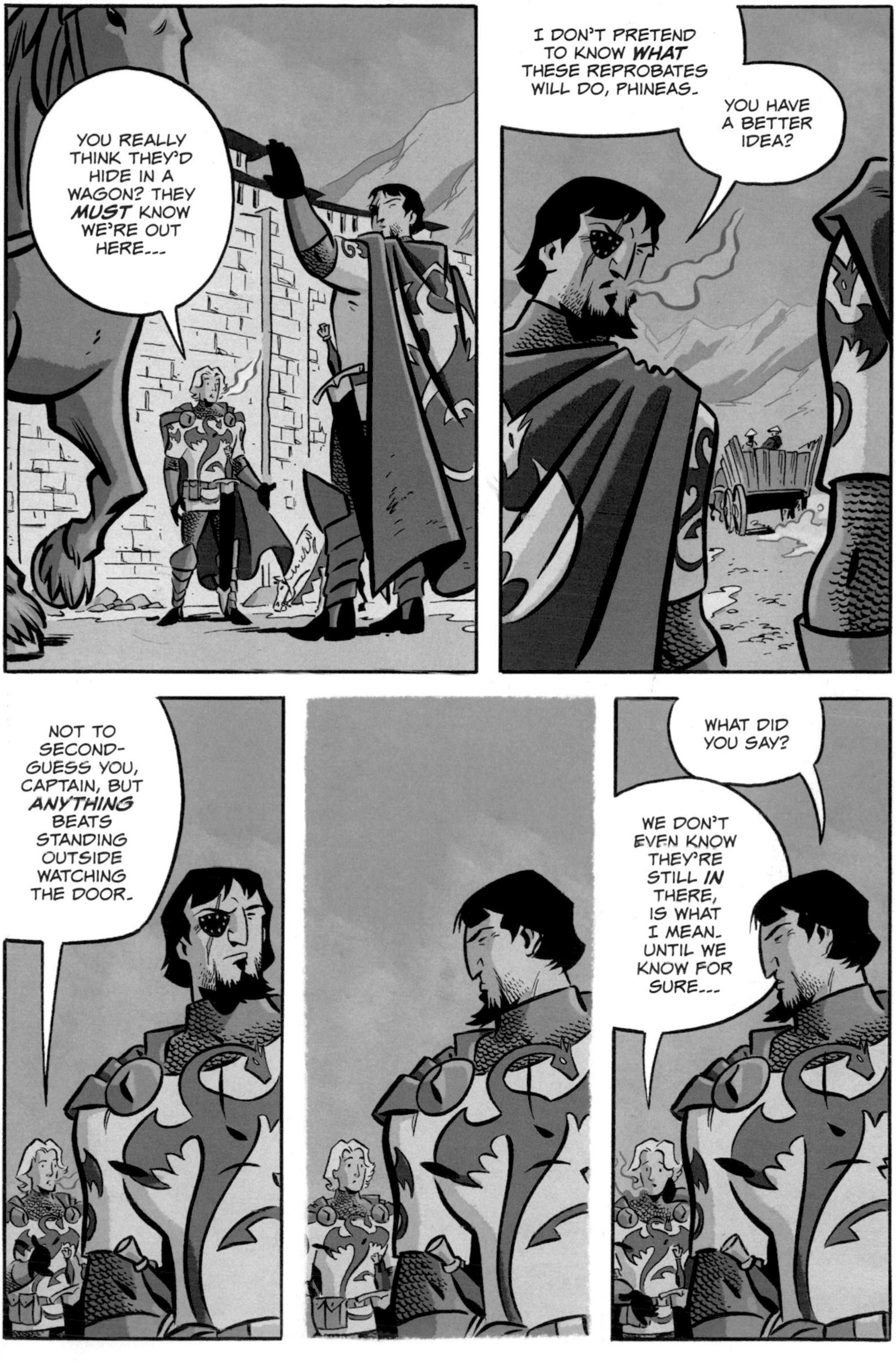
YOU REALLY THINK THEY'D HIDE IN A WAGON? THEY MUST KNOW WE'RE OUT HERE...
I DON'T PRETEND TO KNOW WHAT THESE REPROBATES WILL DO, PHINEAS.
YOU HAVE A BETTER IDEA?
NOT TO SECOND-GUESS YOU, CAPTAIN, BUT ANYTHING BEATS STANDING OUTSIDE WATCHING THE DOOR.
WHAT DID YOU SAY?
WE DON'T EVEN KNOW THEY'RE STILL IN THERE, IS WHAT I MEAN. UNTIL WE KNOW FOR SURE...

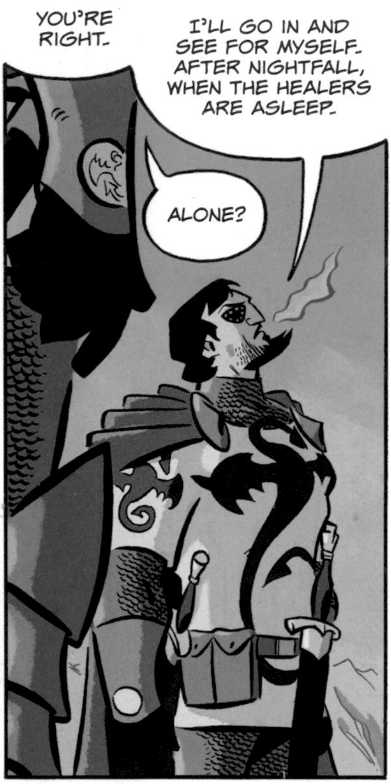
YOU'RE RIGHT.
I'LL GO IN AND SEE FOR MYSELF. AFTER NIGHTFALL, WHEN THE HEALERS ARE ASLEEP.
ALONE?

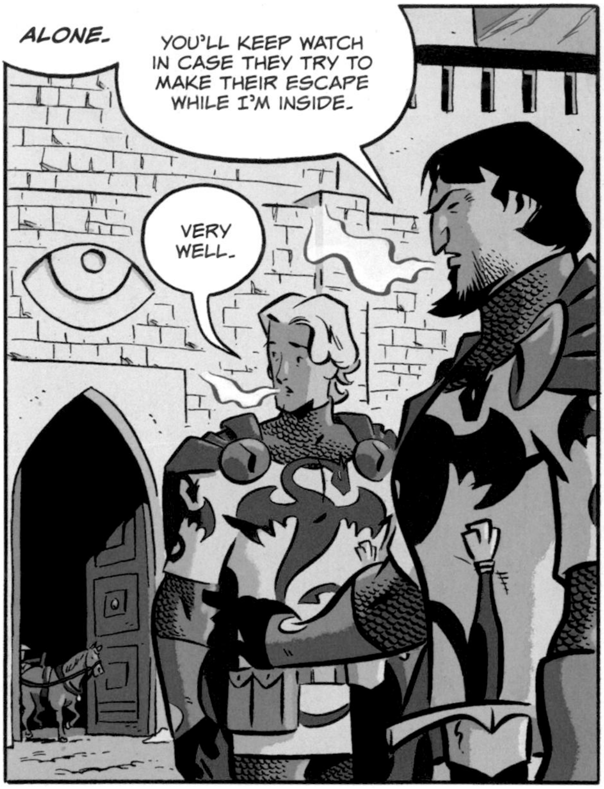
ALONE.
YOU'LL KEEP WATCH IN CASE THEY TRY TO MAKE THEIR ESCAPE WHILE I'M INSIDE.
VERY WELL.

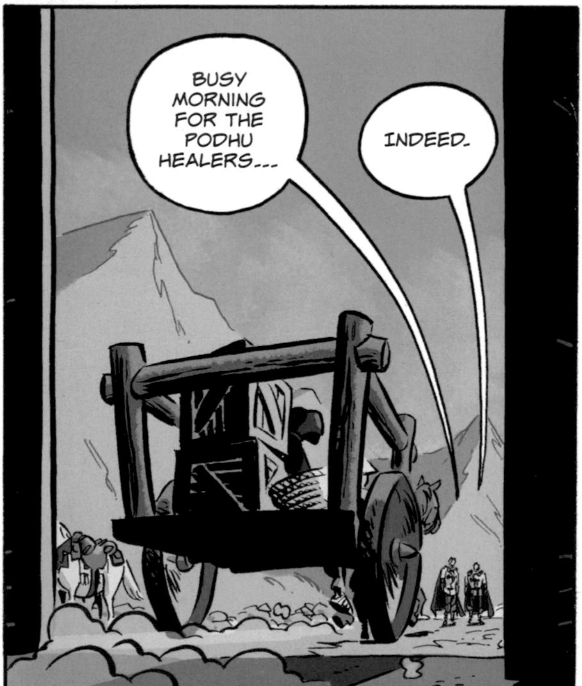
BUSY MORNING FOR THE PODHU HEALERS...
INDEED.

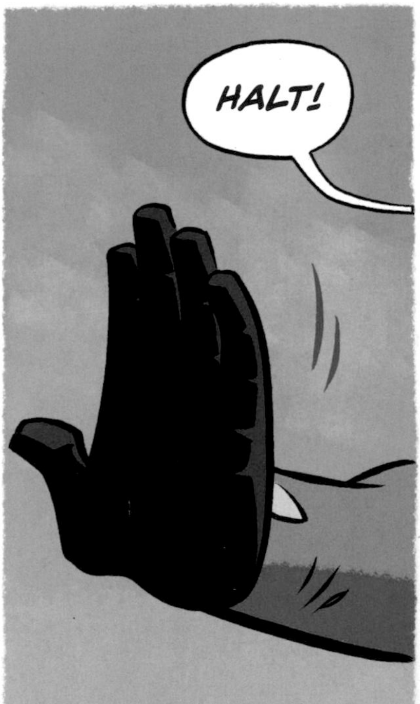
HALT!

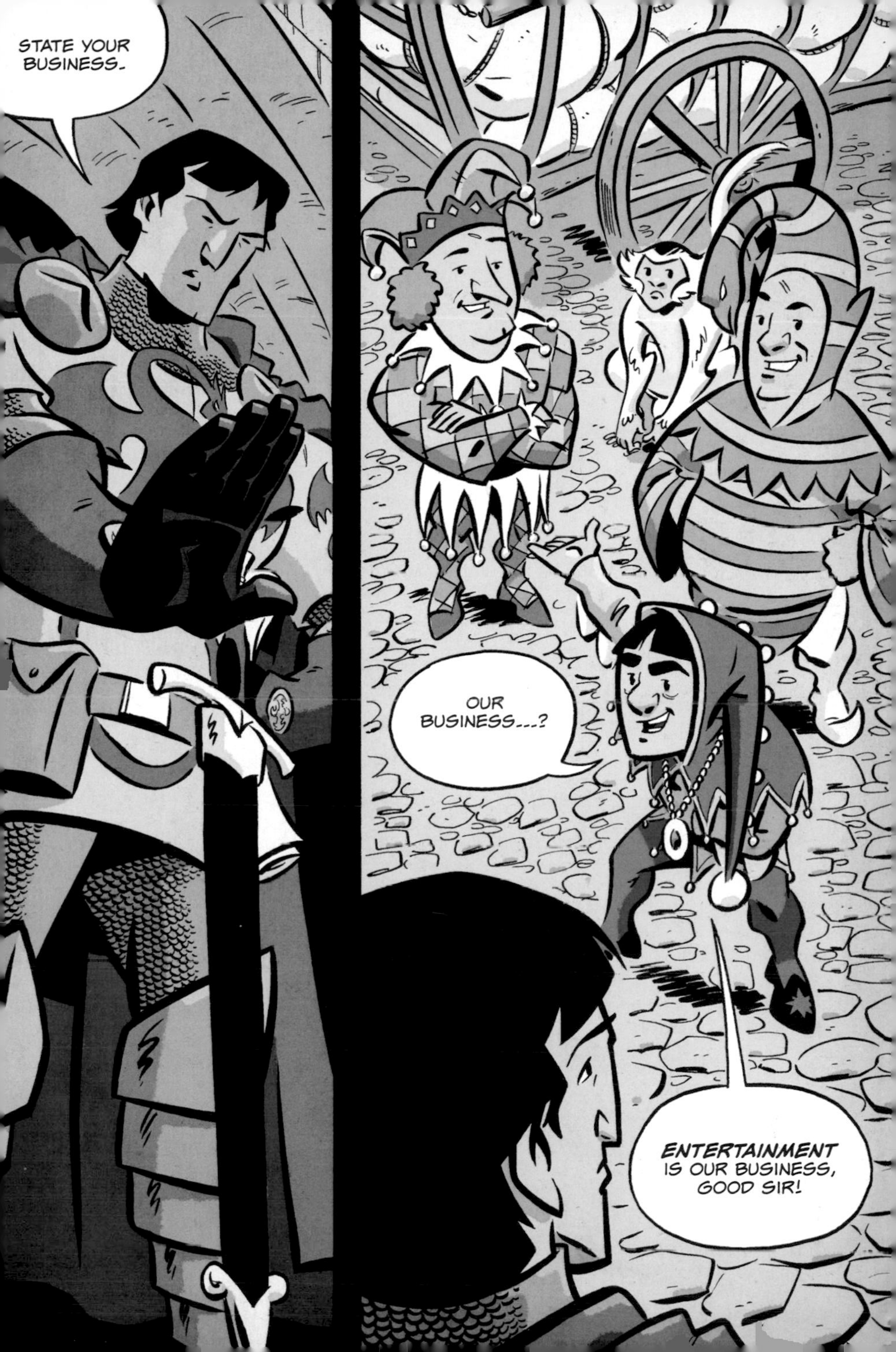
STATE YOUR BUSINESS.
OUR BUSINESS...?
ENTERTAINMENT IS OUR BUSINESS, GOOD SIR!

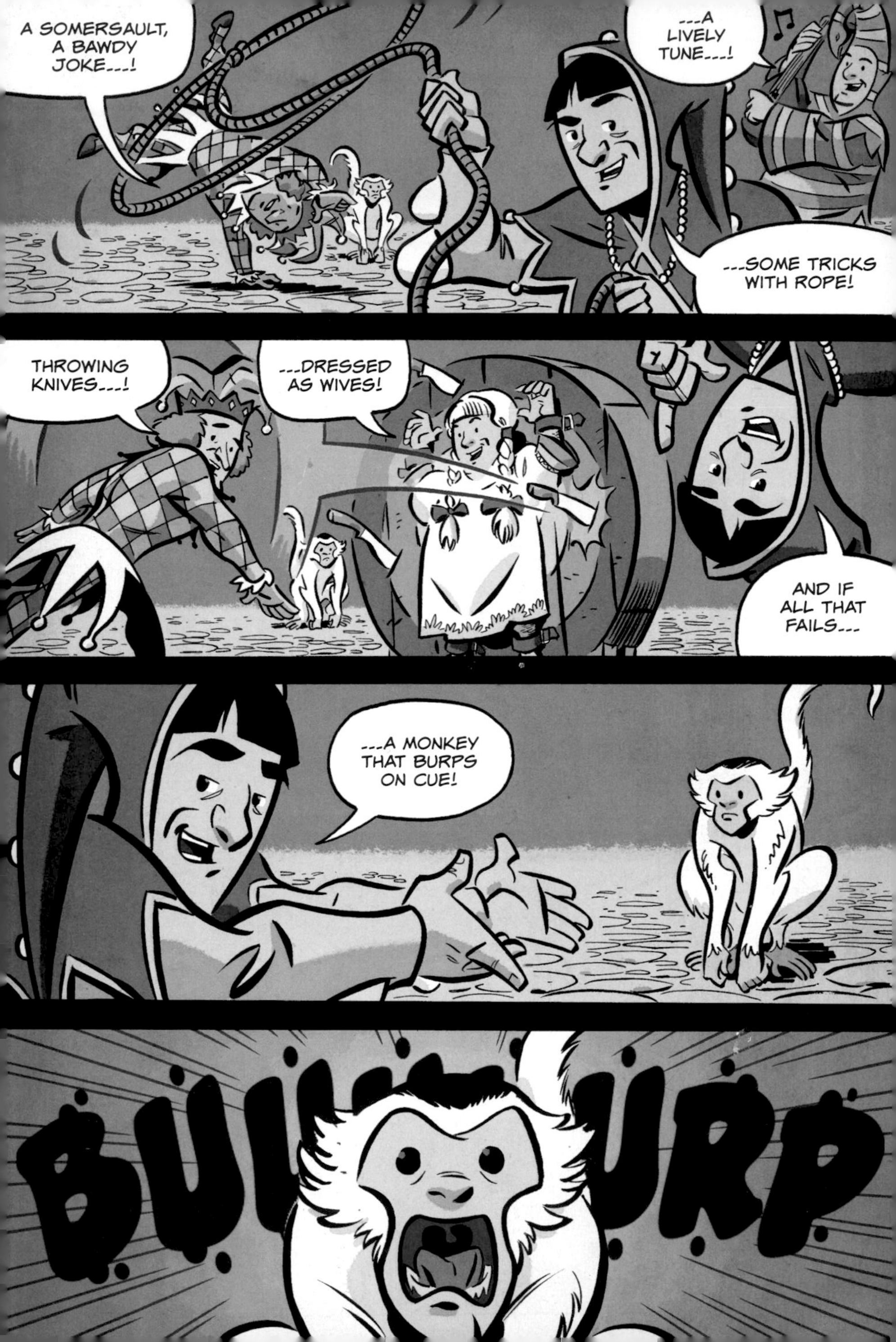
A SOMERSAULT, A BAWDY JOKE...!
...A LIVELY TUNE...!
...SOME TRICKS WITH ROPE!
THROWING KNIVES...!
...DRESSED AS WIVES!
AND IF ALL THAT FAILS...
...A MONKEY THAT BURPS ON CUE!

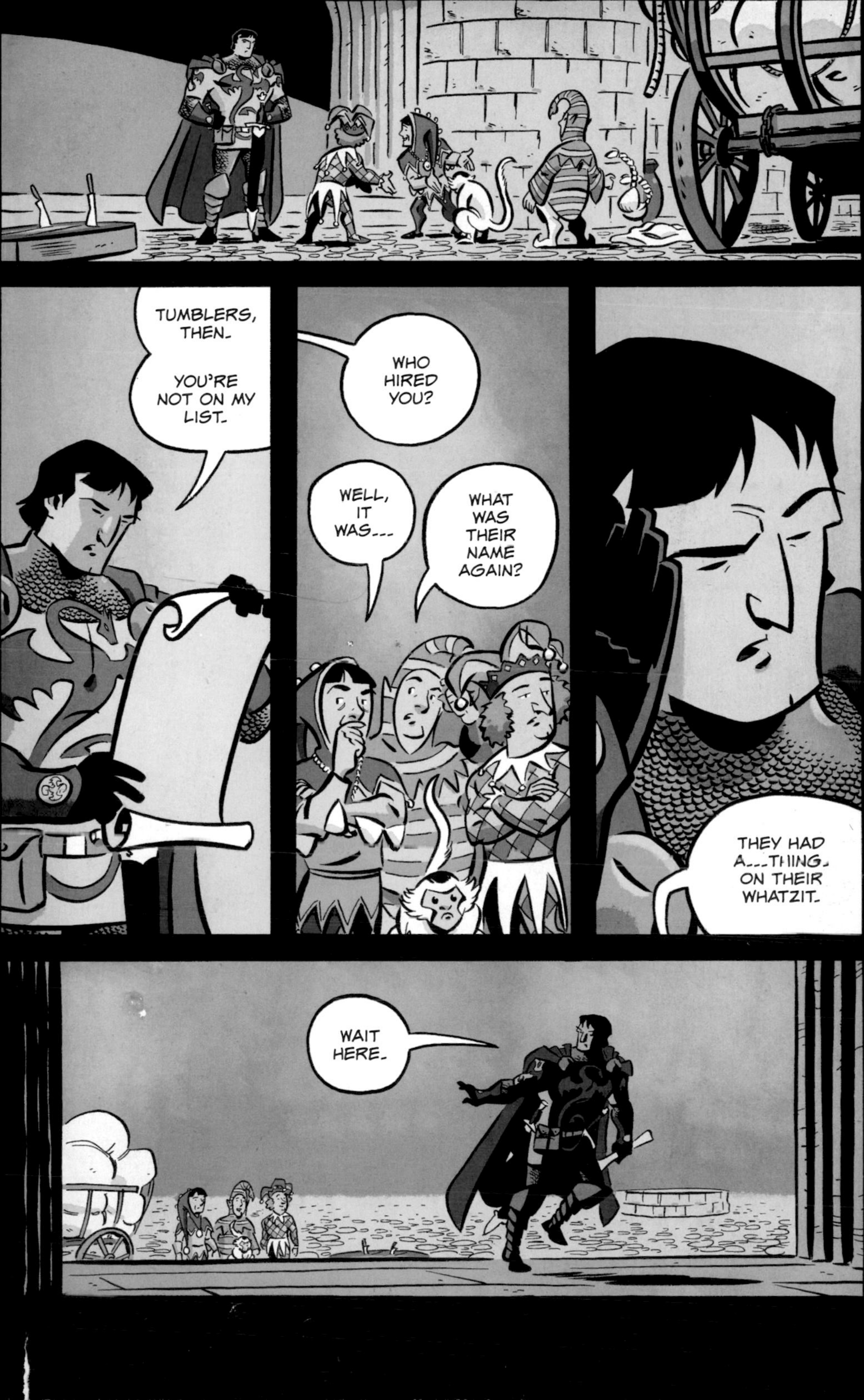
TUMBLERS, THEN.
YOU'RE NOT ON MY LIST.
WHO HIRED YOU?
WELL, IT WAS...
WHAT WAS THEIR NAME AGAIN?
THEY HAD A...THING. ON THEIR WHATZIT.
WAIT HERE.

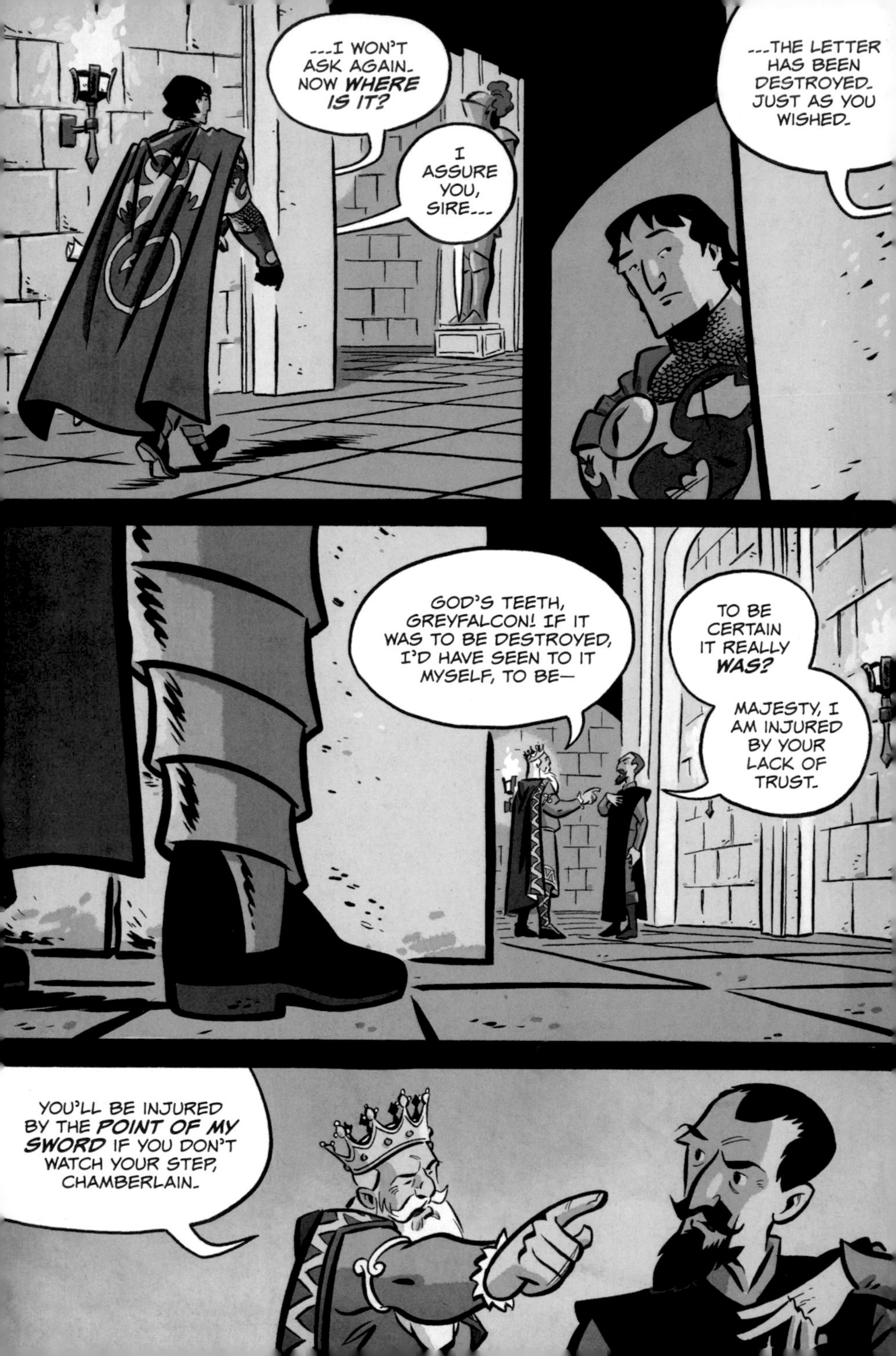
...I WON'T ASK AGAIN. NOW WHERE IS IT?
I ASSURE YOU, SIRE...
...THE LETTER HAS BEEN DESTROYED. JUST AS YOU WISHED.
GOD'S TEETH, GREYFALCON! IF IT WAS TO BE DESTROYED, I'D HAVE SEEN TO IT MYSELF, TO BE—
TO BE CERTAIN IT REALLY WAS?
MAJESTY, I AM INJURED BY YOUR LACK OF TRUST.
YOU'LL BE INJURED BY THE POINT OF MY SWORD IF YOU DON'T WATCH YOUR STEP, CHAMBERLAIN.

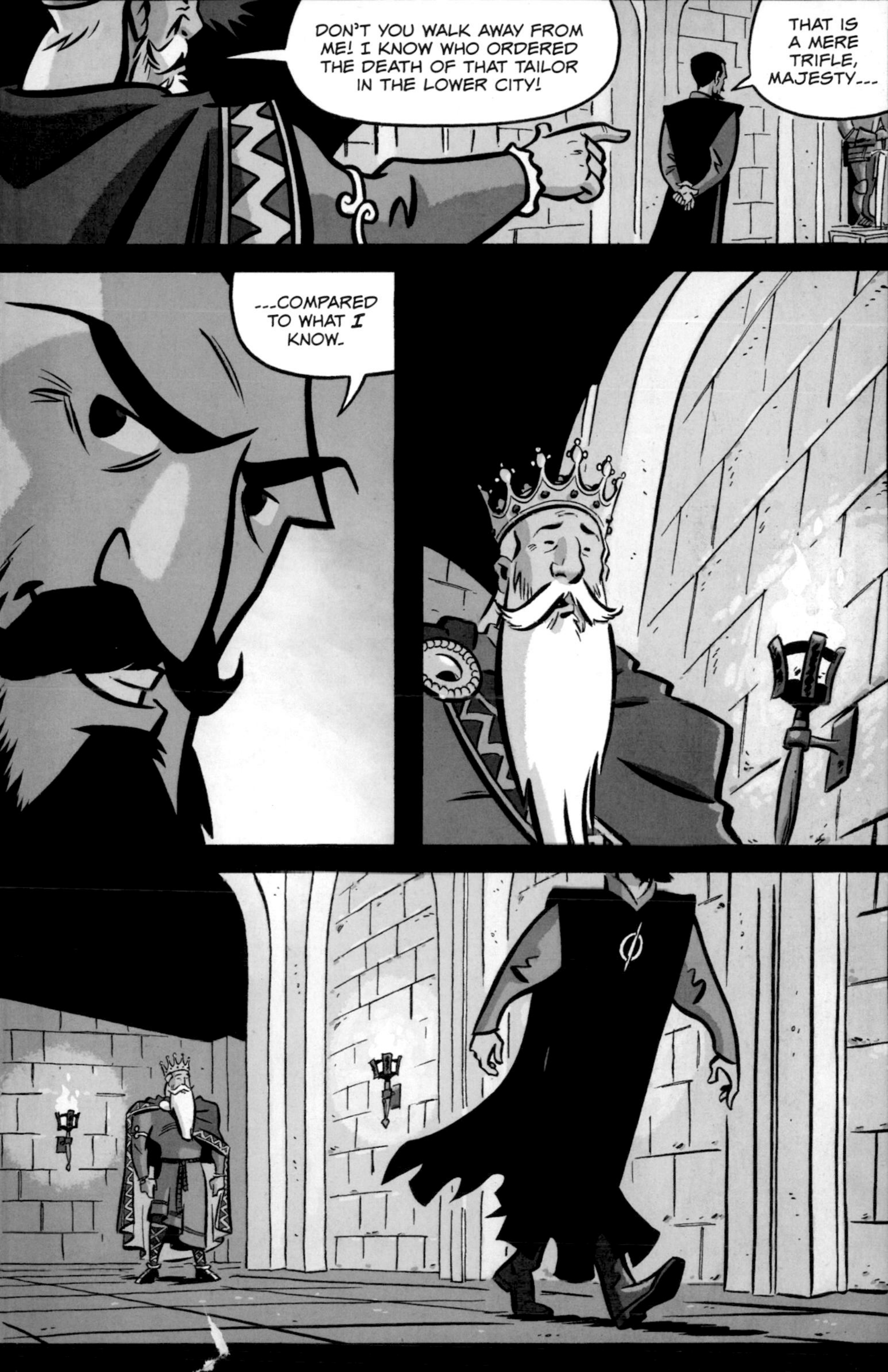
DON'T YOU WALK AWAY FROM ME! I KNOW WHO ORDERED THE DEATH OF THAT TAILOR IN THE LOWER CITY!
THAT IS A MERE TRIFLE, MAJESTY...
...COMPARED TO WHAT I KNOW.

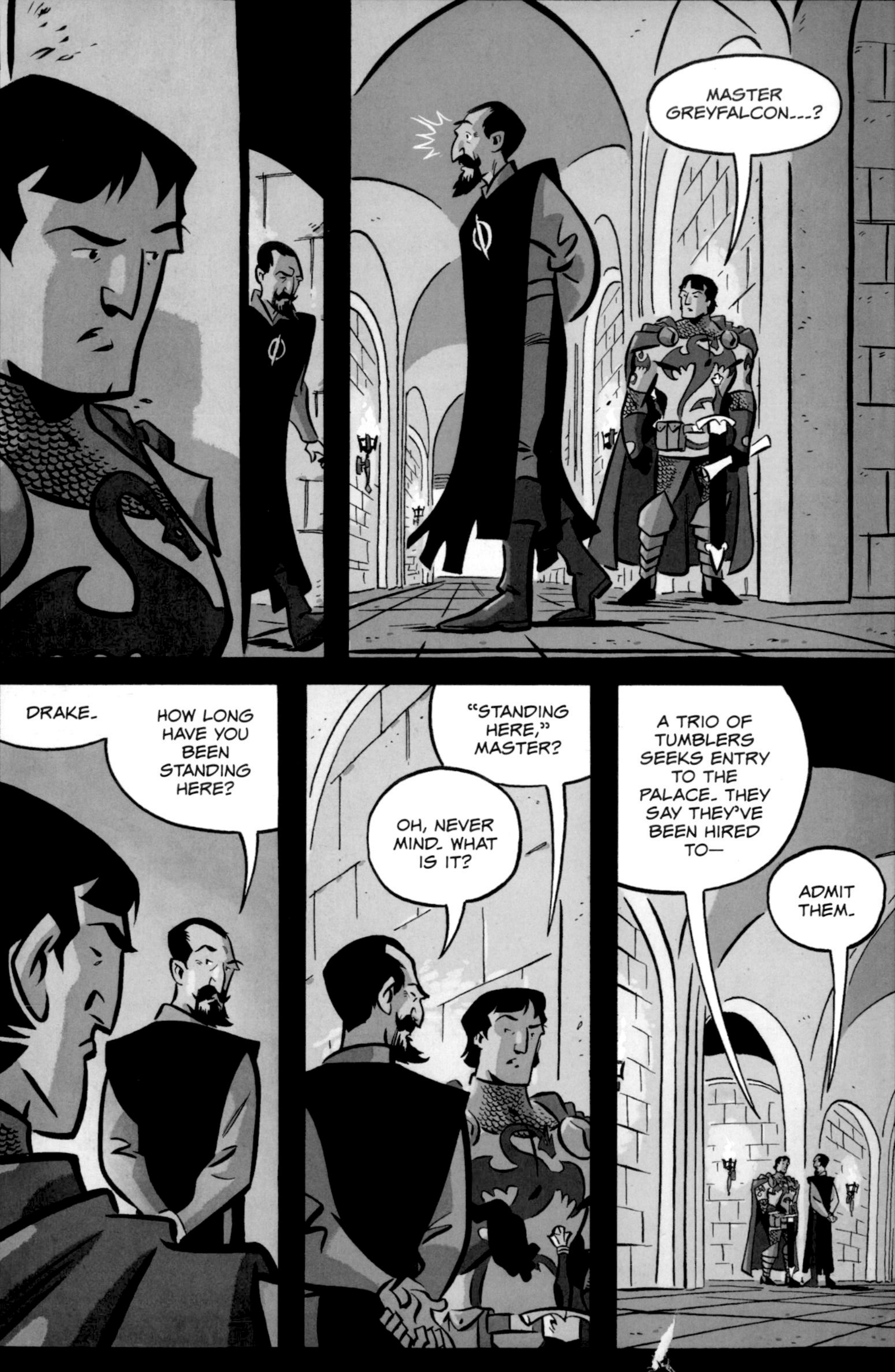
MASTER GREYFALCON...?
DRAKE.
HOW LONG HAVE YOU BEEN STANDING HERE?
"STANDING HERE," MASTER?
OH, NEVER MIND. WHAT IS IT?
A TRIO OF TUMBLERS SEEKS ENTRY TO THE PALACE. THEY SAY THEY'VE BEEN HIRED TO—
ADMIT THEM.

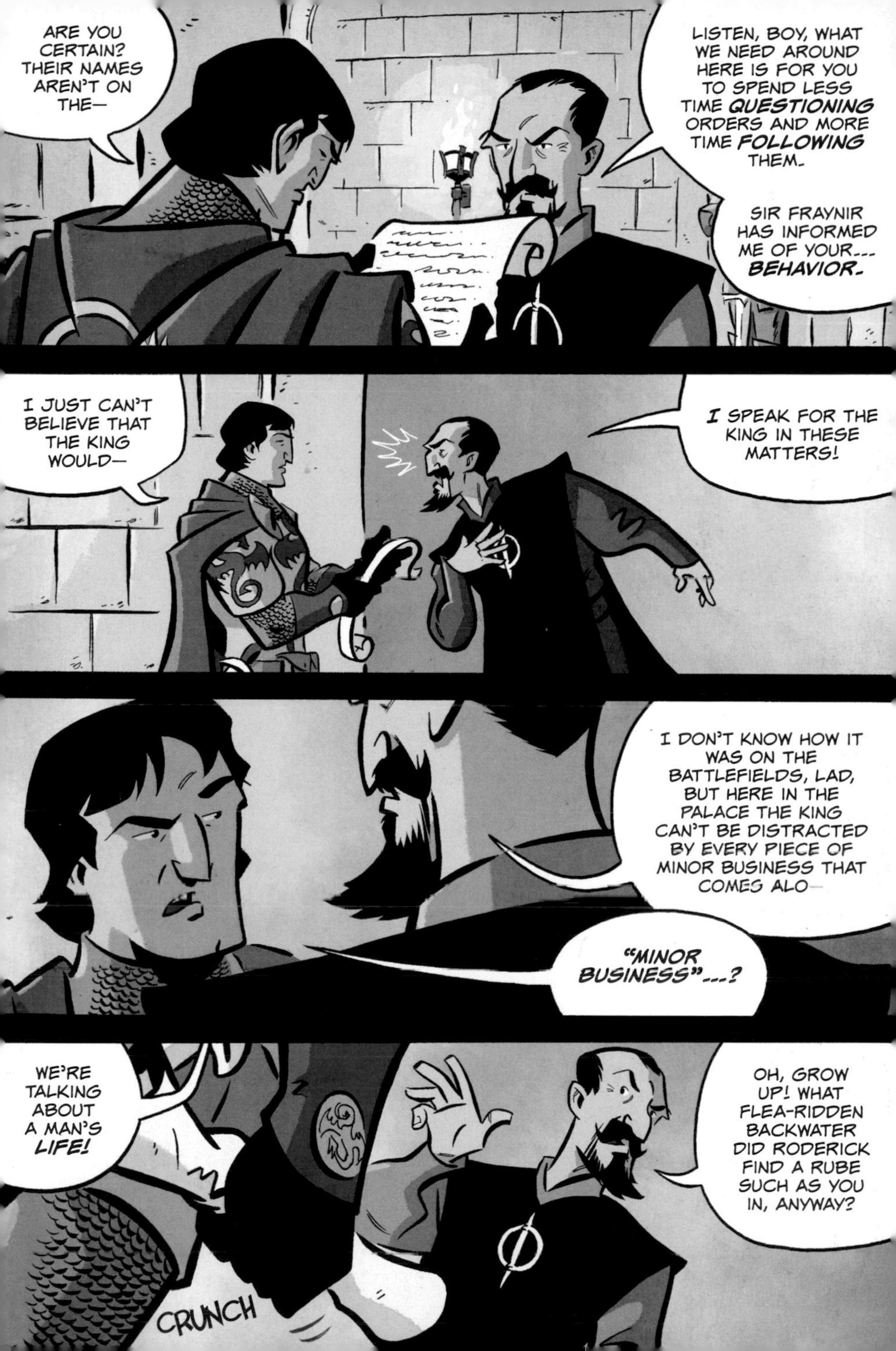
ARE YOU CERTAIN? THEIR NAMES AREN'T ON THE—
LISTEN, BOY, WHAT WE NEED AROUND HERE IS FOR YOU TO SPEND LESS TIME QUESTIONING ORDERS AND MORE TIME FOLLOWING THEM.
SIR FRAYNIR HAS INFORMED ME OF YOUR... BEHAVIOR.
I JUST CAN'T BELIEVE THAT THE KING WOULD—
I SPEAK FOR THE KING IN THESE MATTERS!
I DON'T KNOW HOW IT WAS ON THE BATTLEFIELDS, LAD, BUT HERE IN THE PALACE THE KING CAN'T BE DISTRACTED BY EVERY PIECE OF MINOR BUSINESS THAT COMES ALO—
"MINOR BUSINESS"...?
WE'RE TALKING ABOUT A MAN'S LIFE!
OH, GROW UP! WHAT FLEA-RIDDEN BACKWATER DID RODERICK FIND A RUBE SUCH AS YOU IN, ANYWAY?
CRUNCH

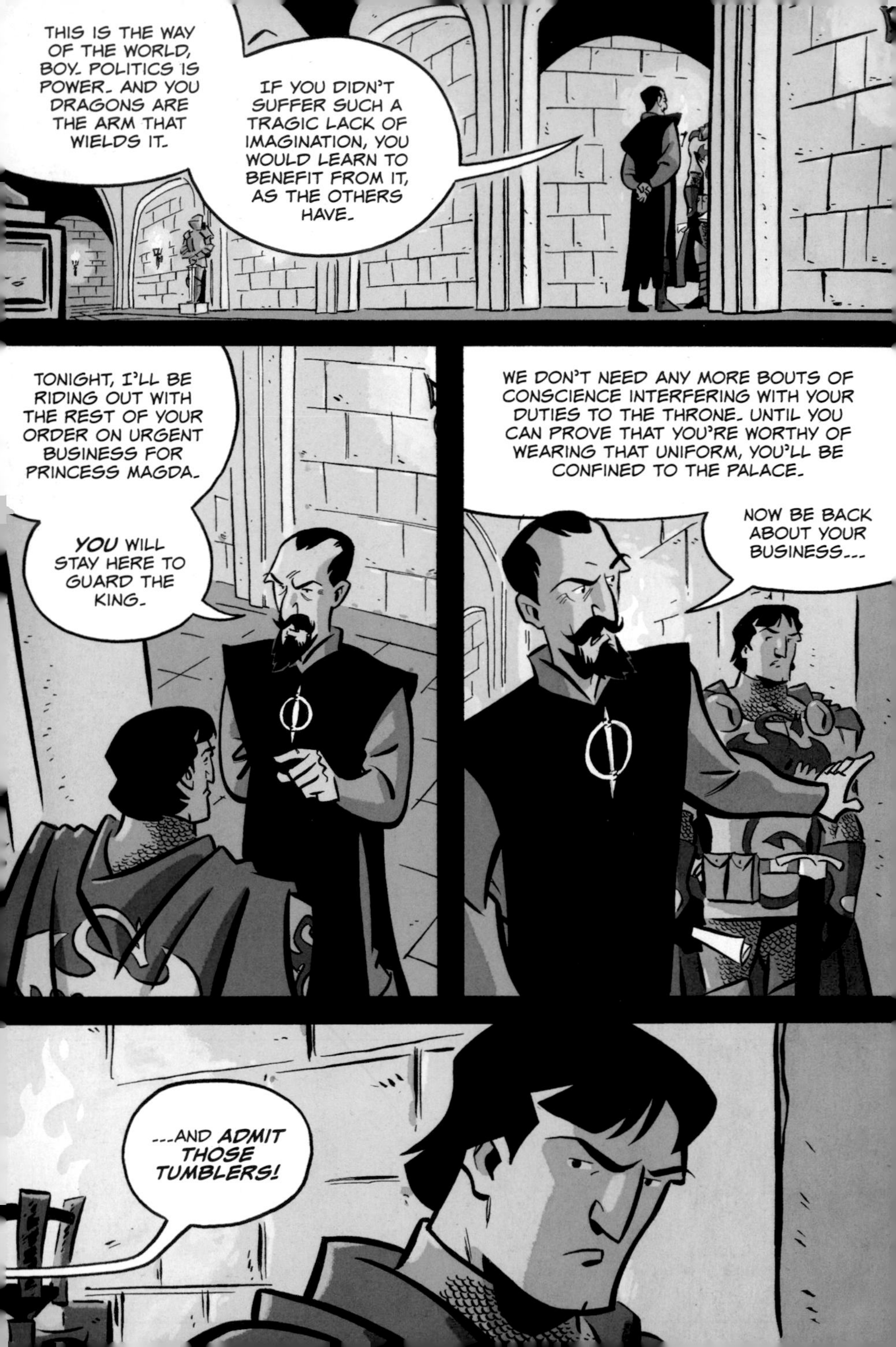
THIS IS THE WAY OF THE WORLD, BOY. POLITICS IS POWER. AND YOU DRAGONS ARE THE ARM THAT WIELDS IT.
IF YOU DIDN'T SUFFER SUCH A TRAGIC LACK OF IMAGINATION, YOU WOULD LEARN TO BENEFIT FROM IT, AS THE OTHERS HAVE.
TONIGHT, I'LL BE RIDING OUT WITH THE REST OF YOUR ORDER ON URGENT BUSINESS FOR PRINCESS MAGDA.
YOU WILL STAY HERE TO GUARD THE KING.
WE DON'T NEED ANY MORE BOUTS OF CONSCIENCE INTERFERING WITH YOUR DUTIES TO THE THRONE. UNTIL YOU CAN PROVE THAT YOU'RE WORTHY OF WEARING THAT UNIFORM, YOU'LL BE CONFINED TO THE PALACE.
NOW BE BACK ABOUT YOUR BUSINESS...
...AND *ADMIT THOSE TUMBLERS!*

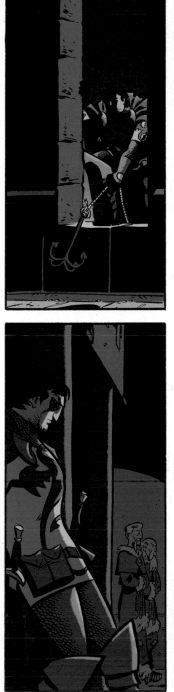

ALL
ALONE,
DRAKE___?

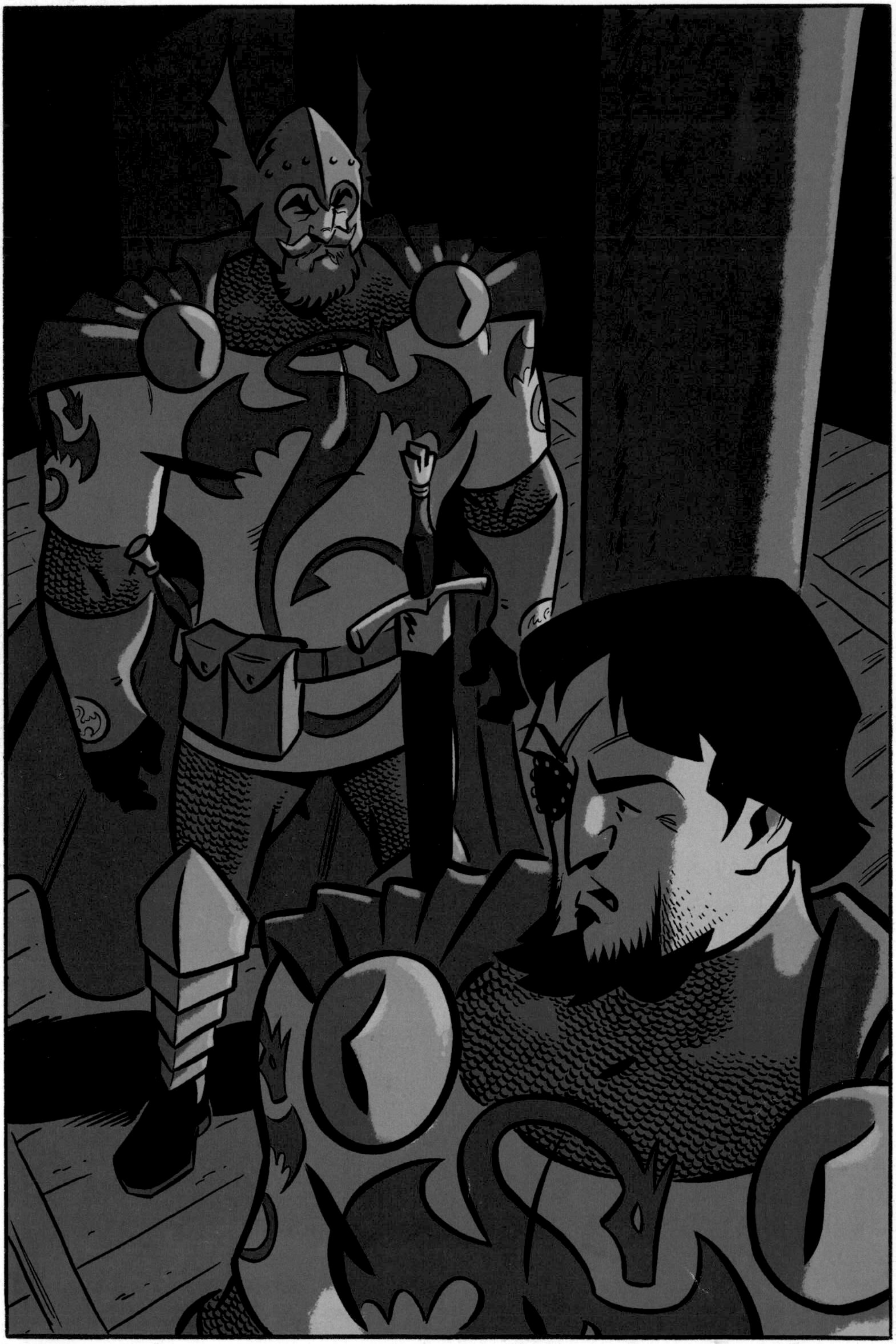

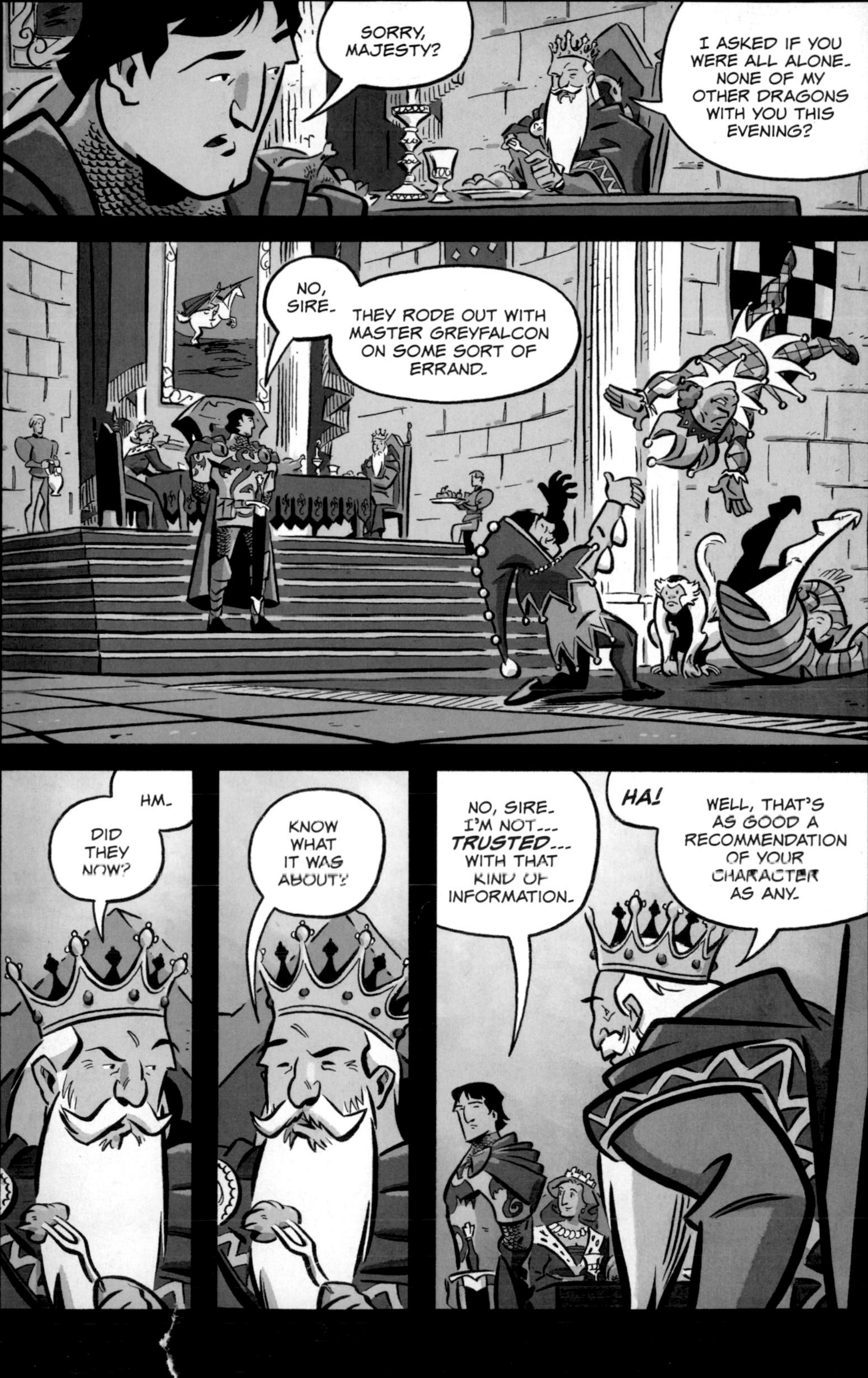
SORRY, MAJESTY?
I ASKED IF YOU WERE ALL ALONE. NONE OF MY OTHER DRAGONS WITH YOU THIS EVENING?
NO, SIRE.
THEY RODE OUT WITH MASTER GREYFALCON ON SOME SORT OF ERRAND.
HM.
DID THEY NOW?
KNOW WHAT IT WAS ABOUT?
NO, SIRE. I'M NOT... TRUSTED... WITH THAT KIND OF INFORMATION.
HA!
WELL, THAT'S AS GOOD A RECOMMENDATION OF YOUR CHARACTER AS ANY.

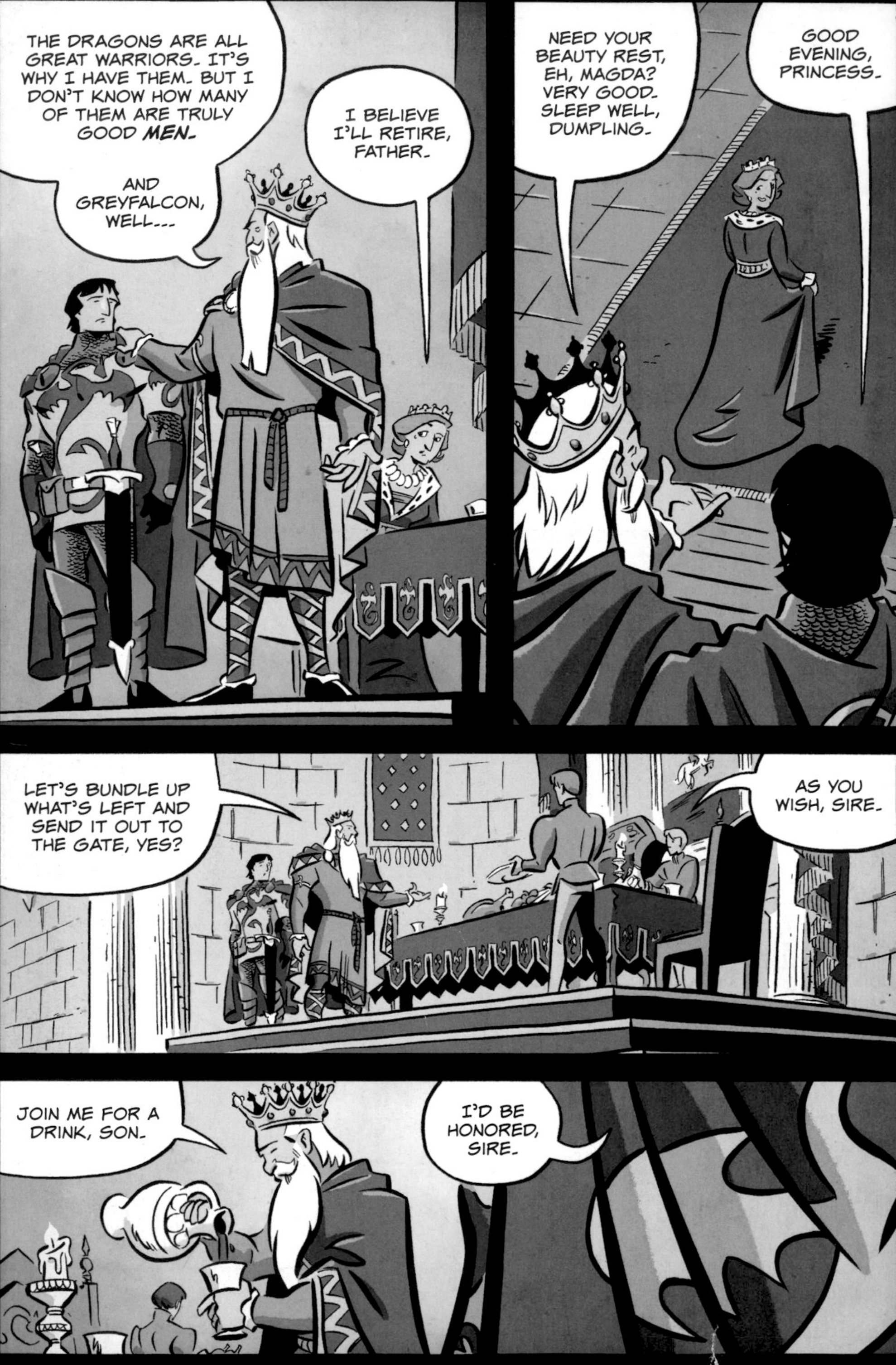
THE DRAGONS ARE ALL GREAT WARRIORS. IT'S WHY I HAVE THEM. BUT I DON'T KNOW HOW MANY OF THEM ARE TRULY GOOD MEN.
AND GREYFALCON, WELL...
I BELIEVE I'LL RETIRE, FATHER.
NEED YOUR BEAUTY REST, EH, MAGDA? VERY GOOD. SLEEP WELL, DUMPLING.
GOOD EVENING, PRINCESS.
LET'S BUNDLE UP WHAT'S LEFT AND SEND IT OUT TO THE GATE, YES?
AS YOU WISH, SIRE.
JOIN ME FOR A DRINK, SON.
I'D BE HONORED, SIRE.

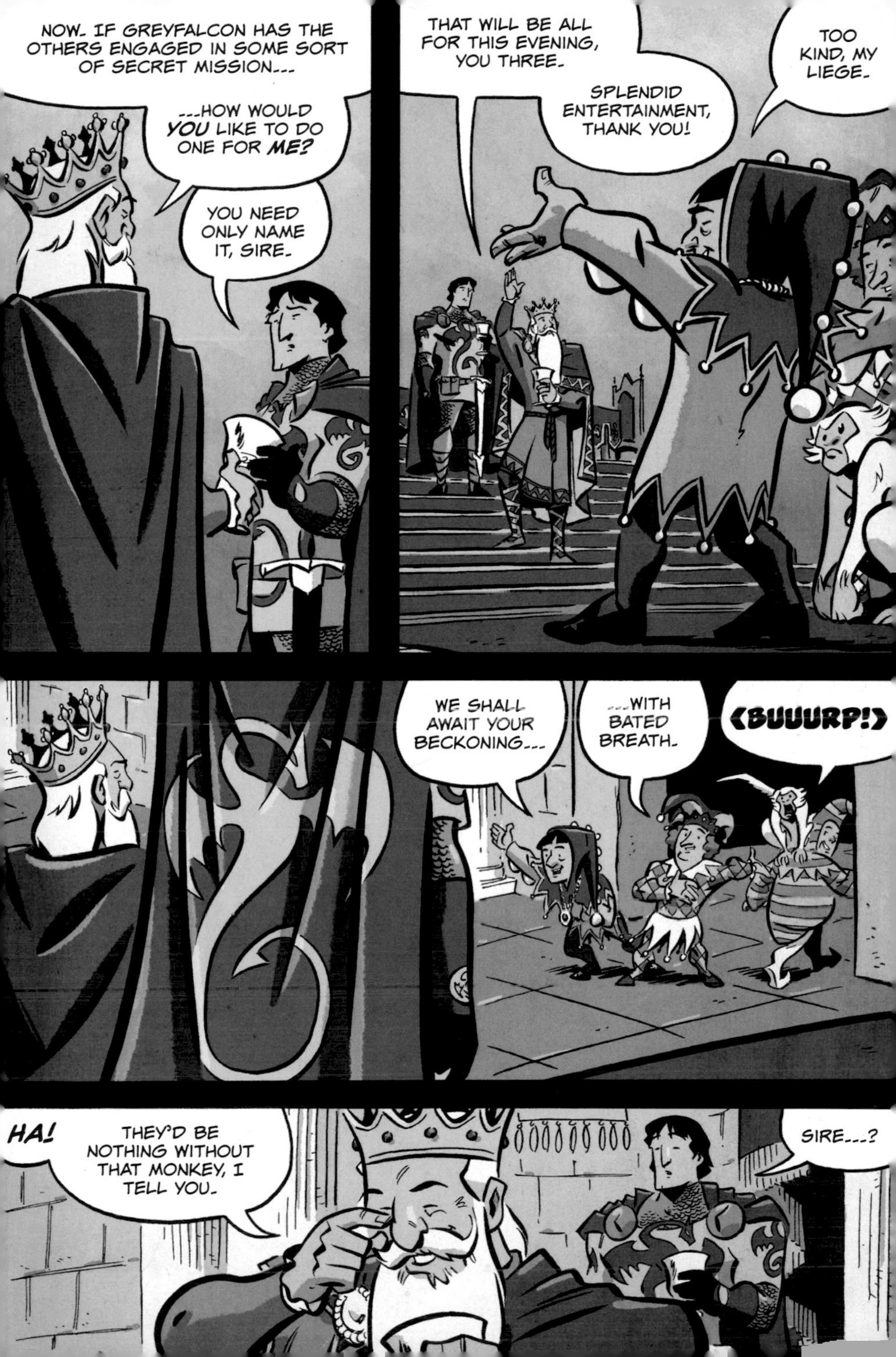
NOW. IF GREYFALCON HAS THE OTHERS ENGAGED IN SOME SORT OF SECRET MISSION...
...HOW WOULD *YOU* LIKE TO DO ONE FOR *ME?*
YOU NEED ONLY NAME IT, SIRE.
THAT WILL BE ALL FOR THIS EVENING, YOU THREE.
SPLENDID ENTERTAINMENT, THANK YOU!
TOO KIND, MY LIEGE.
WE SHALL AWAIT YOUR BECKONING...
...WITH BATED BREATH.
<BUUURP!>
HA!
THEY'D BE NOTHING WITHOUT THAT MONKEY, I TELL YOU.
SIRE...?

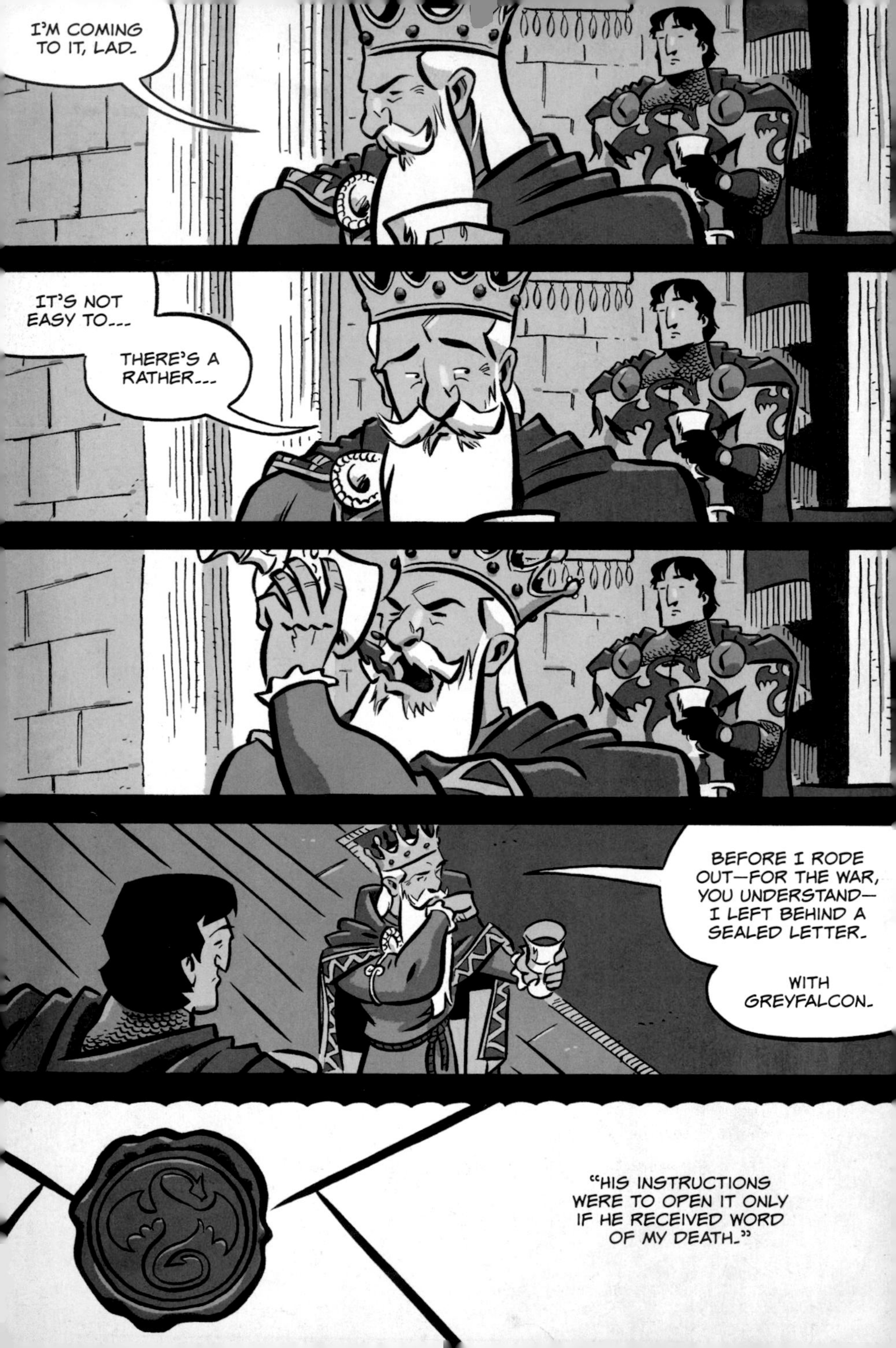
I'M COMING TO IT, LAD.
IT'S NOT EASY TO...
THERE'S A RATHER...
BEFORE I RODE OUT—FOR THE WAR, YOU UNDERSTAND—I LEFT BEHIND A SEALED LETTER.
WITH GREYFALCON.
"HIS INSTRUCTIONS WERE TO OPEN IT ONLY IF HE RECEIVED WORD OF MY DEATH."

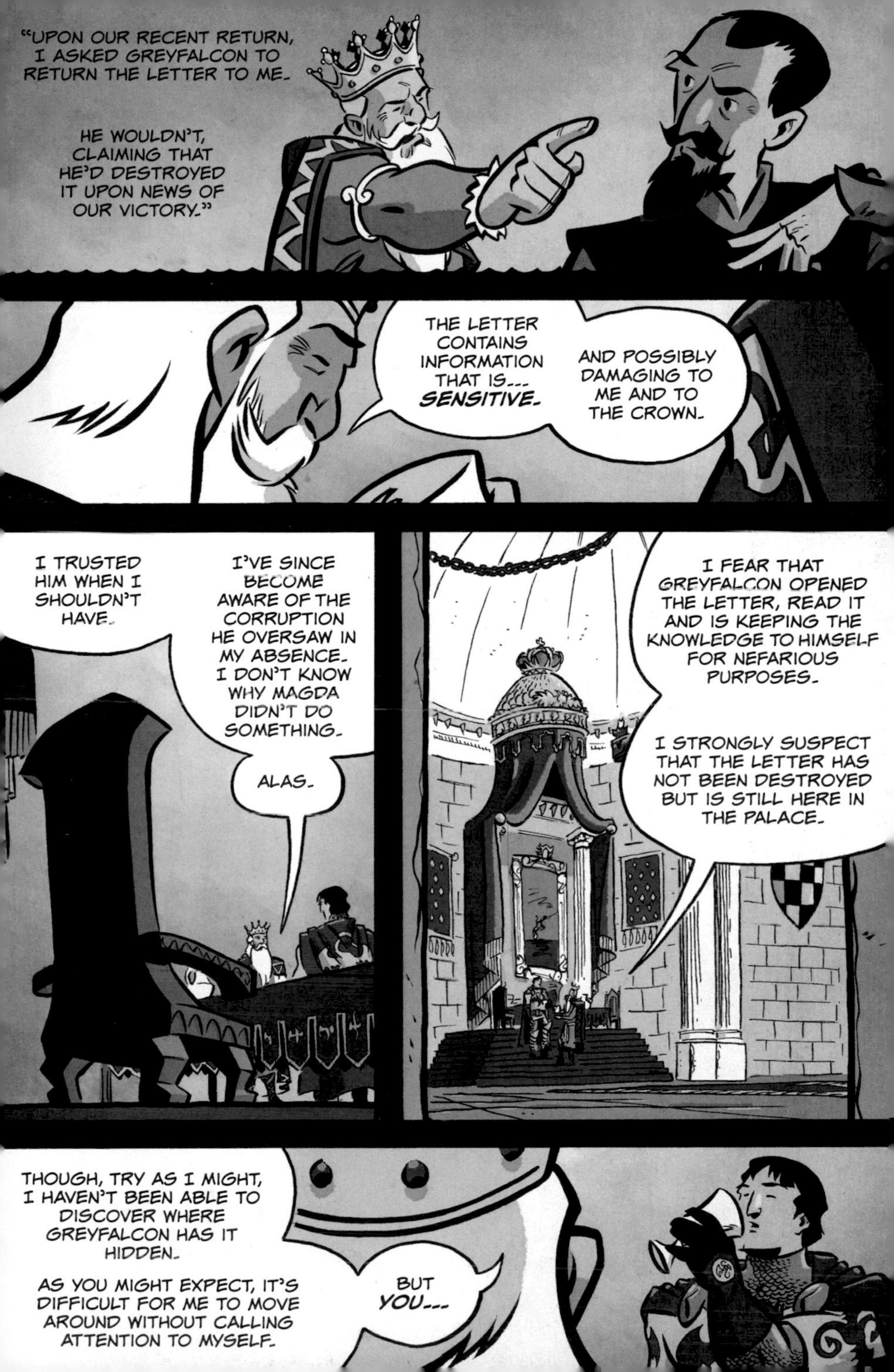
"UPON OUR RECENT RETURN, I ASKED GREYFALCON TO RETURN THE LETTER TO ME.
HE WOULDN'T, CLAIMING THAT HE'D DESTROYED IT UPON NEWS OF OUR VICTORY."
THE LETTER CONTAINS INFORMATION THAT IS... SENSITIVE.
AND POSSIBLY DAMAGING TO ME AND TO THE CROWN.
I TRUSTED HIM WHEN I SHOULDN'T HAVE.
I'VE SINCE BECOME AWARE OF THE CORRUPTION HE OVERSAW IN MY ABSENCE. I DON'T KNOW WHY MAGDA DIDN'T DO SOMETHING.
ALAS.
I FEAR THAT GREYFALCON OPENED THE LETTER, READ IT AND IS KEEPING THE KNOWLEDGE TO HIMSELF FOR NEFARIOUS PURPOSES.
I STRONGLY SUSPECT THAT THE LETTER HAS NOT BEEN DESTROYED BUT IS STILL HERE IN THE PALACE.
THOUGH, TRY AS I MIGHT, I HAVEN'T BEEN ABLE TO DISCOVER WHERE GREYFALCON HAS IT HIDDEN.
AS YOU MIGHT EXPECT, IT'S DIFFICULT FOR ME TO MOVE AROUND WITHOUT CALLING ATTENTION TO MYSELF.
BUT YOU...

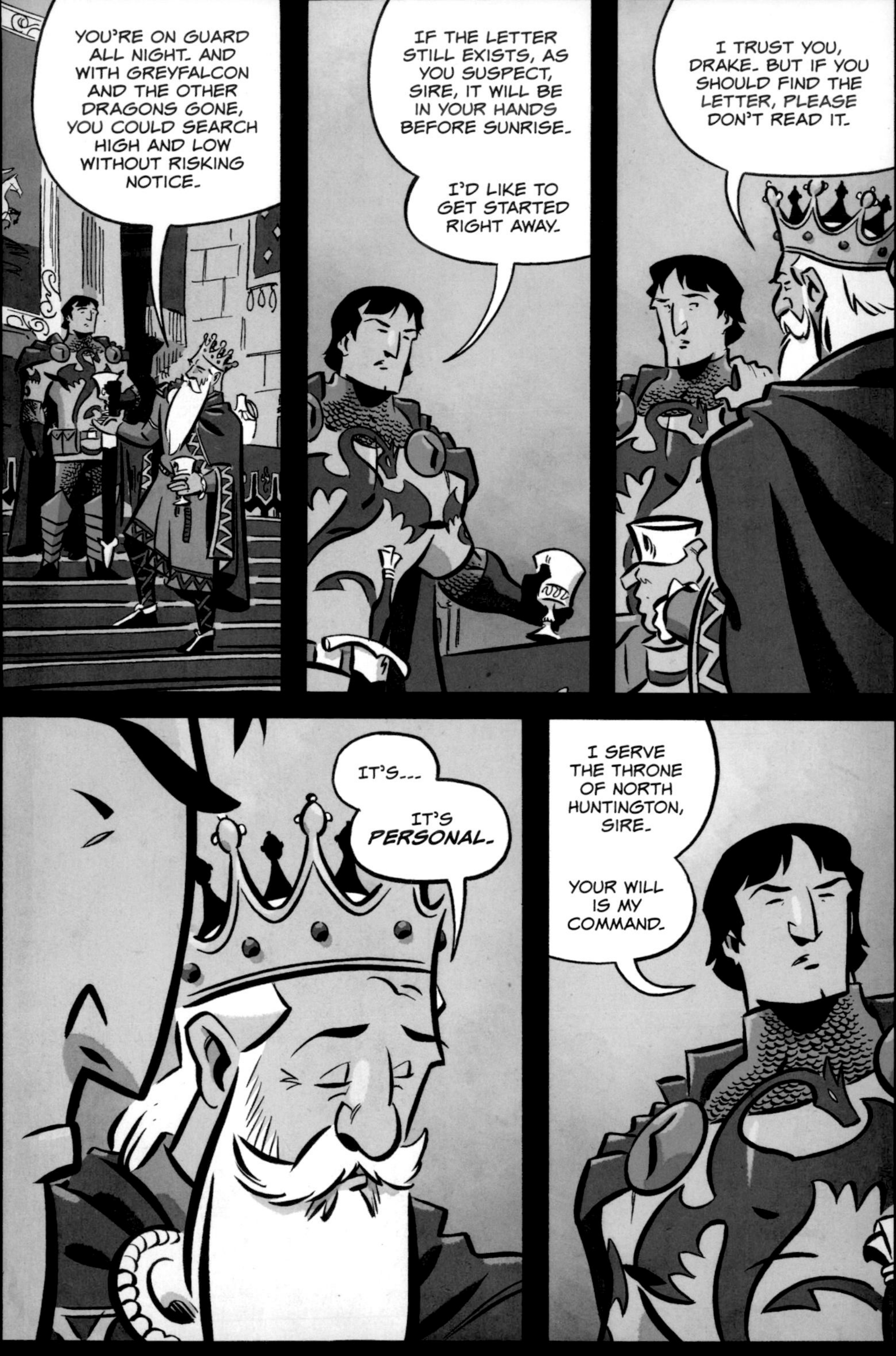
YOU'RE ON GUARD ALL NIGHT. AND WITH GREYFALCON AND THE OTHER DRAGONS GONE, YOU COULD SEARCH HIGH AND LOW WITHOUT RISKING NOTICE.
IF THE LETTER STILL EXISTS, AS YOU SUSPECT, SIRE, IT WILL BE IN YOUR HANDS BEFORE SUNRISE.
I'D LIKE TO GET STARTED RIGHT AWAY.
I TRUST YOU, DRAKE. BUT IF YOU SHOULD FIND THE LETTER, PLEASE DON'T READ IT.
IT'S...
IT'S PERSONAL.
I SERVE THE THRONE OF NORTH HUNTINGTON, SIRE.
YOUR WILL IS MY COMMAND.

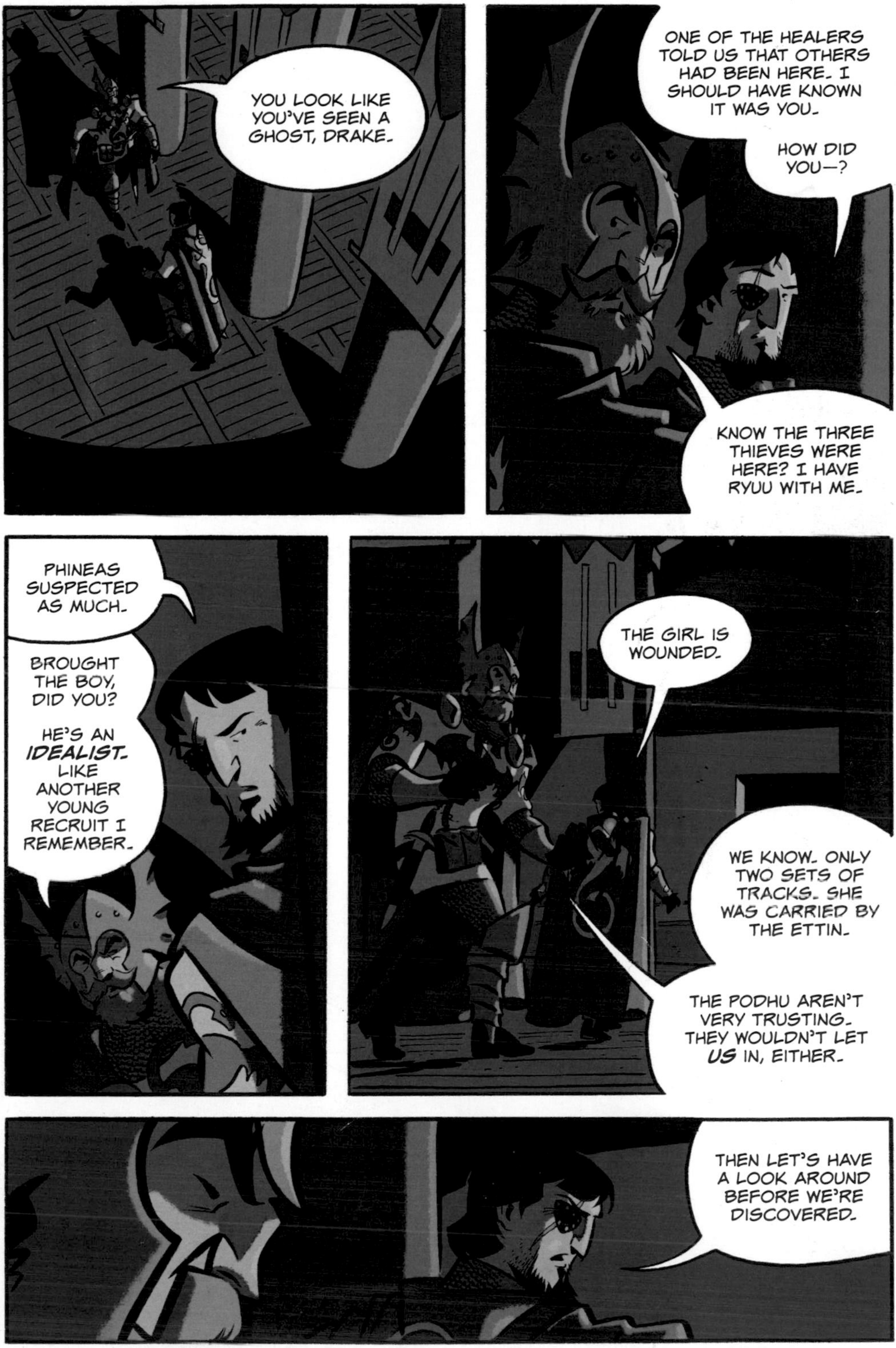
YOU LOOK LIKE YOU'VE SEEN A GHOST, DRAKE.
ONE OF THE HEALERS TOLD US THAT OTHERS HAD BEEN HERE. I SHOULD HAVE KNOWN IT WAS YOU.
HOW DID YOU—?
KNOW THE THREE THIEVES WERE HERE? I HAVE RYUU WITH ME.
PHINEAS SUSPECTED AS MUCH.
BROUGHT THE BOY, DID YOU?
HE'S AN *IDEALIST.* LIKE ANOTHER YOUNG RECRUIT I REMEMBER.
THE GIRL IS WOUNDED.
WE KNOW. ONLY TWO SETS OF TRACKS. SHE WAS CARRIED BY THE ETTIN.
THE PODHU AREN'T VERY TRUSTING. THEY WOULDN'T LET *US* IN, EITHER.
THEN LET'S HAVE A LOOK AROUND BEFORE WE'RE DISCOVERED.

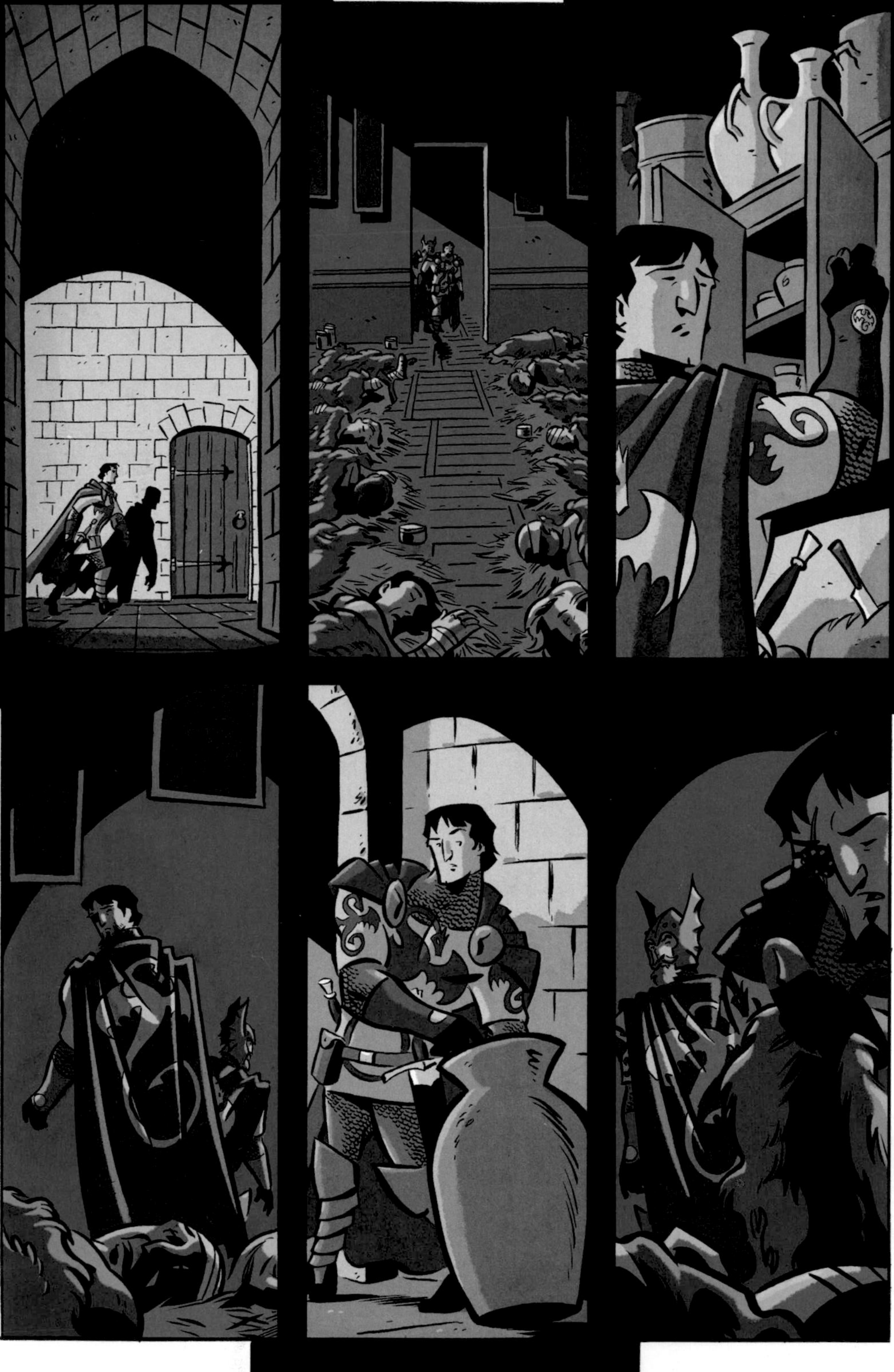

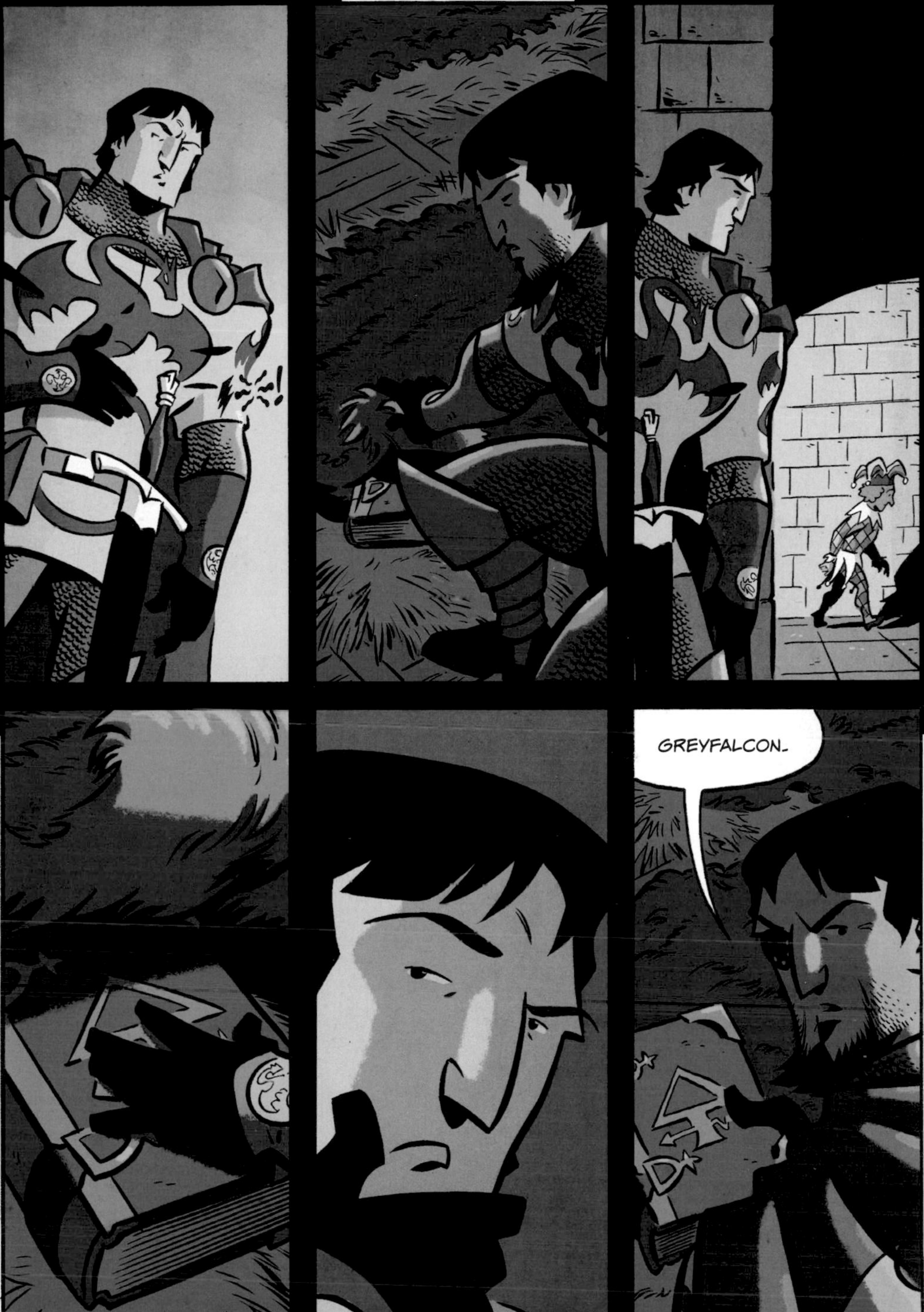
GREYFALCON.

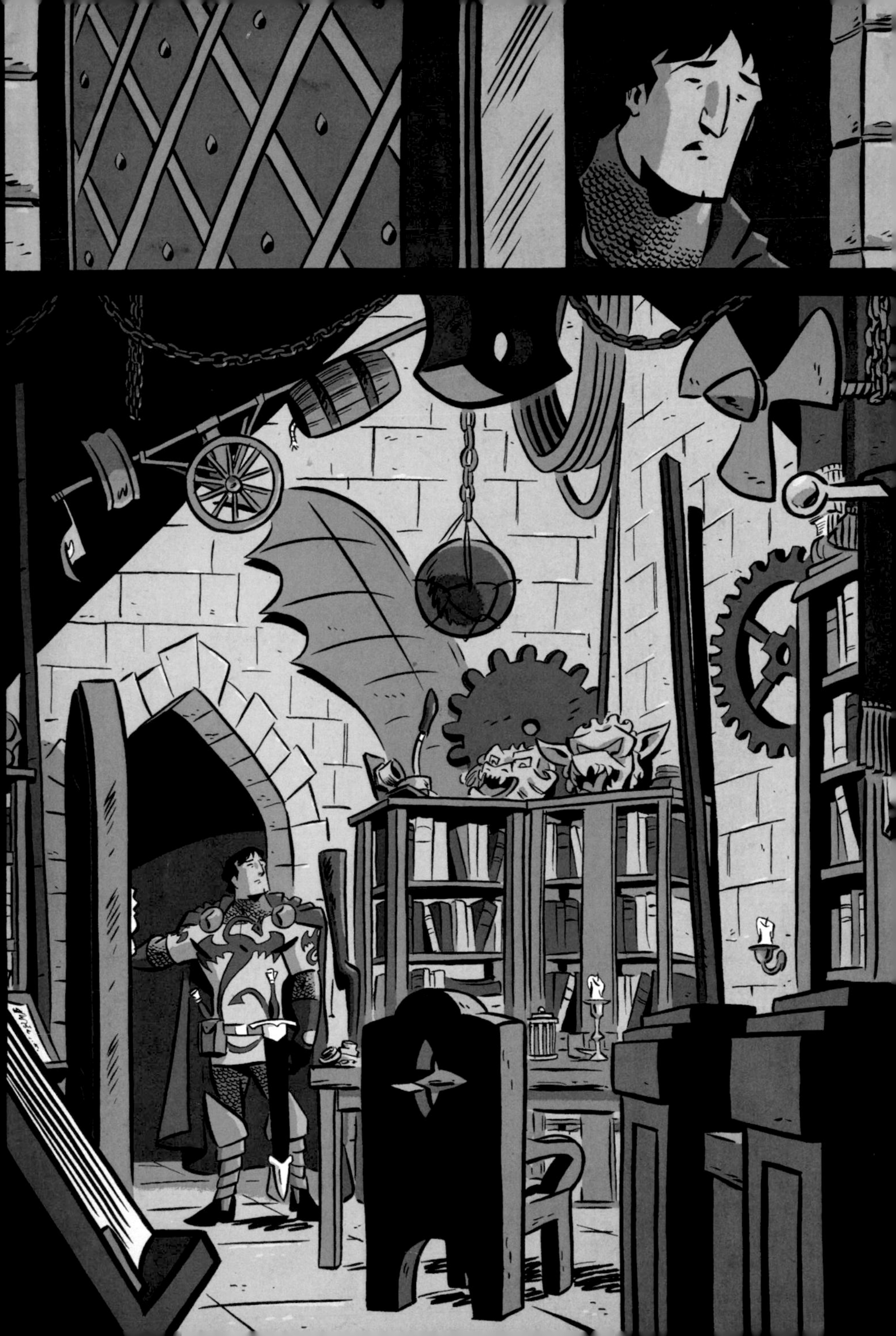

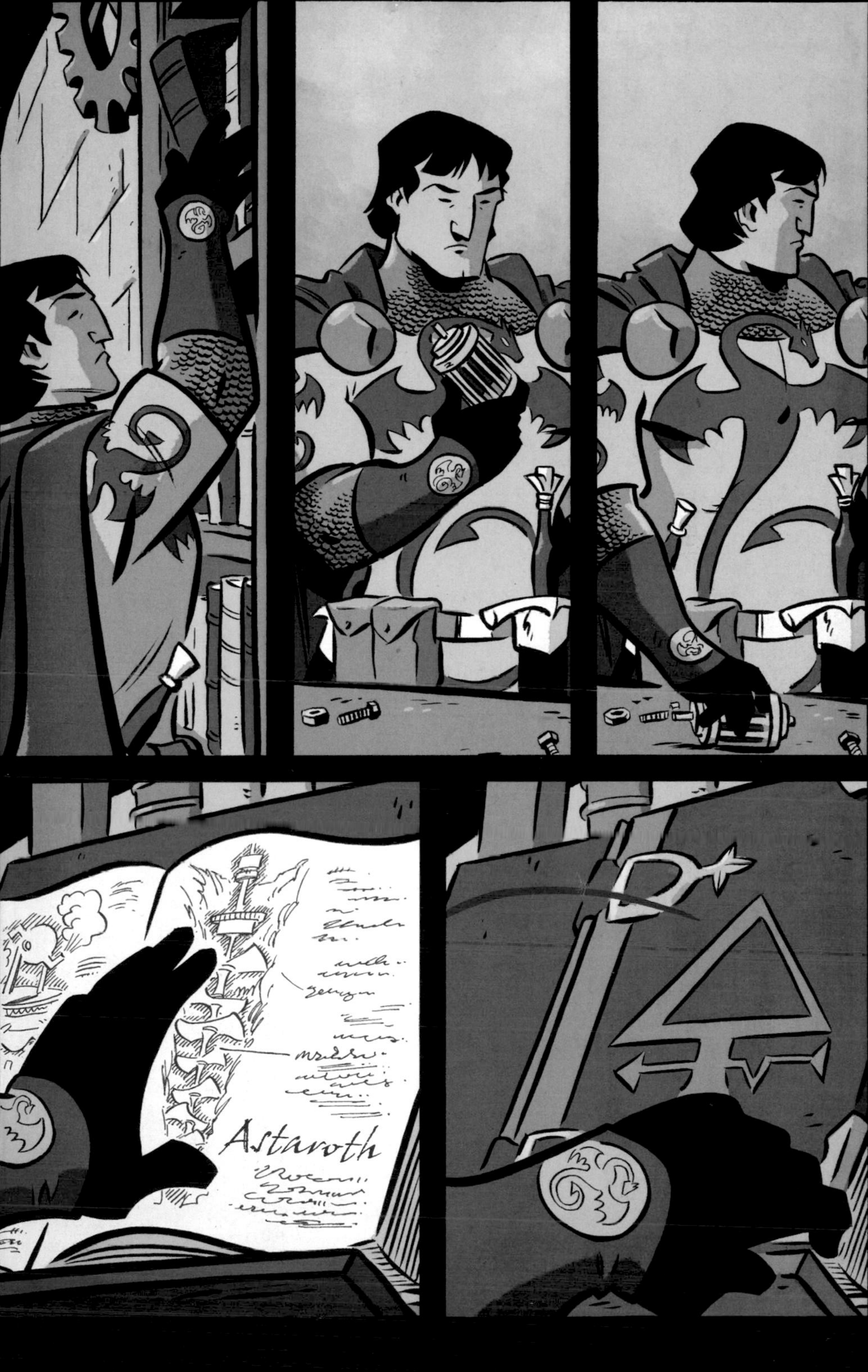
Astaroth

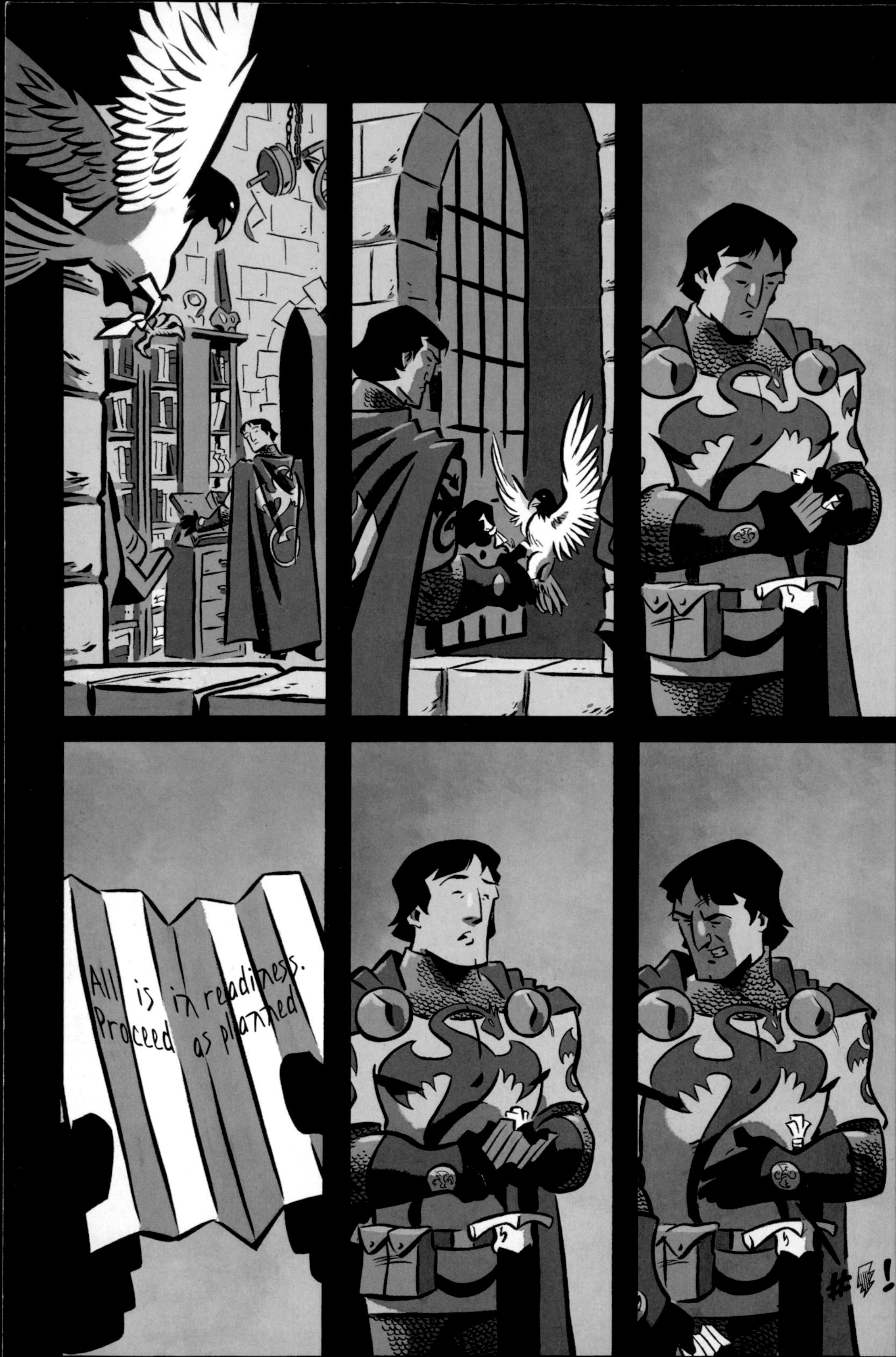
All is in readiness.
Proceed as planned

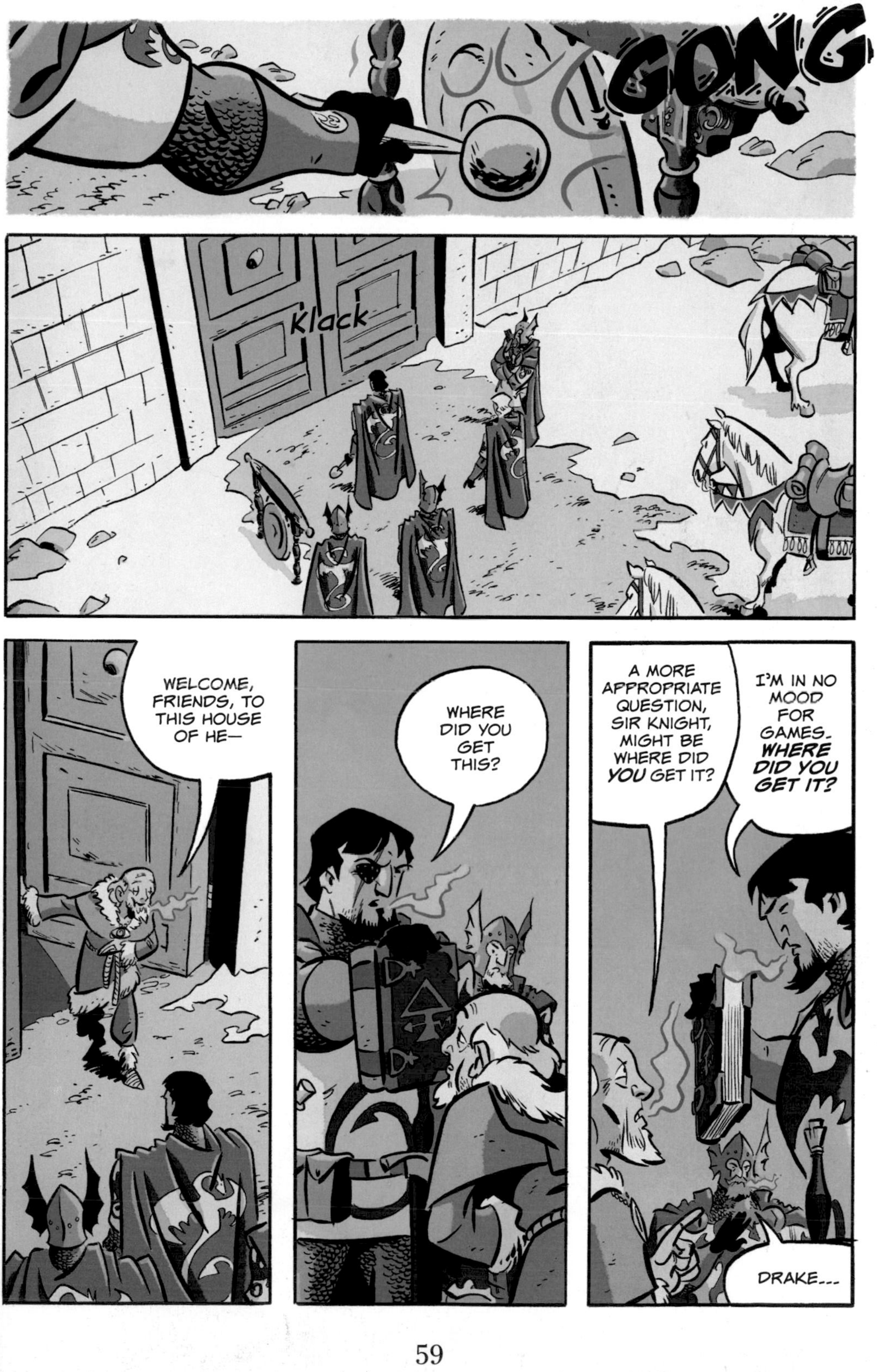
GONG
Klack
WELCOME, FRIENDS, TO THIS HOUSE OF HE—
WHERE DID YOU GET THIS?
A MORE APPROPRIATE QUESTION, SIR KNIGHT, MIGHT BE WHERE DID YOU GET IT?
I'M IN NO MOOD FOR GAMES. WHERE DID YOU GET IT?
DRAKE...

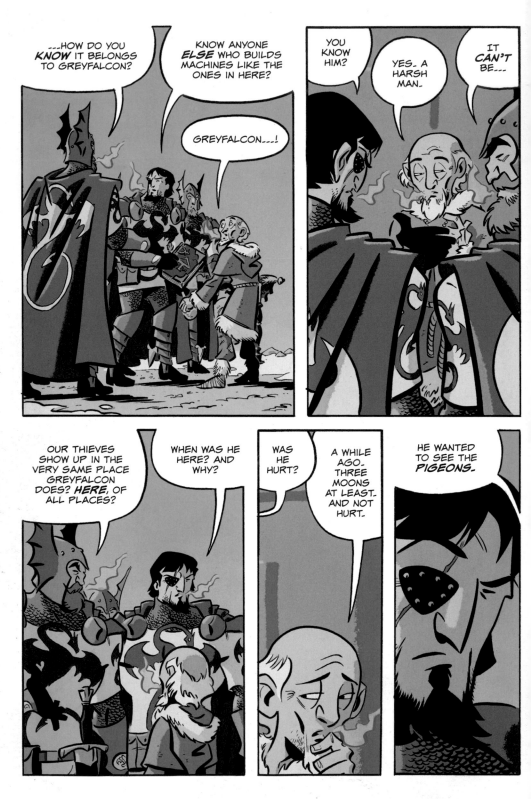

---HOW DO YOU **KNOW** IT BELONGS TO GREYFALCON?

KNOW ANYONE **ELSE** WHO BUILDS MACHINES LIKE THE ONES IN HERE?

GREYFALCON...!

YOU KNOW HIM?

YES. A HARSH MAN.

IT **CAN'T** BE...

OUR THIEVES SHOW UP IN THE VERY SAME PLACE GREYFALCON DOES? **HERE**, OF ALL PLACES?

WHEN WAS HE HERE? AND WHY?

WAS HE HURT?

A WHILE AGO. THREE MOONS AT LEAST. AND NOT HURT.

HE WANTED TO SEE THE **PIGEONS.**

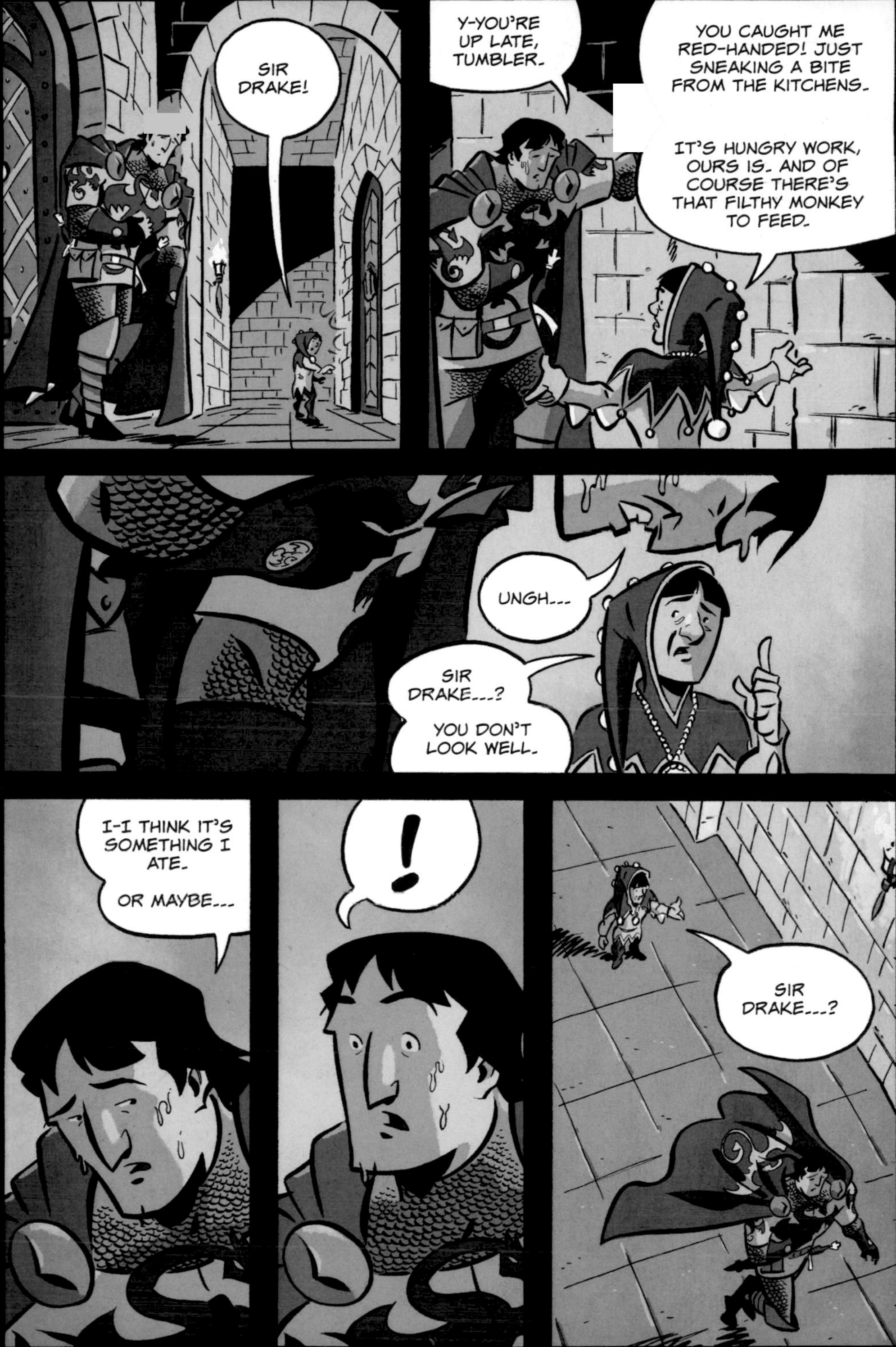
SIR DRAKE!
Y-YOU'RE UP LATE, TUMBLER.
YOU CAUGHT ME RED-HANDED! JUST SNEAKING A BITE FROM THE KITCHENS.
IT'S HUNGRY WORK, OURS IS. AND OF COURSE THERE'S THAT FILTHY MONKEY TO FEED.
UNGH...
SIR DRAKE...?
YOU DON'T LOOK WELL.
I-I THINK IT'S SOMETHING I ATE.
OR MAYBE...
!
SIR DRAKE...?

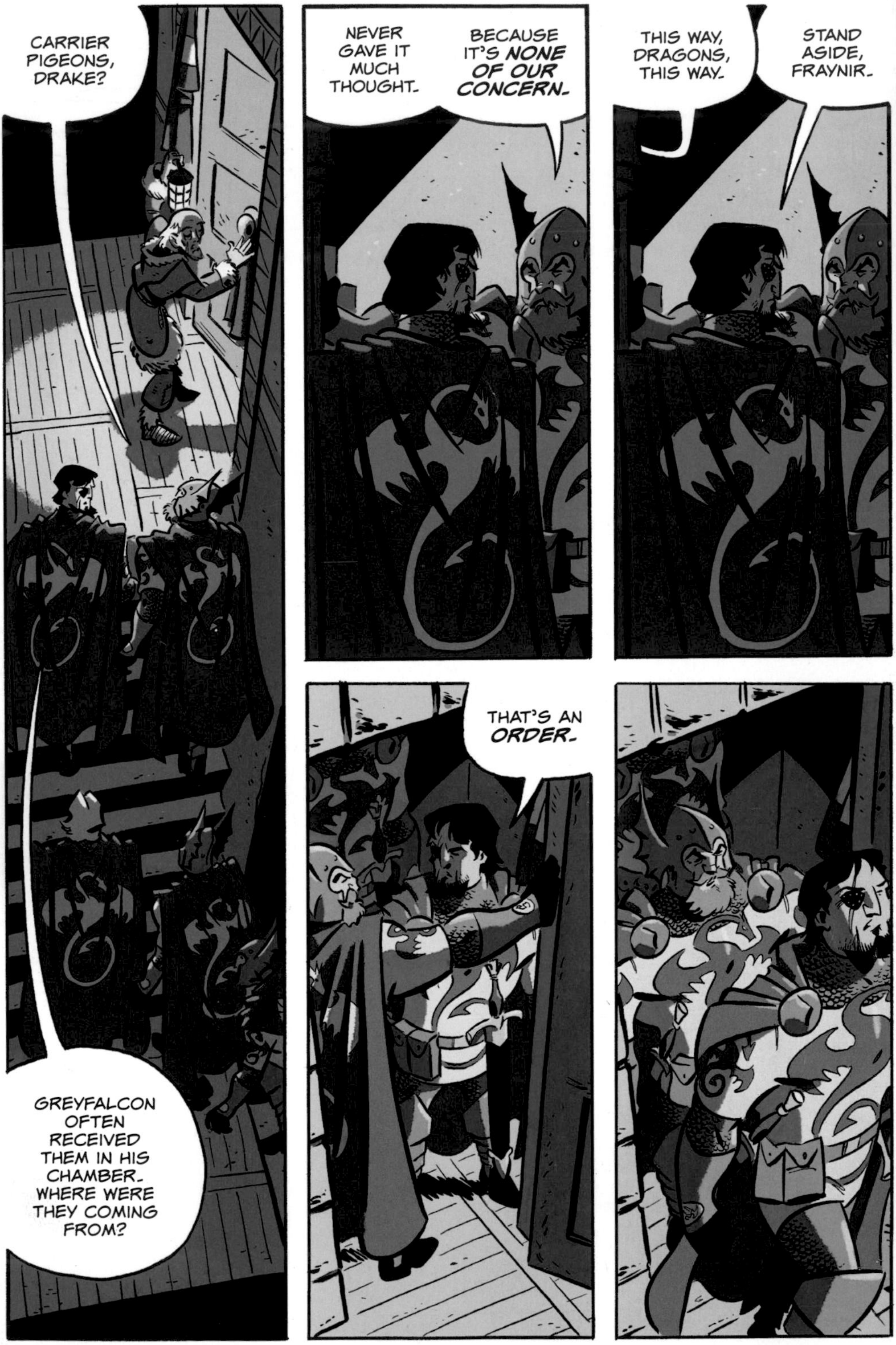

CARRIER PIGEONS, DRAKE?
GREYFALCON OFTEN RECEIVED THEM IN HIS CHAMBER. WHERE WERE THEY COMING FROM?
NEVER GAVE IT MUCH THOUGHT.
BECAUSE IT'S *NONE OF OUR CONCERN.*
THIS WAY, DRAGONS, THIS WAY.
STAND ASIDE, FRAYNIR.
THAT'S AN *ORDER.*

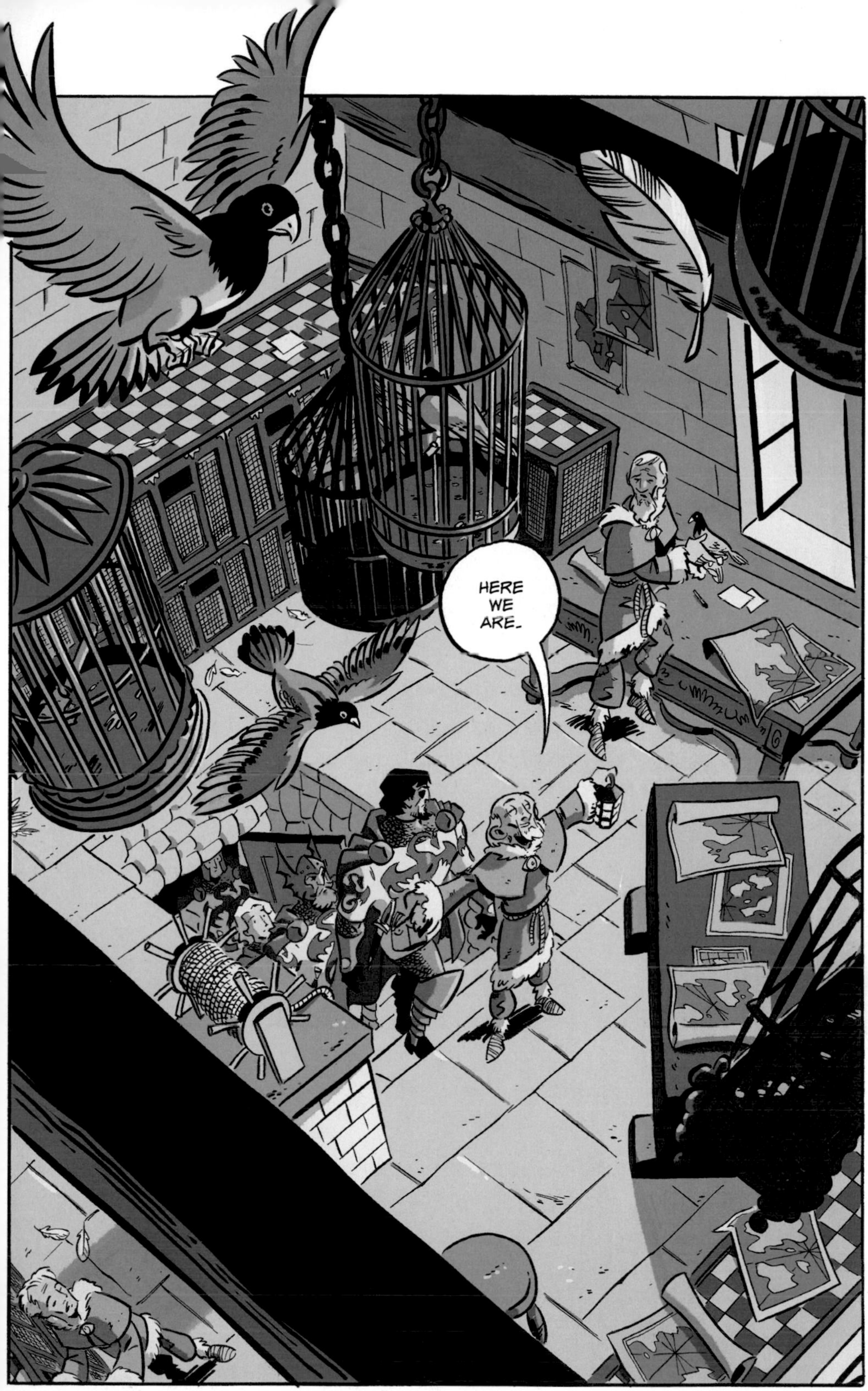
HERE WE ARE.

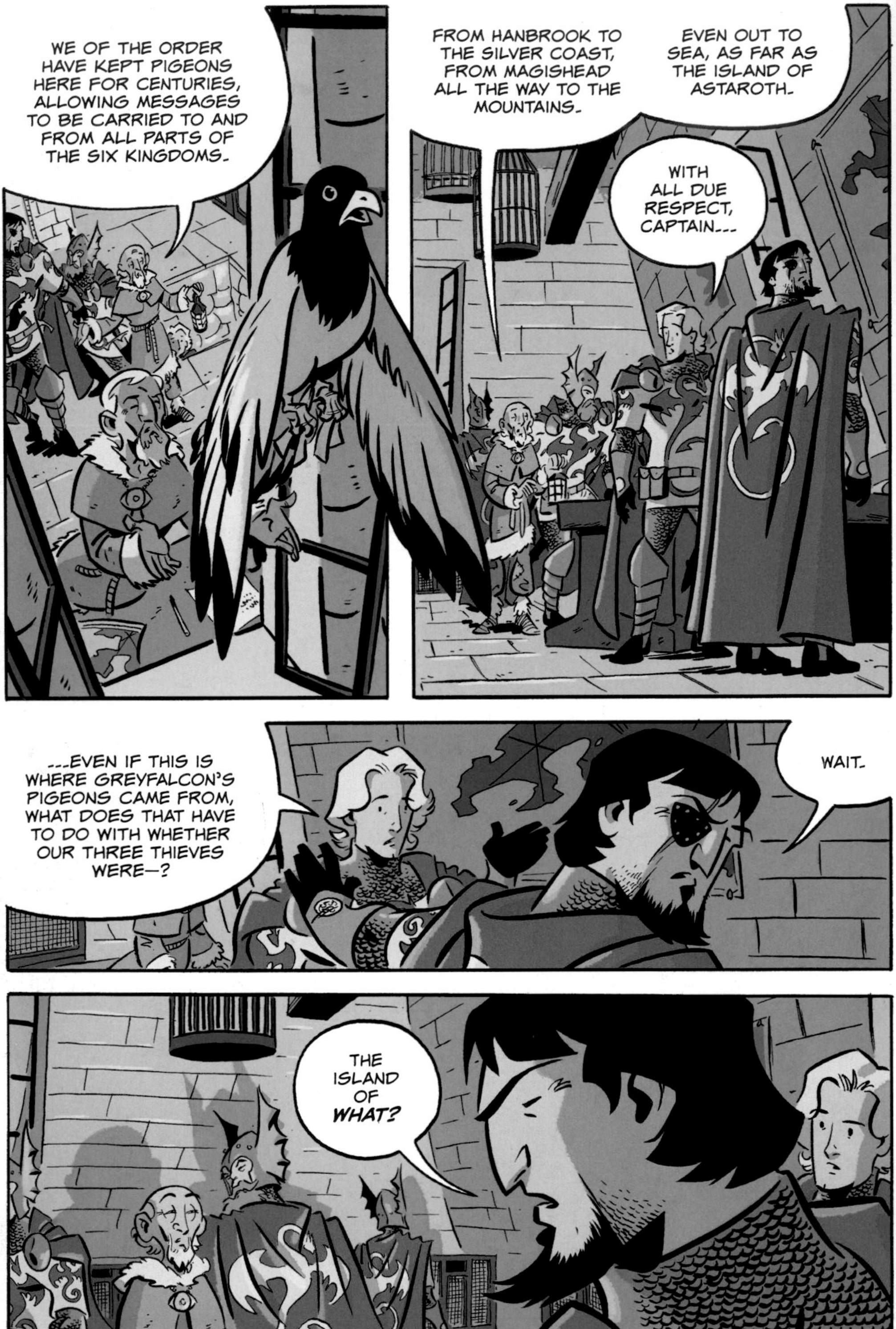
WE OF THE ORDER HAVE KEPT PIGEONS HERE FOR CENTURIES, ALLOWING MESSAGES TO BE CARRIED TO AND FROM ALL PARTS OF THE SIX KINGDOMS.
FROM HANBROOK TO THE SILVER COAST, FROM MAGISHEAD ALL THE WAY TO THE MOUNTAINS.
EVEN OUT TO SEA, AS FAR AS THE ISLAND OF ASTAROTH.
WITH ALL DUE RESPECT, CAPTAIN...
...EVEN IF THIS IS WHERE GREYFALCON'S PIGEONS CAME FROM, WHAT DOES THAT HAVE TO DO WITH WHETHER OUR THREE THIEVES WERE—?
WAIT.
THE ISLAND OF *WHAT?*

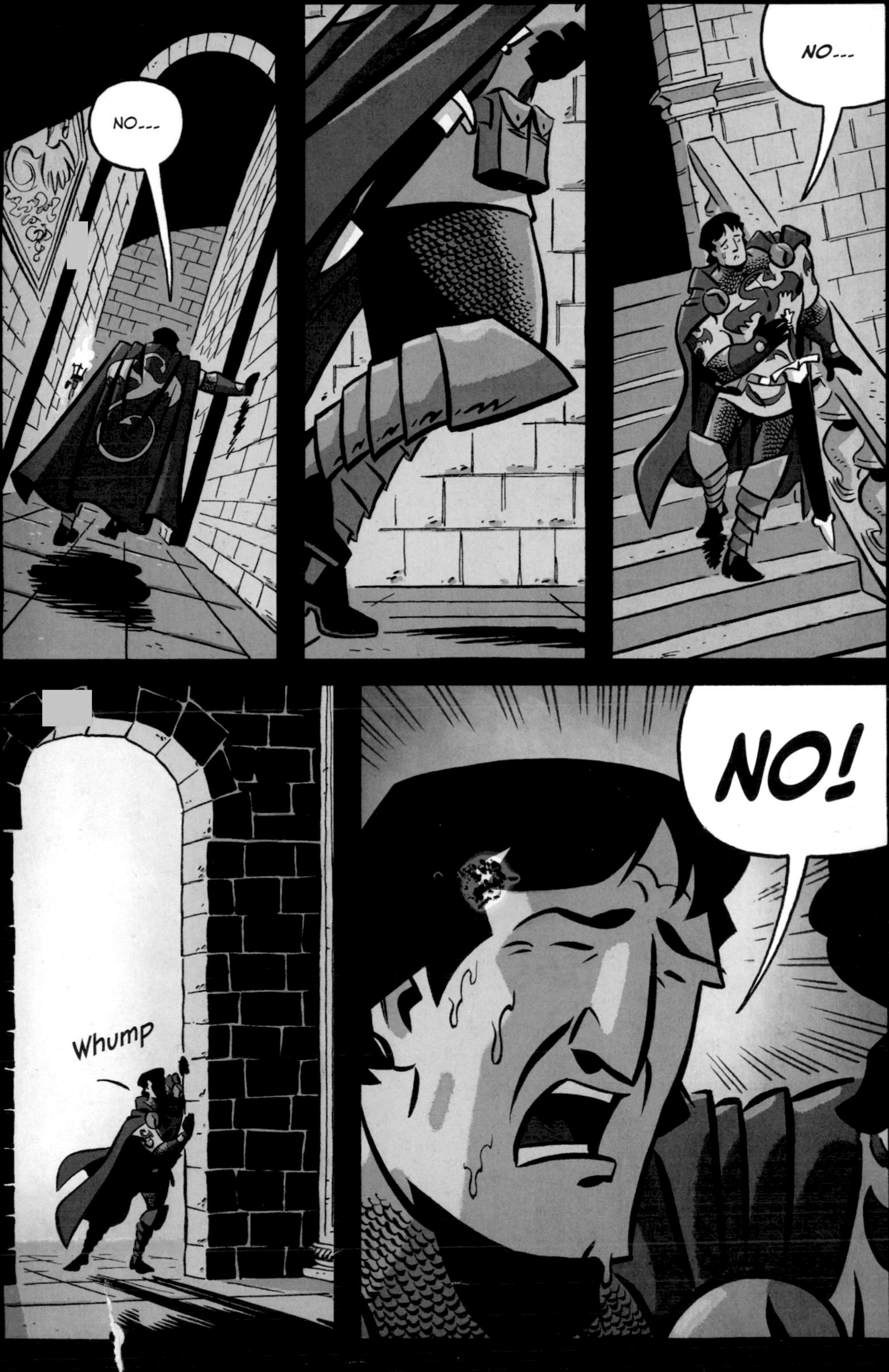
NO---
NO---
Whump
NO!

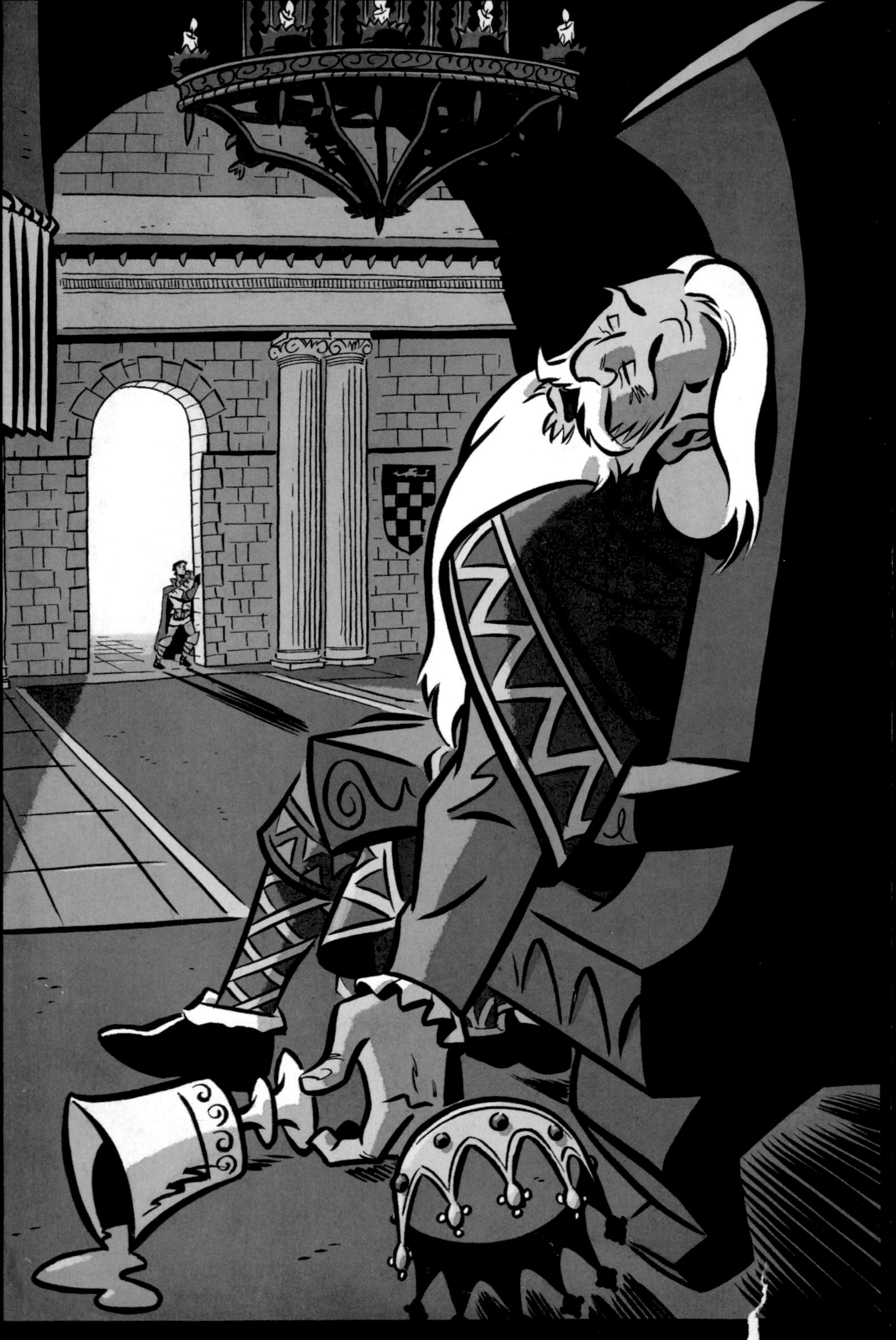

ACT THREE

Blinded

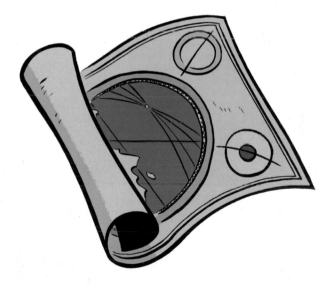

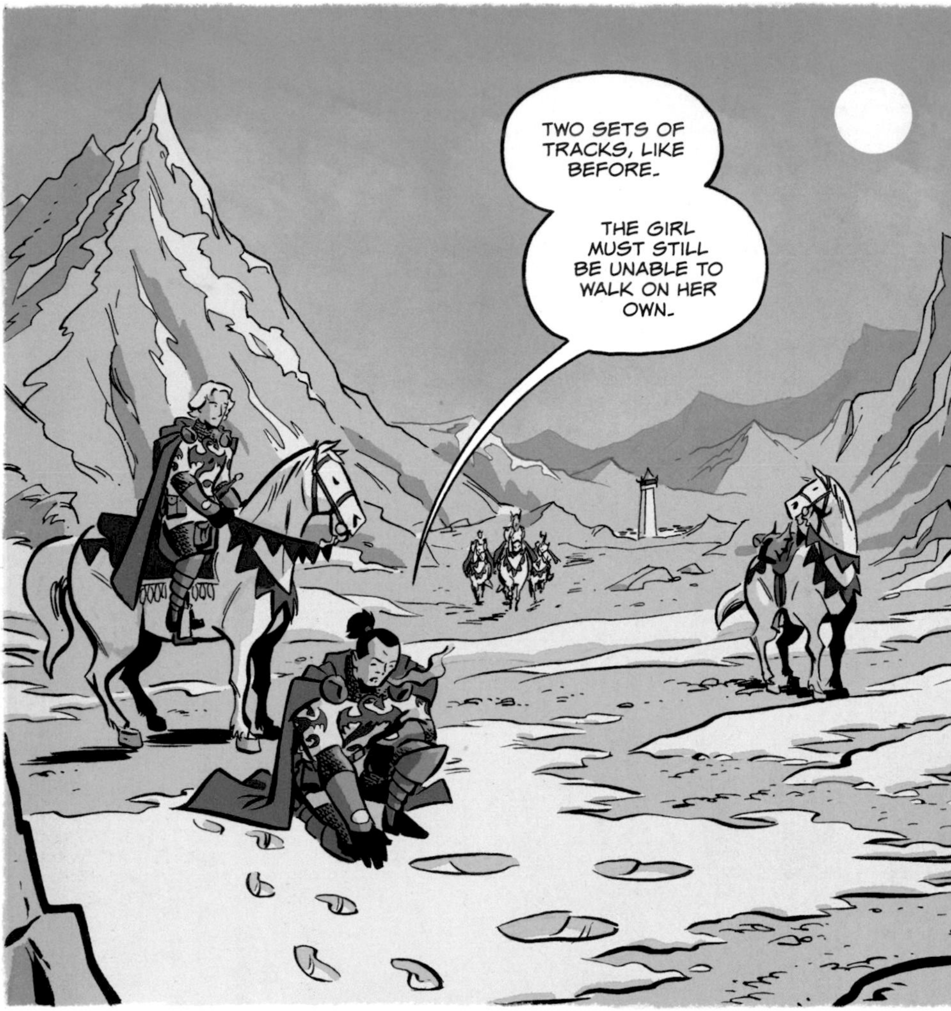
TWO SETS OF TRACKS, LIKE BEFORE.
THE GIRL MUST STILL BE UNABLE TO WALK ON HER OWN.

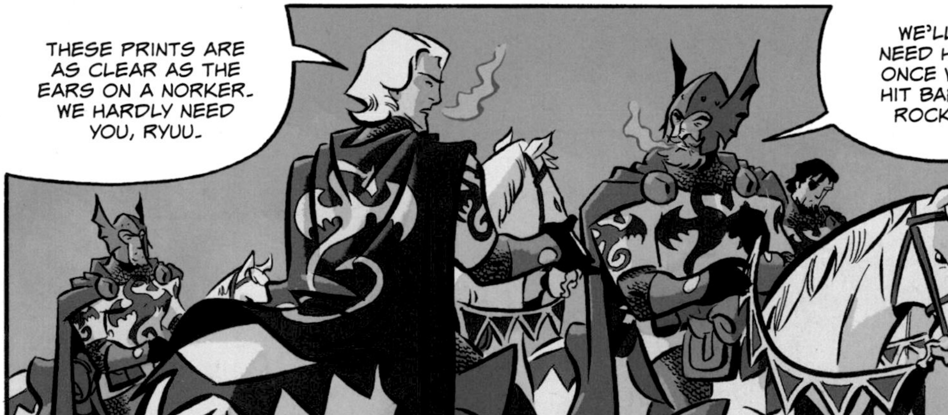
THESE PRINTS ARE AS CLEAR AS THE EARS ON A NORKER. WE HARDLY NEED YOU, RYUU.
WE'LL NEED HIM ONCE WE HIT BARE ROCK.

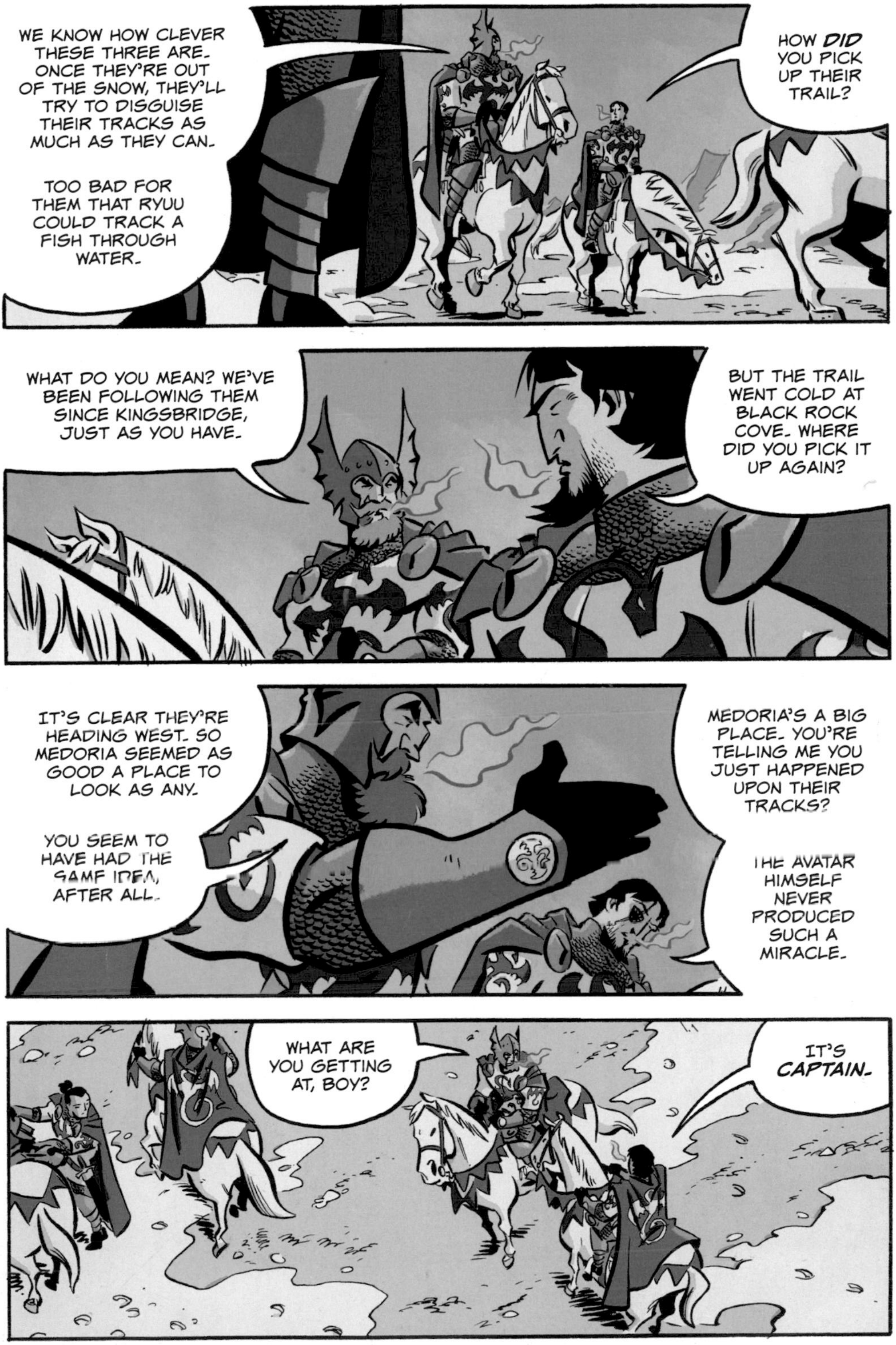
WE KNOW HOW CLEVER THESE THREE ARE. ONCE THEY'RE OUT OF THE SNOW, THEY'LL TRY TO DISGUISE THEIR TRACKS AS MUCH AS THEY CAN.
TOO BAD FOR THEM THAT RYUU COULD TRACK A FISH THROUGH WATER.
HOW *DID* YOU PICK UP THEIR TRAIL?
WHAT DO YOU MEAN? WE'VE BEEN FOLLOWING THEM SINCE KINGSBRIDGE, JUST AS YOU HAVE.
BUT THE TRAIL WENT COLD AT BLACK ROCK COVE. WHERE DID YOU PICK IT UP AGAIN?
IT'S CLEAR THEY'RE HEADING WEST. SO MEDORIA SEEMED AS GOOD A PLACE TO LOOK AS ANY.
YOU SEEM TO HAVE HAD THE SAME IDEA, AFTER ALL.
MEDORIA'S A BIG PLACE. YOU'RE TELLING ME YOU JUST HAPPENED UPON THEIR TRACKS?
THE AVATAR HIMSELF NEVER PRODUCED SUCH A MIRACLE.
WHAT ARE YOU GETTING AT, BOY?
IT'S *CAPTAIN*.

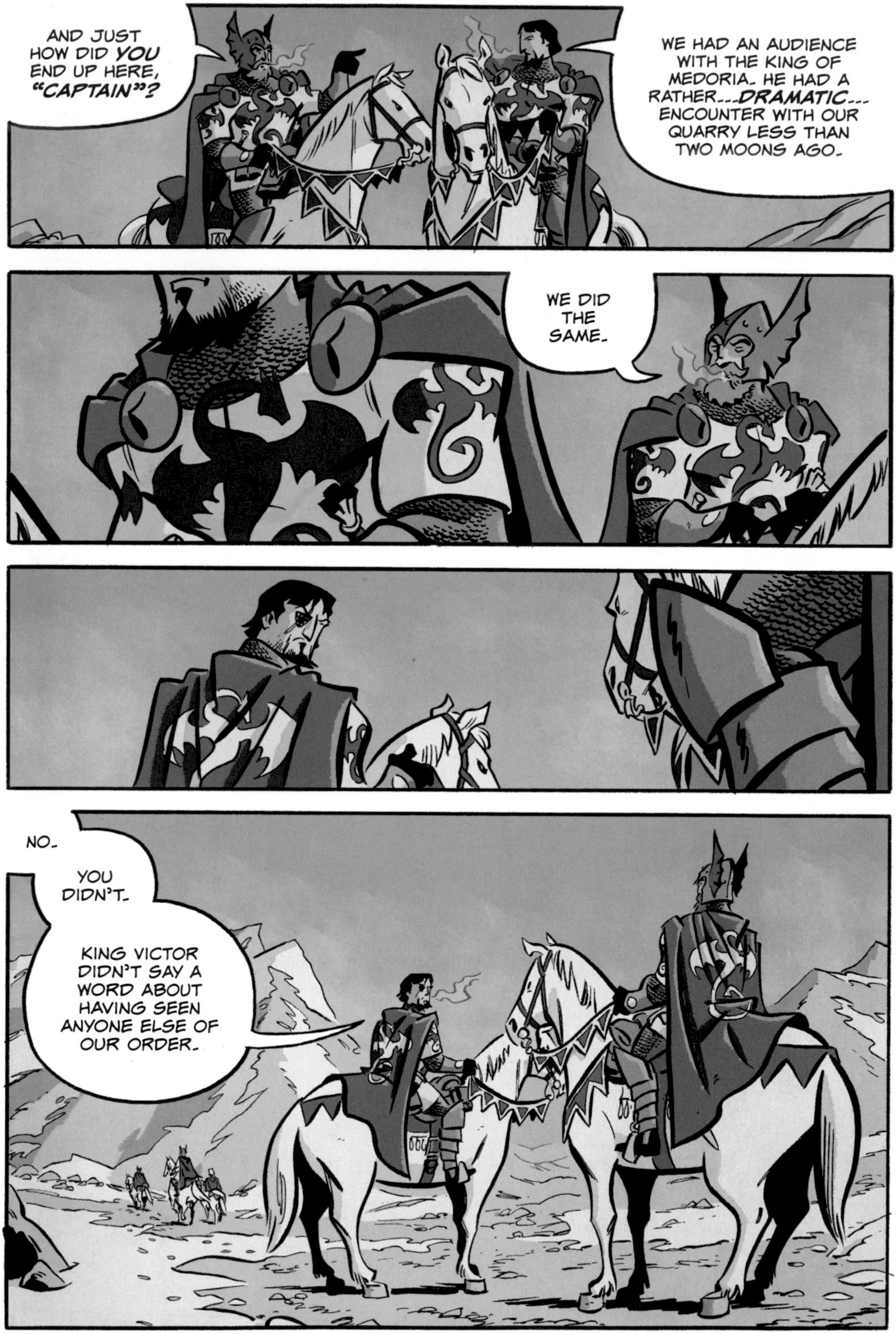
AND JUST HOW DID YOU END UP HERE, "CAPTAIN"?
WE HAD AN AUDIENCE WITH THE KING OF MEDORIA. HE HAD A RATHER...DRAMATIC... ENCOUNTER WITH OUR QUARRY LESS THAN TWO MOONS AGO.
WE DID THE SAME.
NO.
YOU DIDN'T.
KING VICTOR DIDN'T SAY A WORD ABOUT HAVING SEEN ANYONE ELSE OF OUR ORDER.

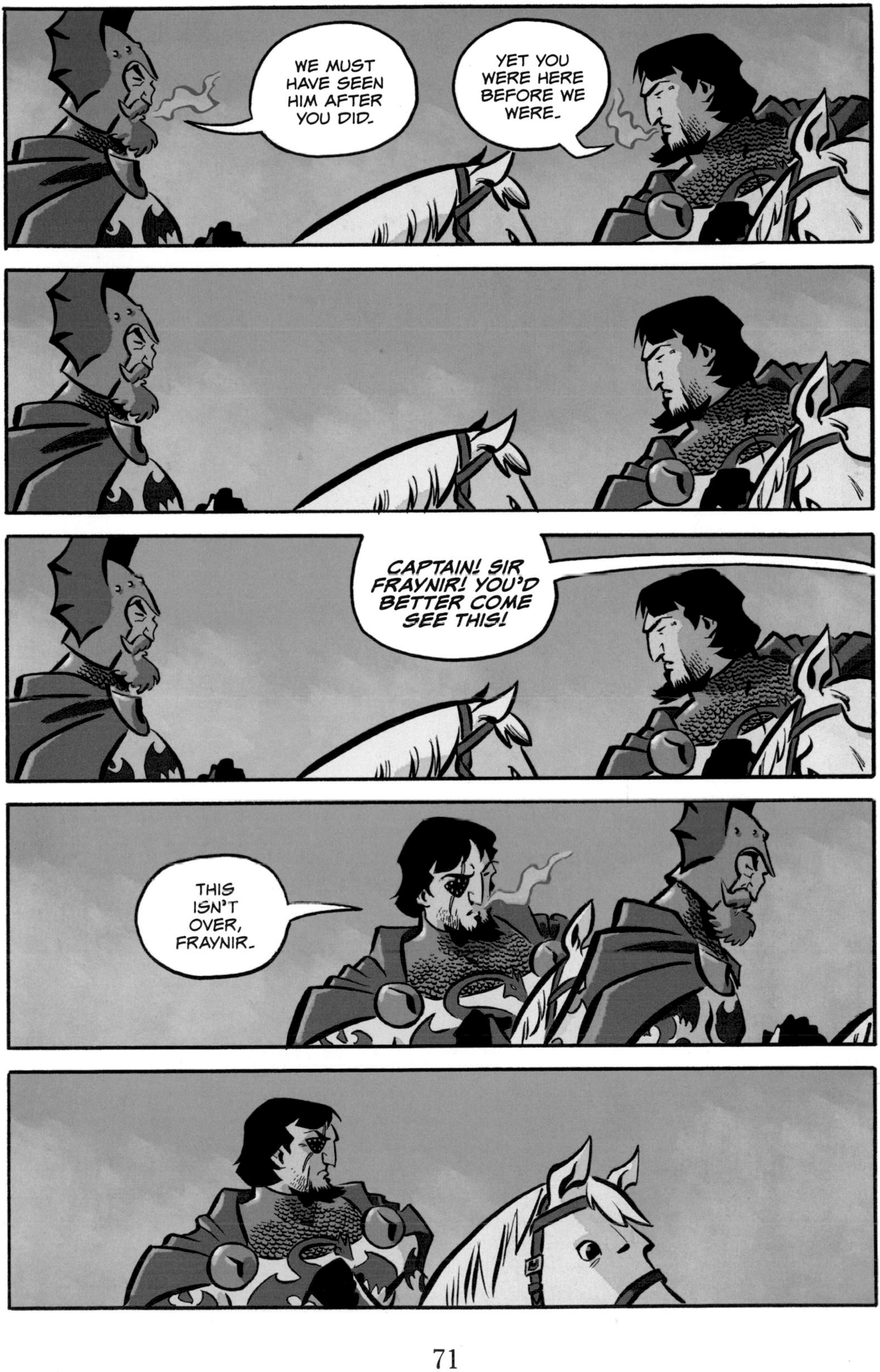
WE MUST HAVE SEEN HIM AFTER YOU DID.
YET YOU WERE HERE BEFORE WE WERE.
CAPTAIN! SIR FRAYNIR! YOU'D BETTER COME SEE THIS!
THIS ISN'T OVER, FRAYNIR.

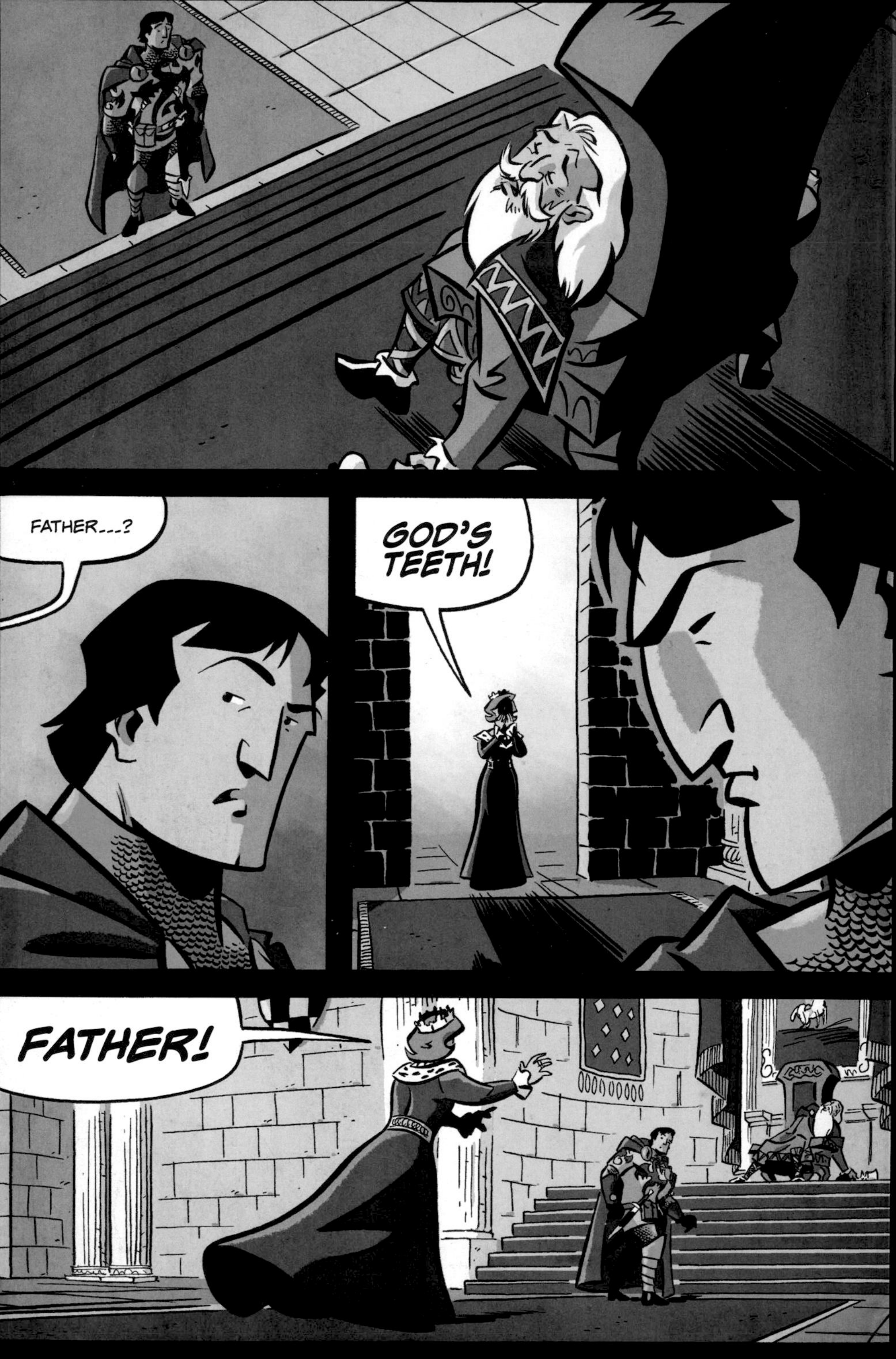
FATHER...?
GOD'S TEETH!
FATHER!

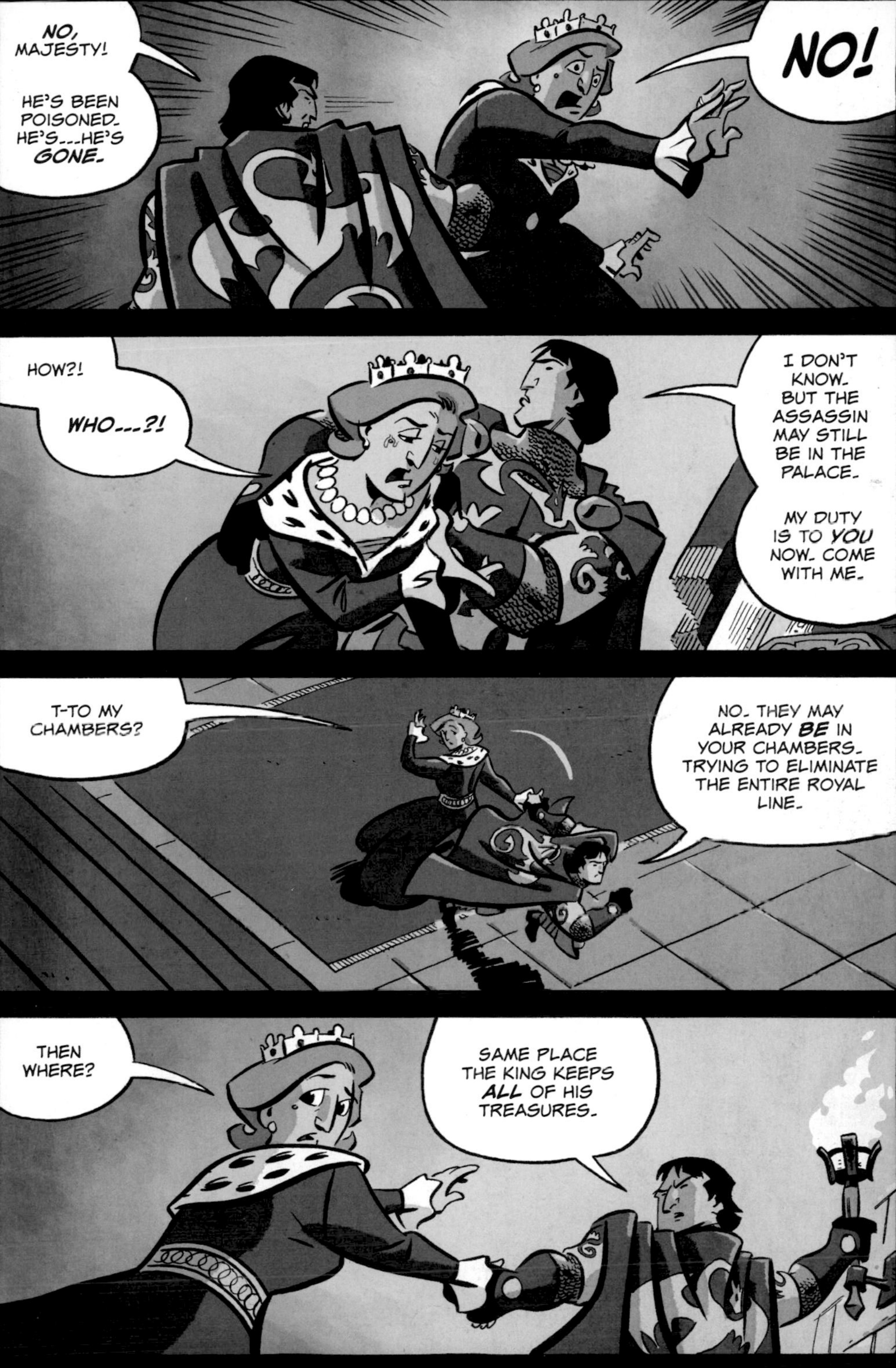
NO, MAJESTY!
HE'S BEEN POISONED. HE'S...HE'S GONE.
NO!
HOW?!
WHO...?!
I DON'T KNOW. BUT THE ASSASSIN MAY STILL BE IN THE PALACE.
MY DUTY IS TO YOU NOW. COME WITH ME.
T-TO MY CHAMBERS?
NO. THEY MAY ALREADY BE IN YOUR CHAMBERS. TRYING TO ELIMINATE THE ENTIRE ROYAL LINE.
THEN WHERE?
SAME PLACE THE KING KEEPS ALL OF HIS TREASURES.

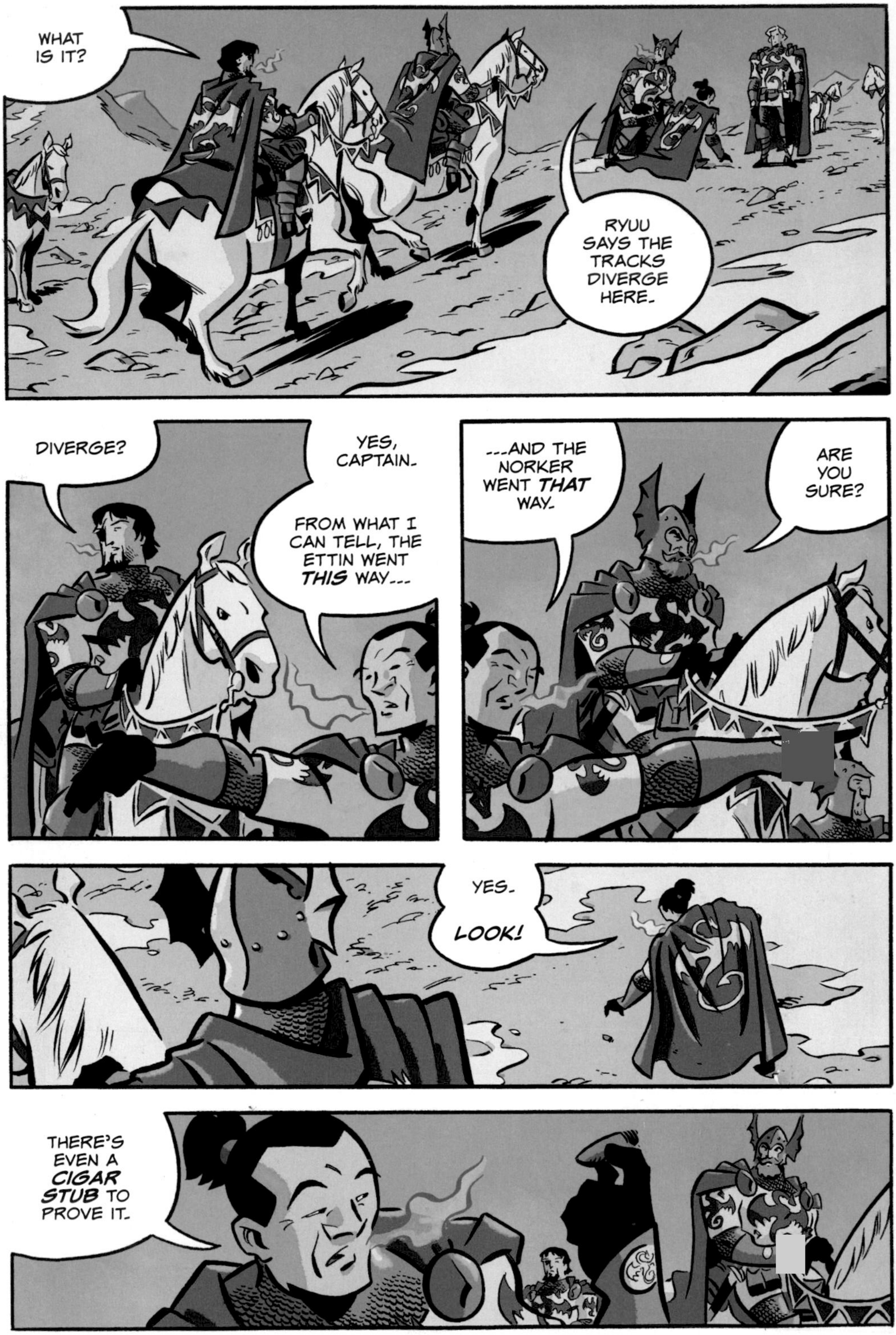
WHAT IS IT?
RYUU SAYS THE TRACKS DIVERGE HERE.
DIVERGE?
YES, CAPTAIN.
FROM WHAT I CAN TELL, THE ETTIN WENT THIS WAY...
...AND THE NORKER WENT THAT WAY.
ARE YOU SURE?
YES.
LOOK!
THERE'S EVEN A CIGAR STUB TO PROVE IT.

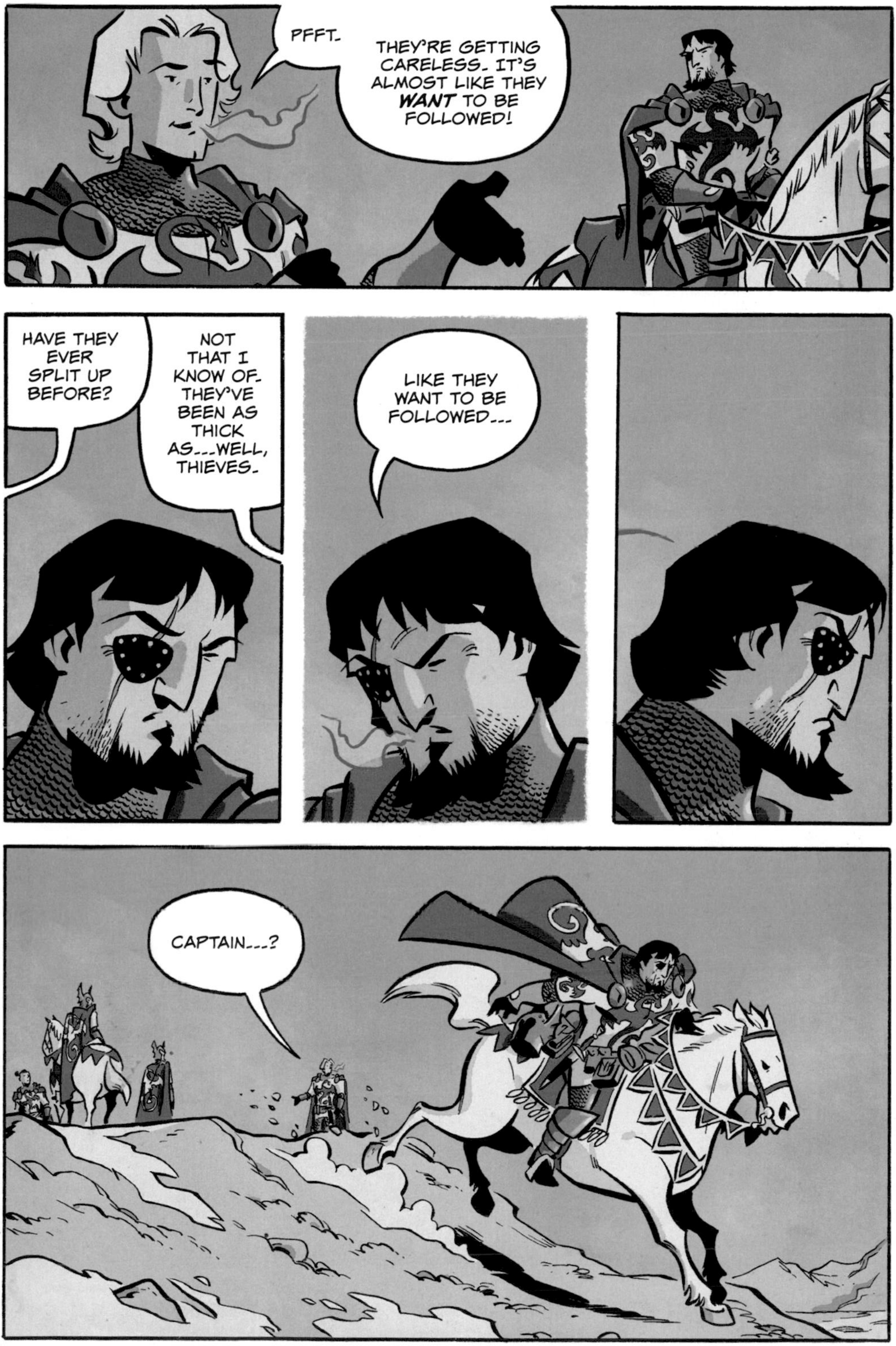
PFFT.
THEY'RE GETTING CARELESS. IT'S ALMOST LIKE THEY *WANT* TO BE FOLLOWED!
HAVE THEY EVER SPLIT UP BEFORE?
NOT THAT I KNOW OF. THEY'VE BEEN AS THICK AS...WELL, THIEVES.
LIKE THEY WANT TO BE FOLLOWED...
CAPTAIN...?

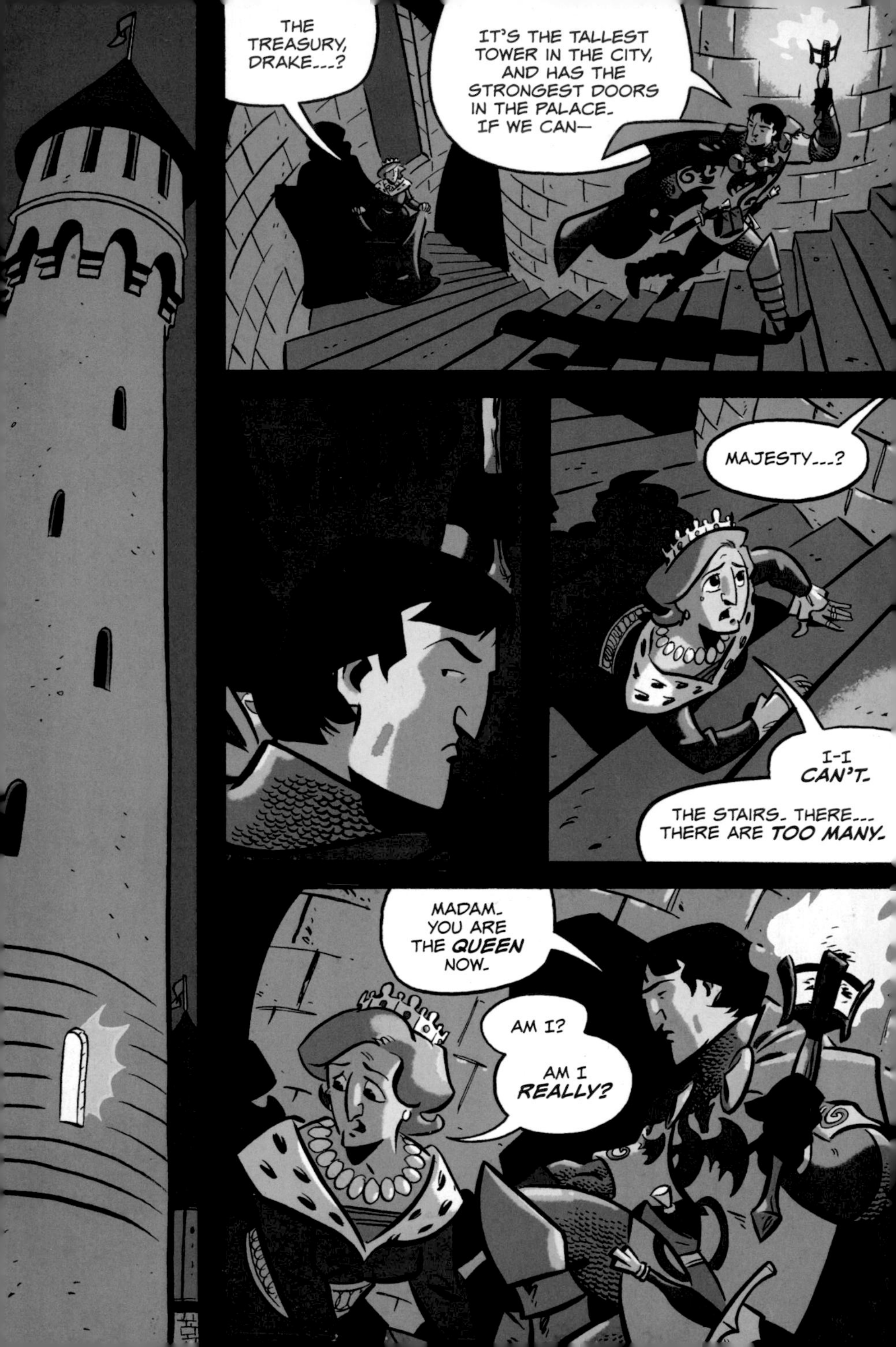

THE TREASURY, DRAKE...?
IT'S THE TALLEST TOWER IN THE CITY, AND HAS THE STRONGEST DOORS IN THE PALACE. IF WE CAN—
MAJESTY...?
I-I *CAN'T.*
THE STAIRS. THERE... THERE ARE *TOO MANY.*
MADAM. YOU ARE THE *QUEEN* NOW.
AM I?
AM I *REALLY?*

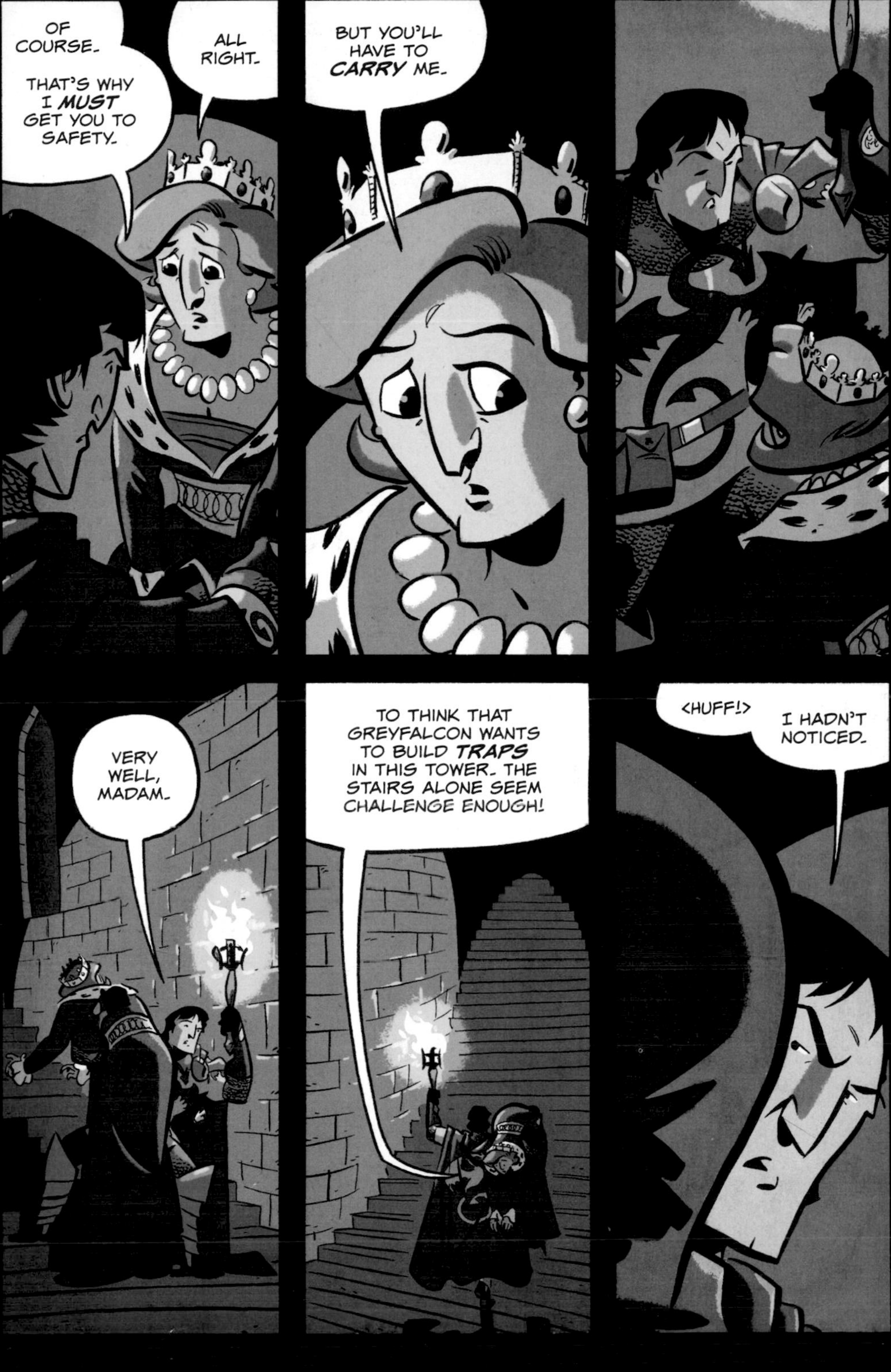

OF COURSE.
THAT'S WHY I MUST GET YOU TO SAFETY.
ALL RIGHT.
BUT YOU'LL HAVE TO CARRY ME.
VERY WELL, MADAM.
TO THINK THAT GREYFALCON WANTS TO BUILD TRAPS IN THIS TOWER. THE STAIRS ALONE SEEM CHALLENGE ENOUGH!
<HUFF!>
I HADN'T NOTICED.

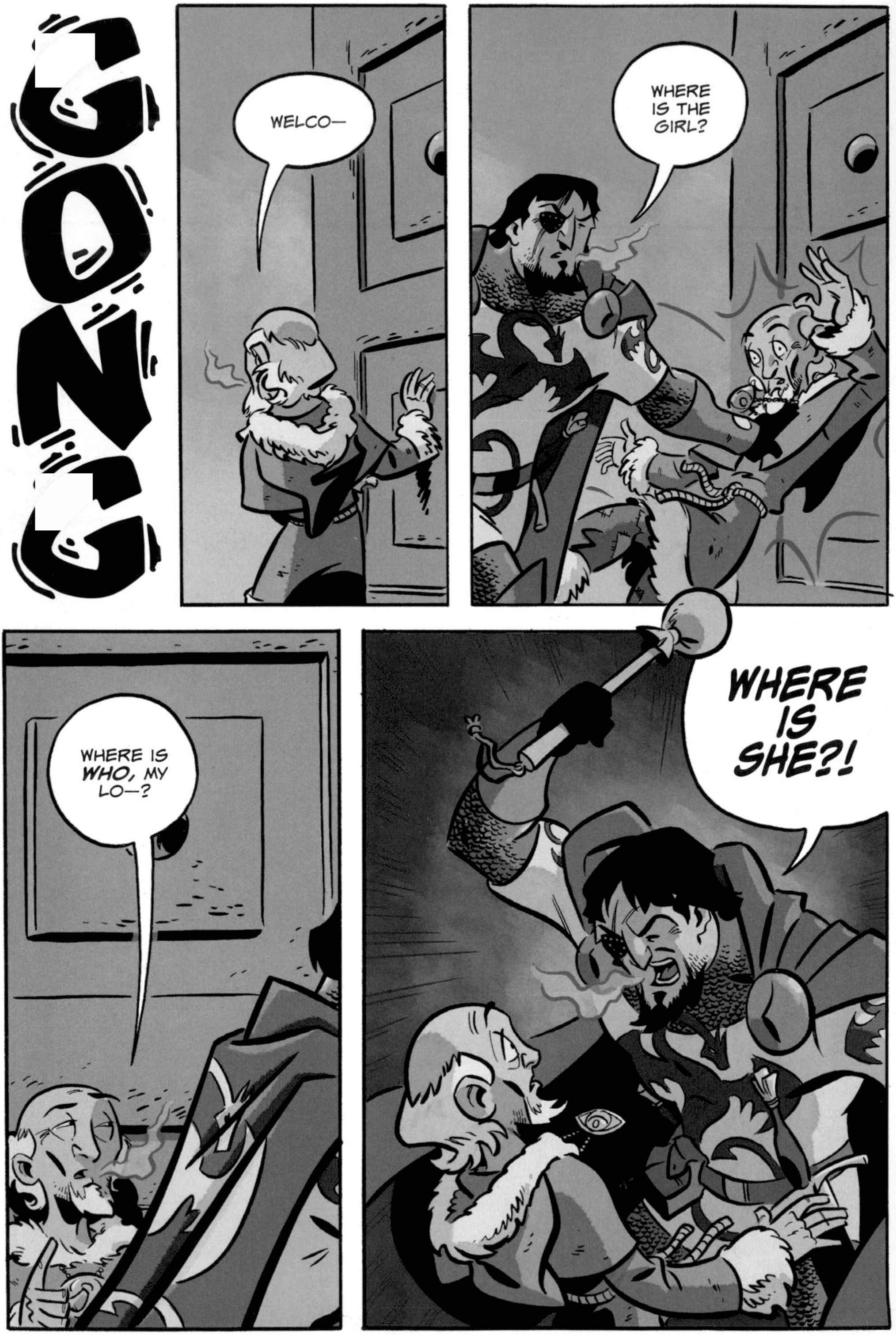
GONG
WELCO—
WHERE IS THE GIRL?
WHERE IS WHO, MY LO—?
WHERE IS SHE?!

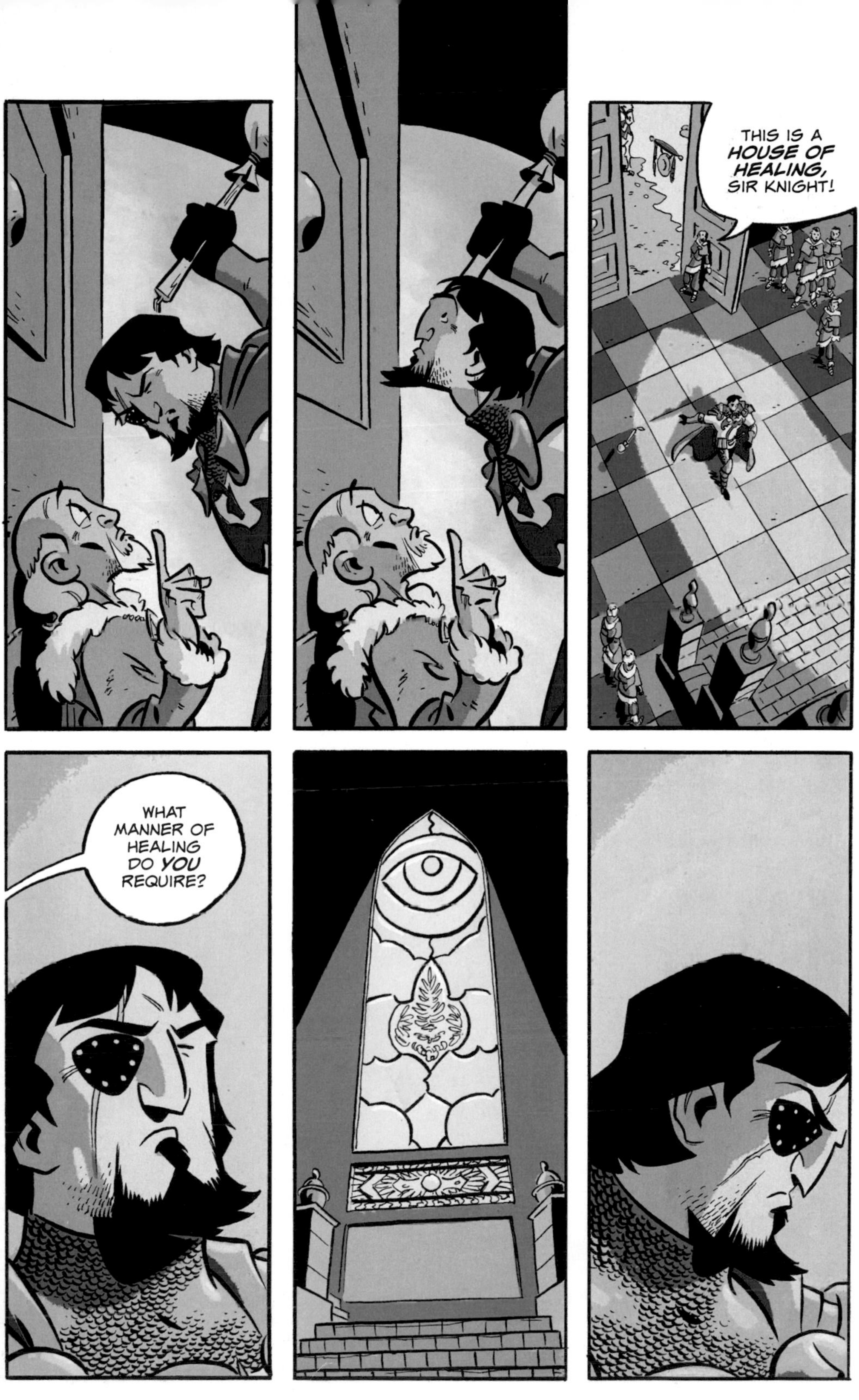
THIS IS A HOUSE OF HEALING, SIR KNIGHT!
WHAT MANNER OF HEALING DO YOU REQUIRE?

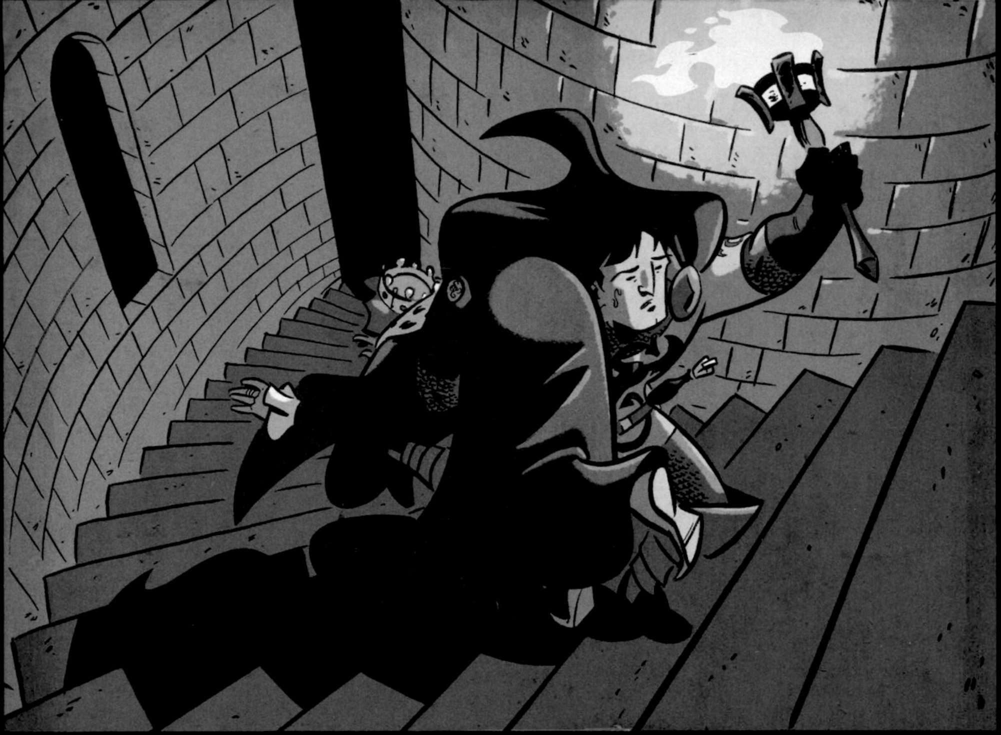

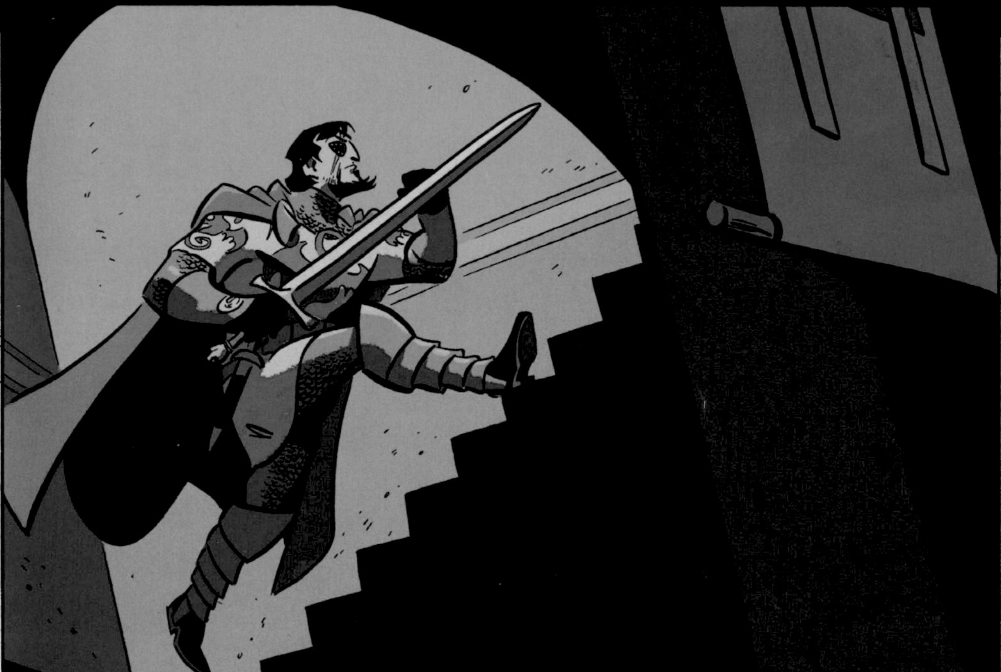

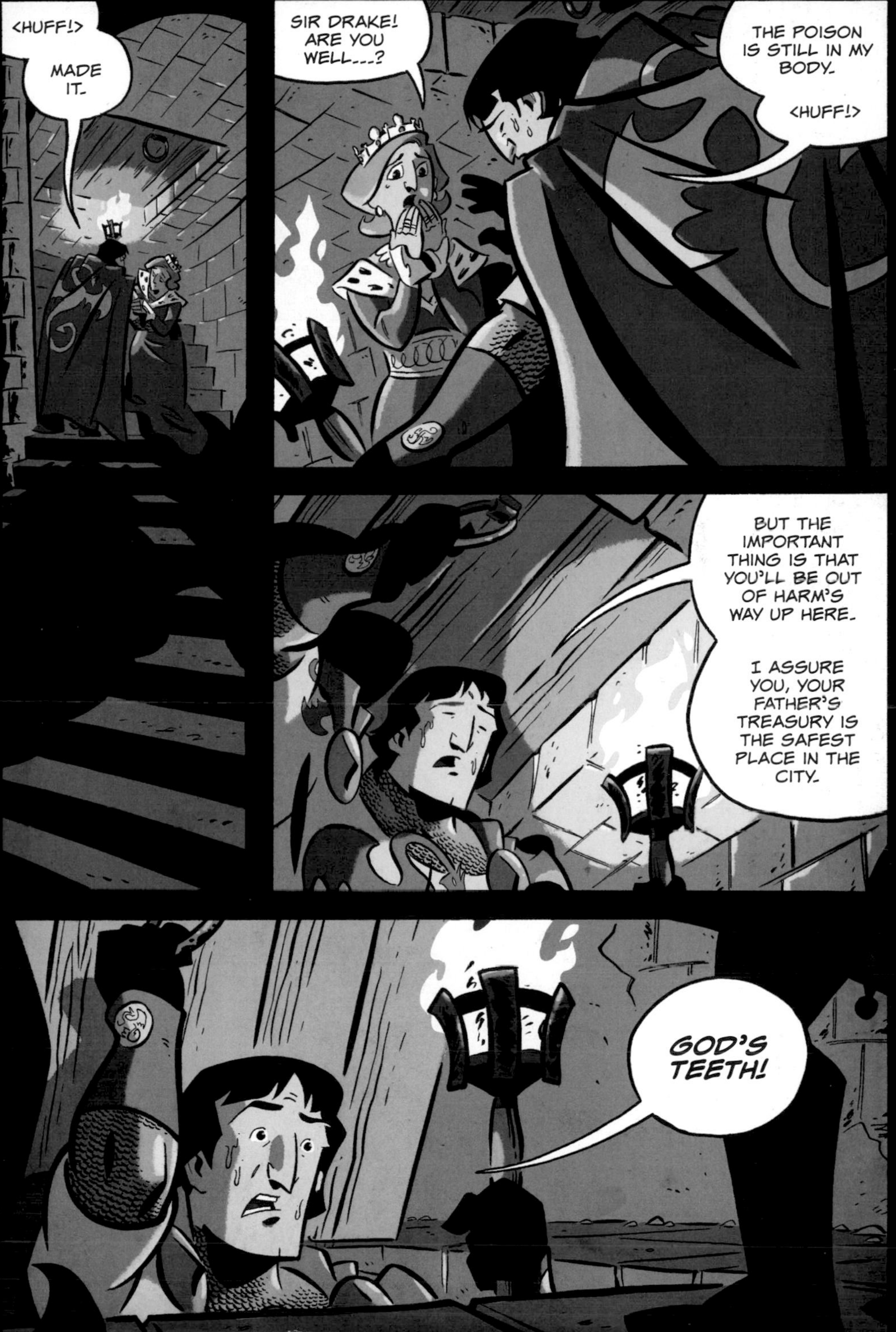
<HUFF!>
MADE IT.
SIR DRAKE! ARE YOU WELL...?
THE POISON IS STILL IN MY BODY.
<HUFF!>
BUT THE IMPORTANT THING IS THAT YOU'LL BE OUT OF HARM'S WAY UP HERE.
I ASSURE YOU, YOUR FATHER'S TREASURY IS THE SAFEST PLACE IN THE CITY.
GOD'S TEETH!

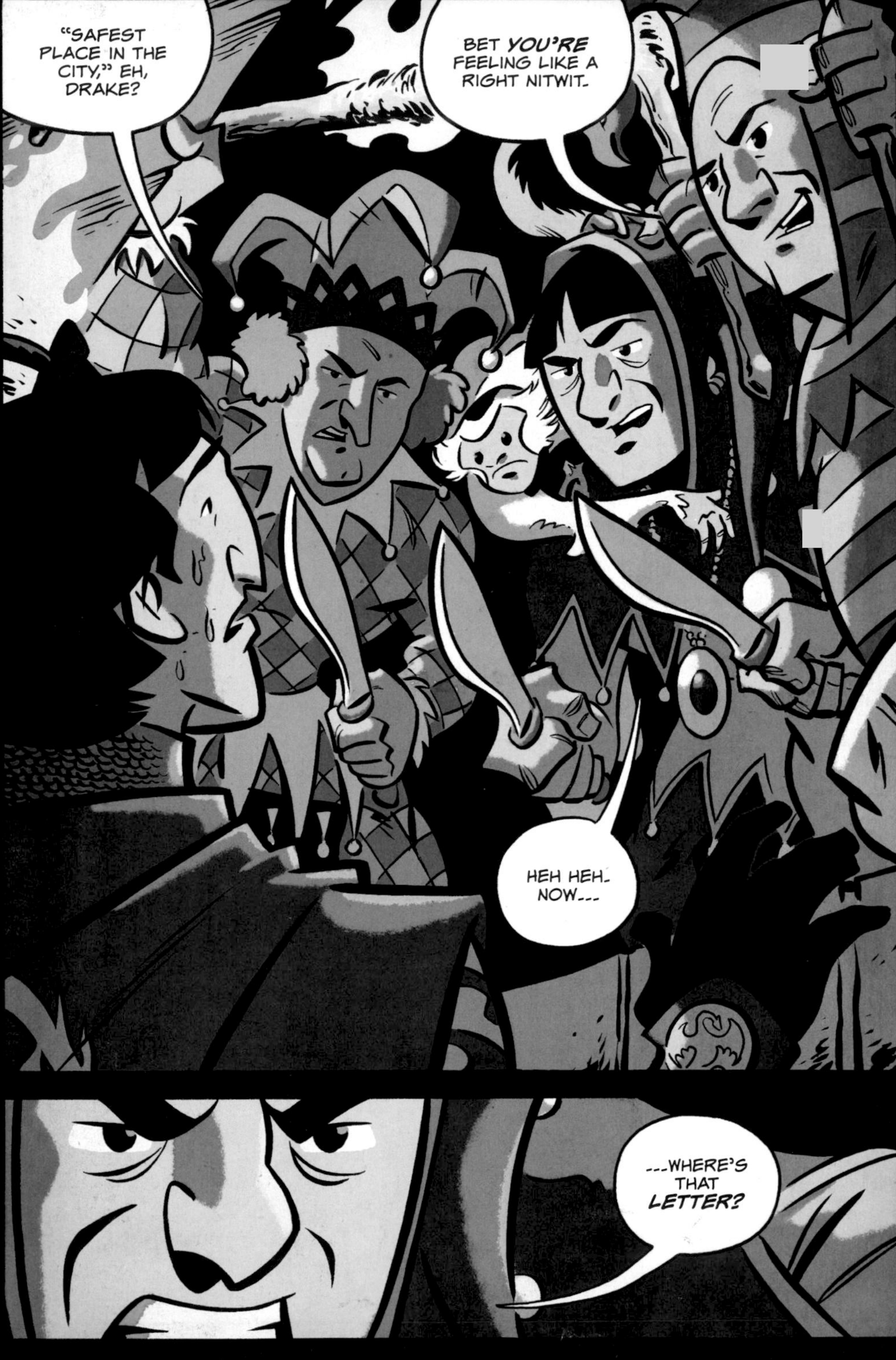
"SAFEST PLACE IN THE CITY," EH, DRAKE?
BET YOU'RE FEELING LIKE A RIGHT NITWIT.
HEH HEH. NOW...
...WHERE'S THAT LETTER?

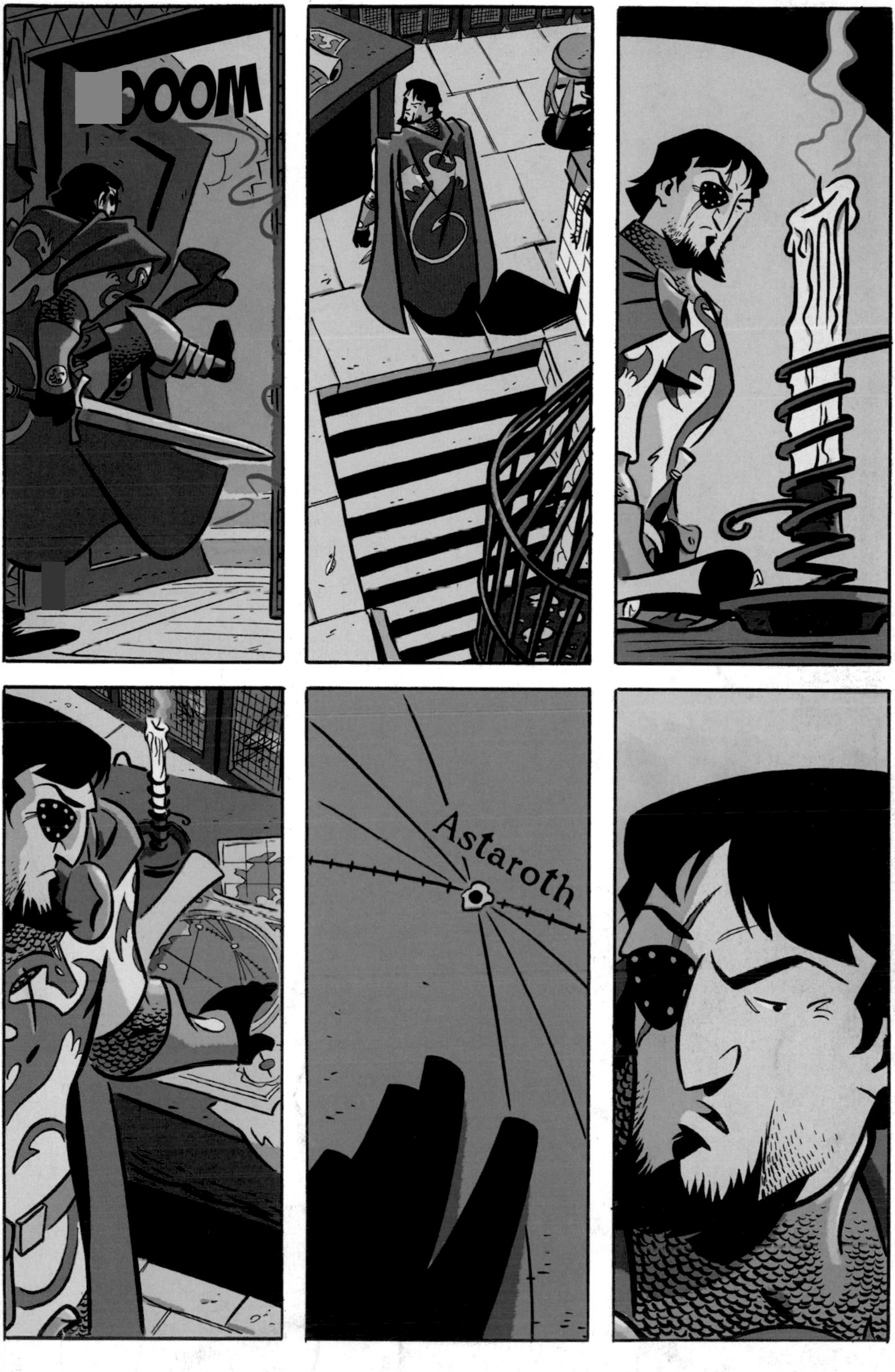
OOM
Astaroth

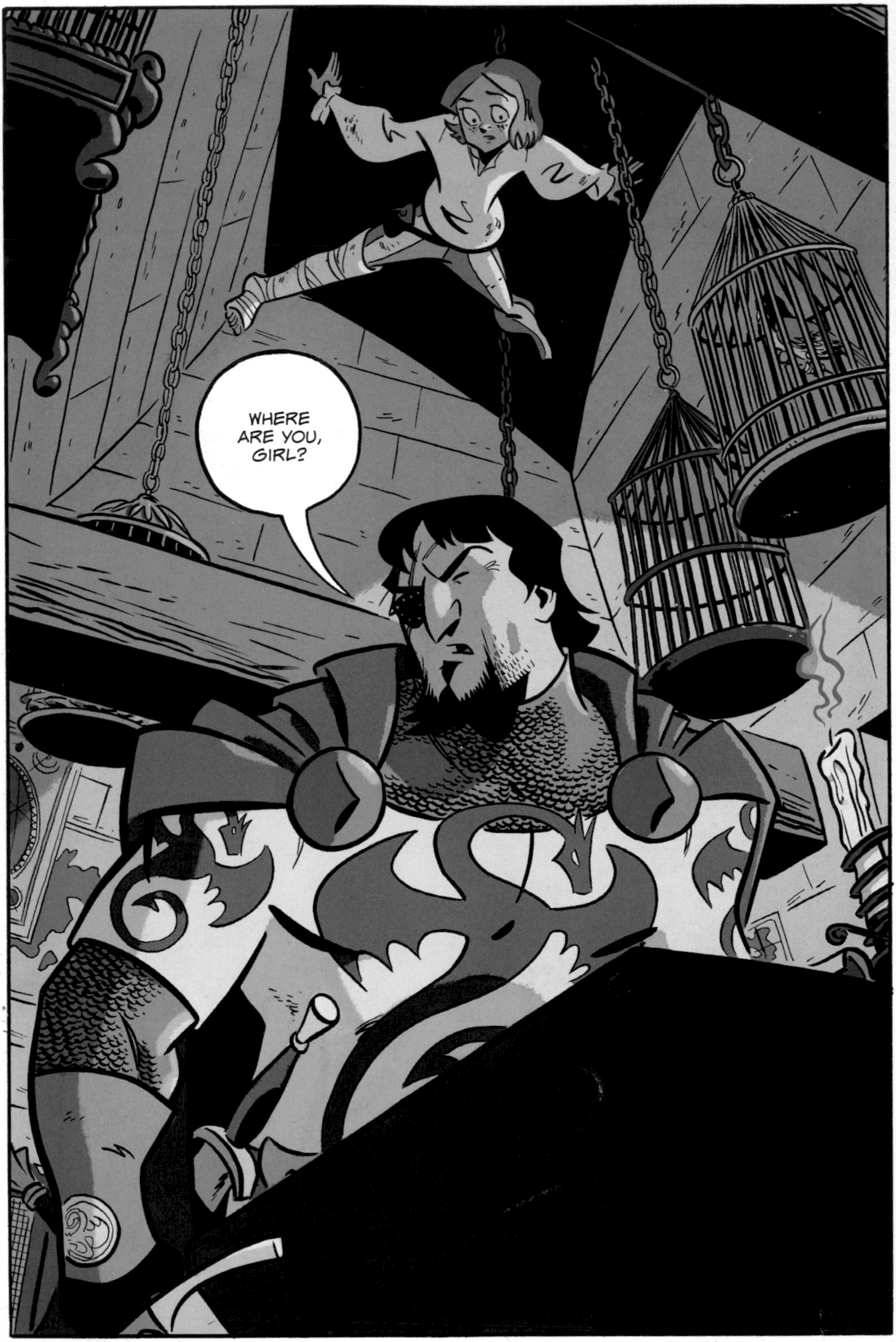
WHERE ARE YOU, GIRL?

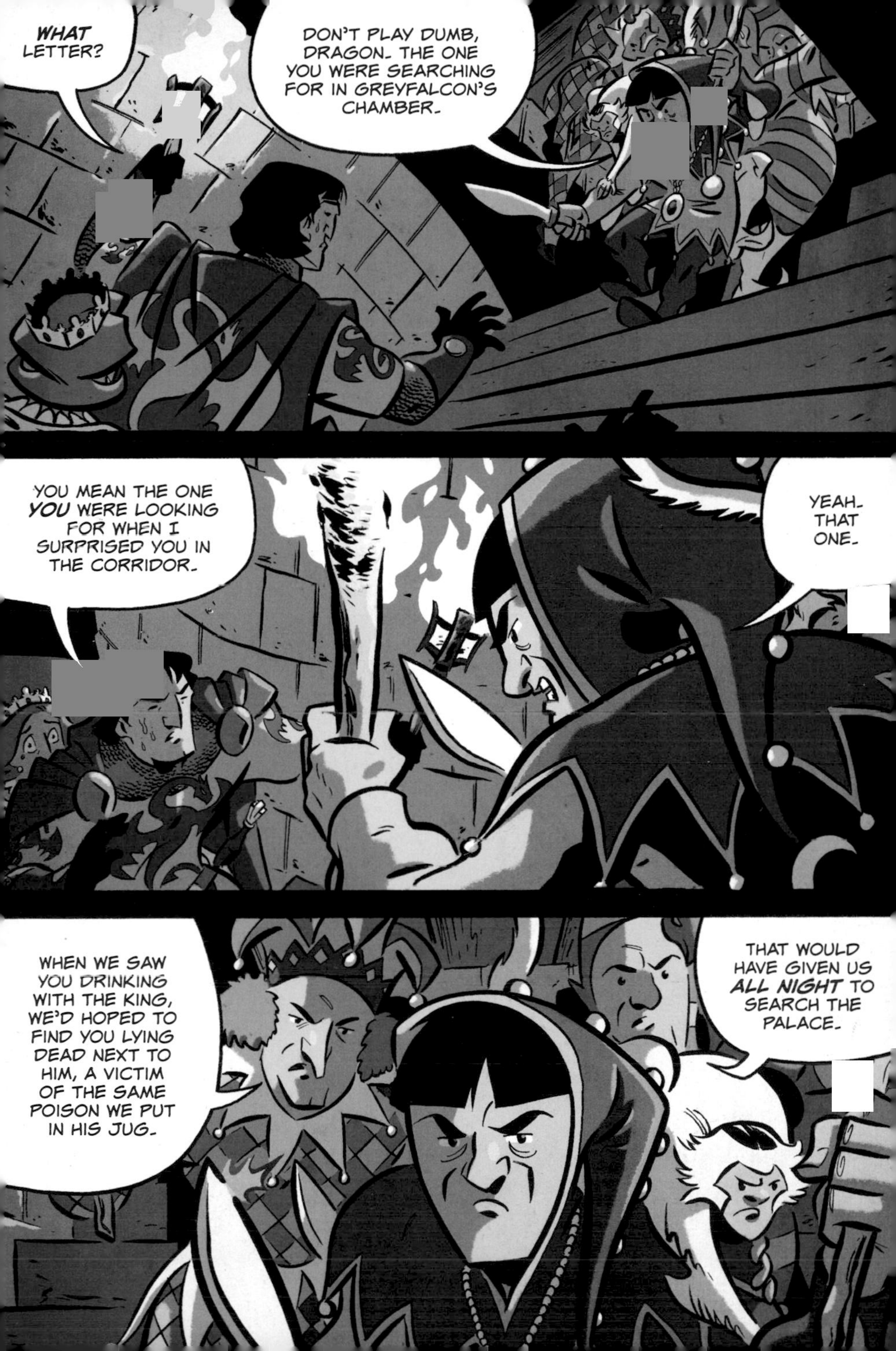
WHAT LETTER?
DON'T PLAY DUMB, DRAGON. THE ONE YOU WERE SEARCHING FOR IN GREYFALCON'S CHAMBER.
YOU MEAN THE ONE YOU WERE LOOKING FOR WHEN I SURPRISED YOU IN THE CORRIDOR.
YEAH. THAT ONE.
WHEN WE SAW YOU DRINKING WITH THE KING, WE'D HOPED TO FIND YOU LYING DEAD NEXT TO HIM, A VICTIM OF THE SAME POISON WE PUT IN HIS JUG.
THAT WOULD HAVE GIVEN US ALL NIGHT TO SEARCH THE PALACE.

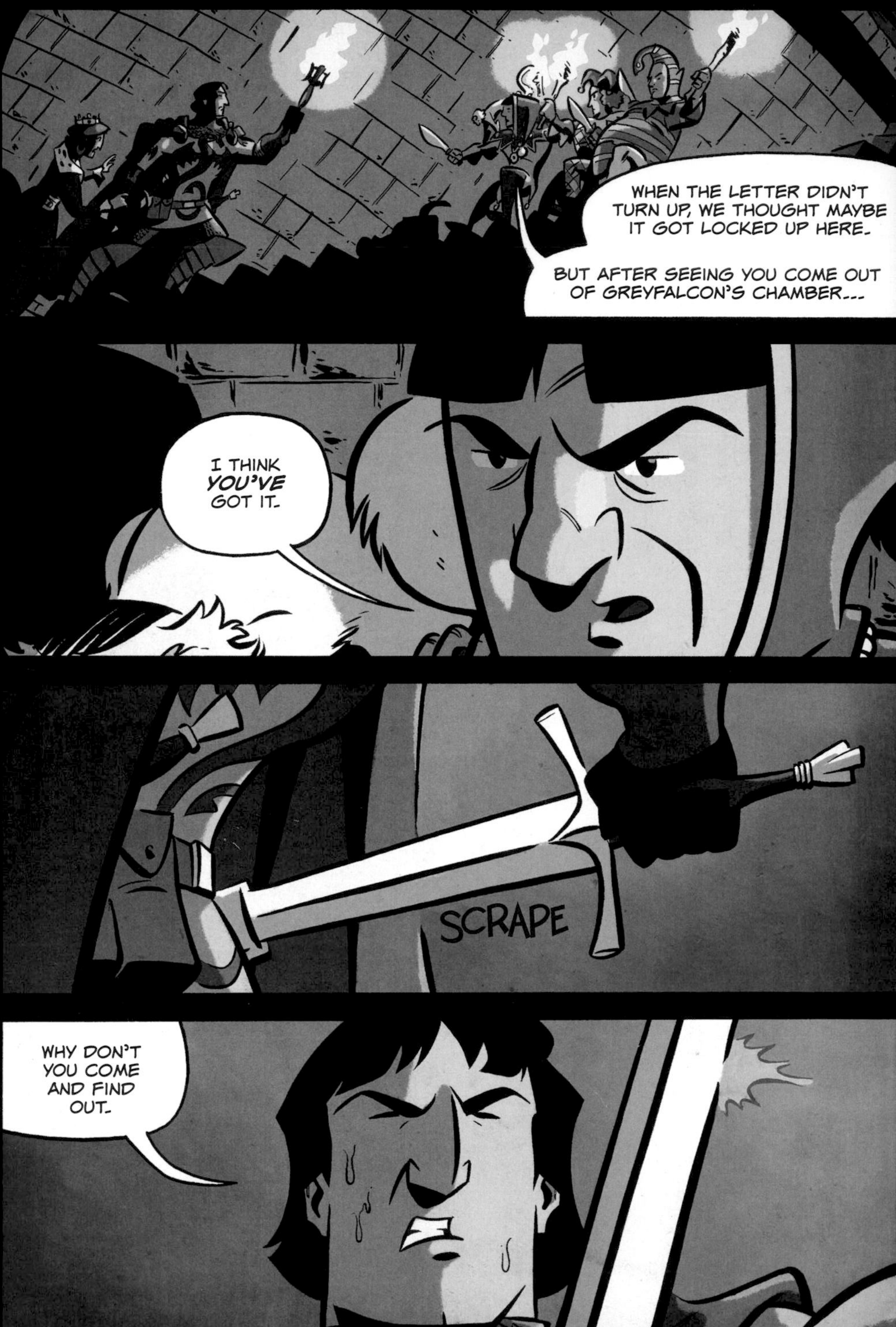
WHEN THE LETTER DIDN'T TURN UP, WE THOUGHT MAYBE IT GOT LOCKED UP HERE.
BUT AFTER SEEING YOU COME OUT OF GREYFALCON'S CHAMBER...
I THINK *YOU'VE* GOT IT.
SCRAPE
WHY DON'T YOU COME AND FIND OUT.

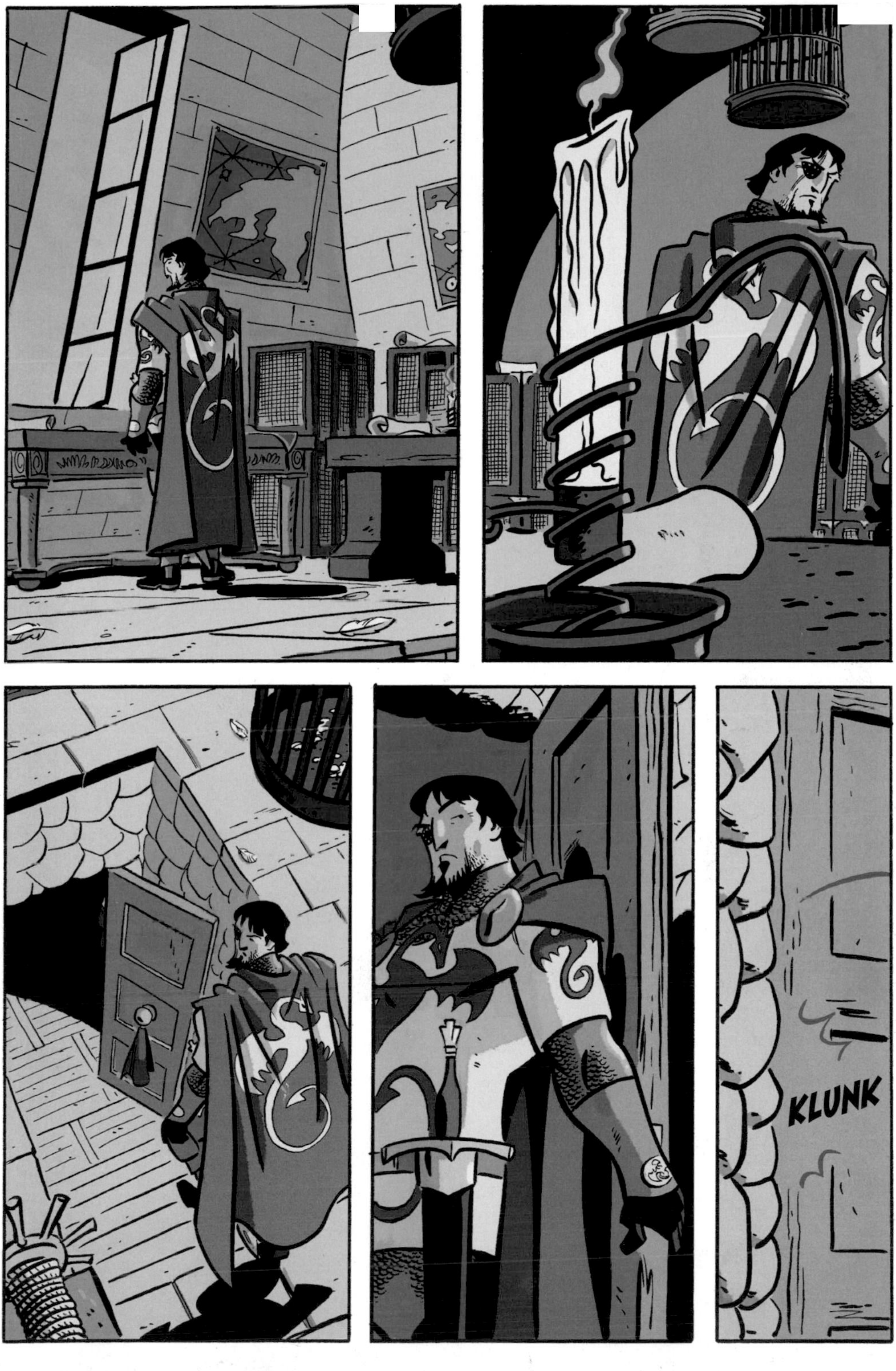
KLUNK

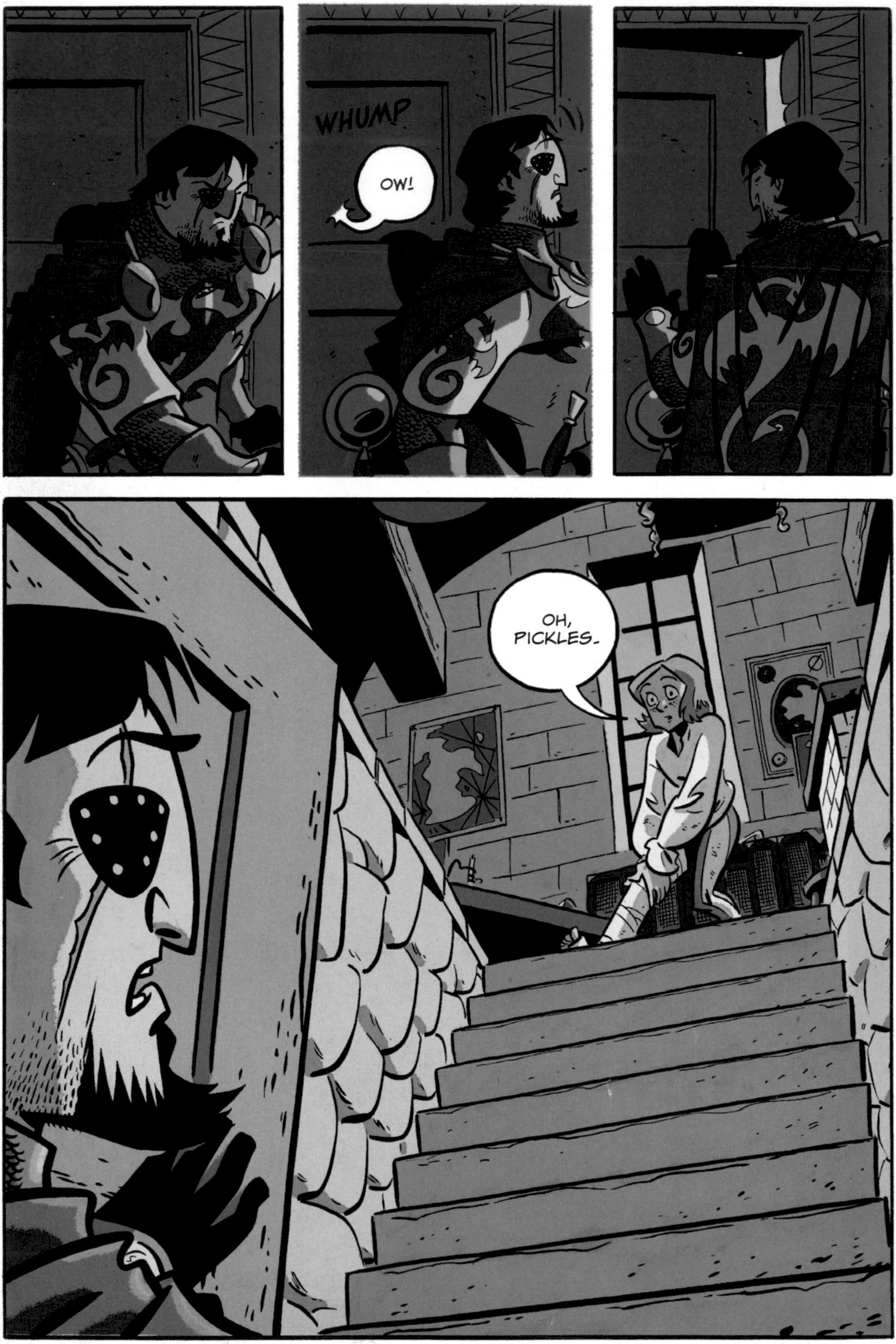
WHUMP
OW!
OH, PICKLES.

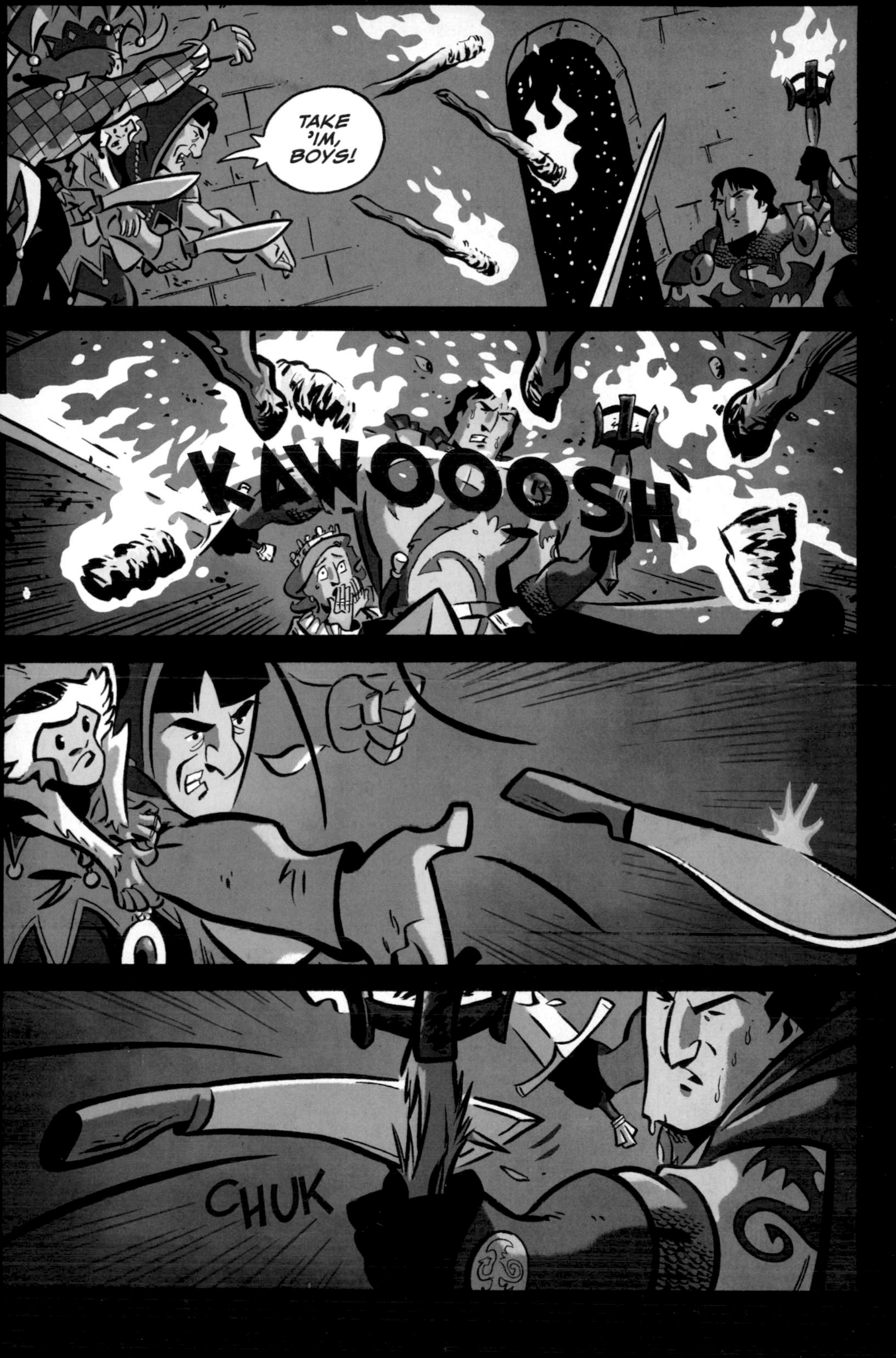
TAKE 'IM, BOYS!
KAWOOOSH
CHUK

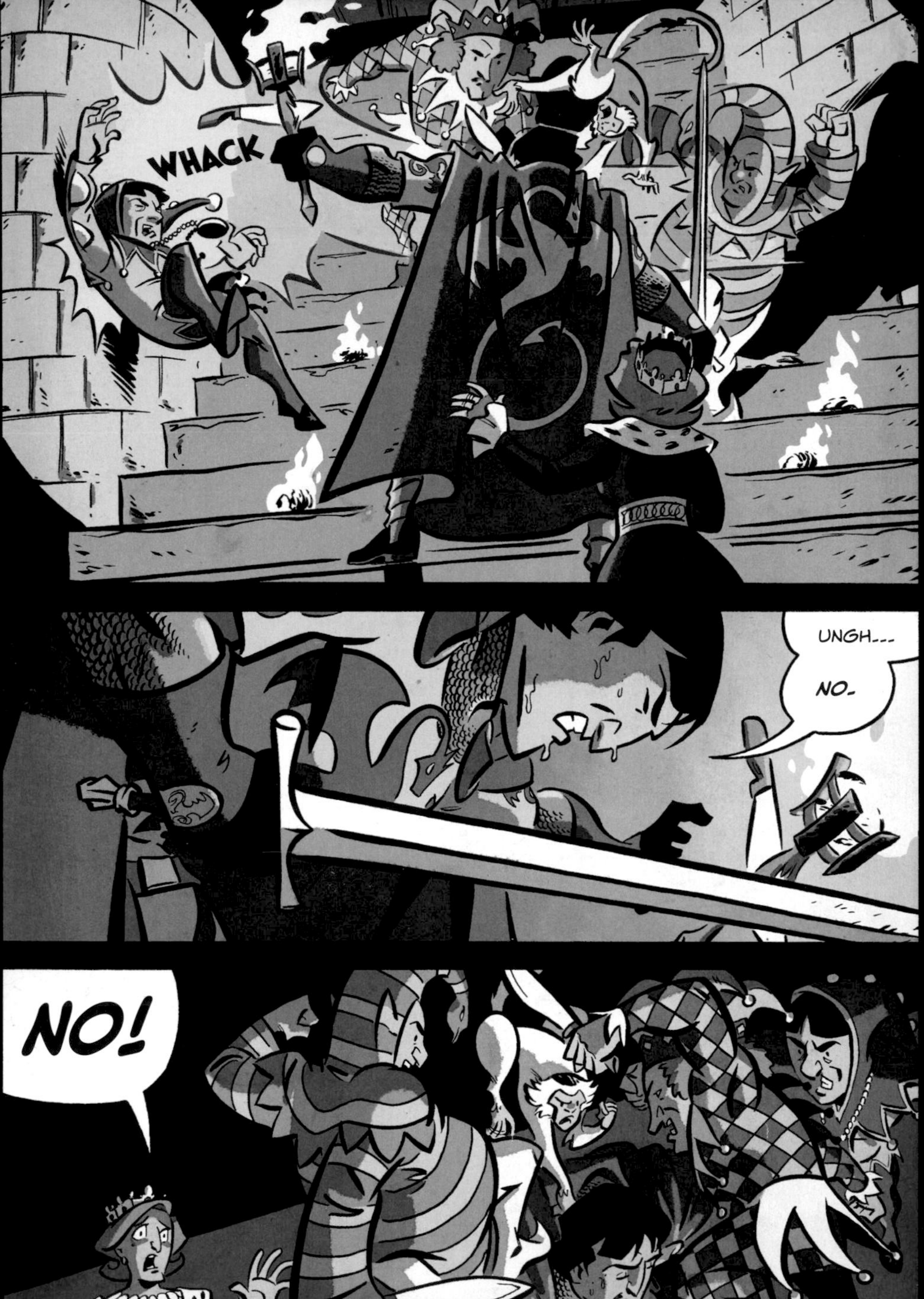
WHACK
UNGH---
NO-
NO!

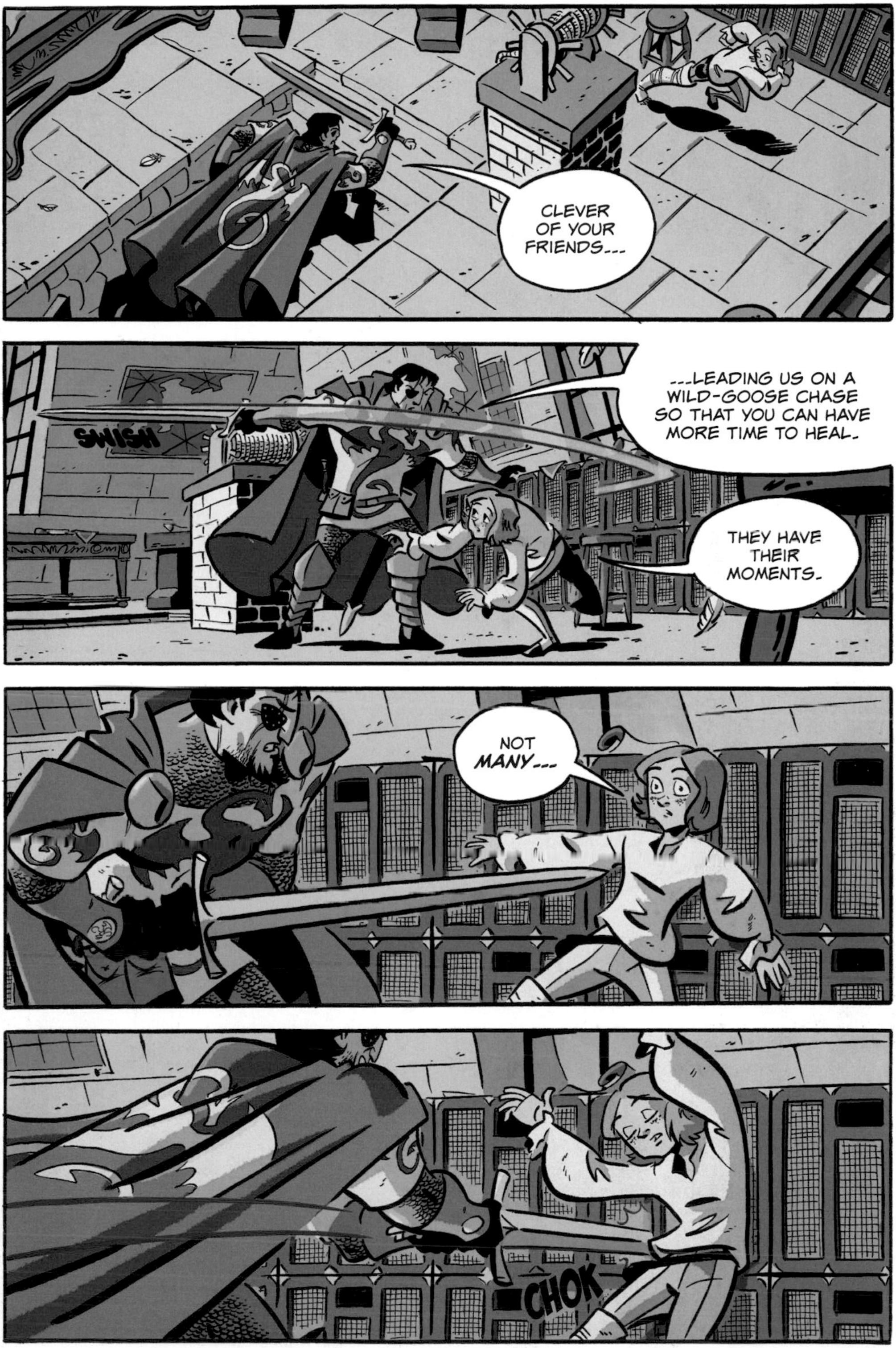
CLEVER OF YOUR FRIENDS...
SWISH
...LEADING US ON A WILD-GOOSE CHASE SO THAT YOU CAN HAVE MORE TIME TO HEAL.
THEY HAVE THEIR MOMENTS.
NOT *MANY*...
CHOK

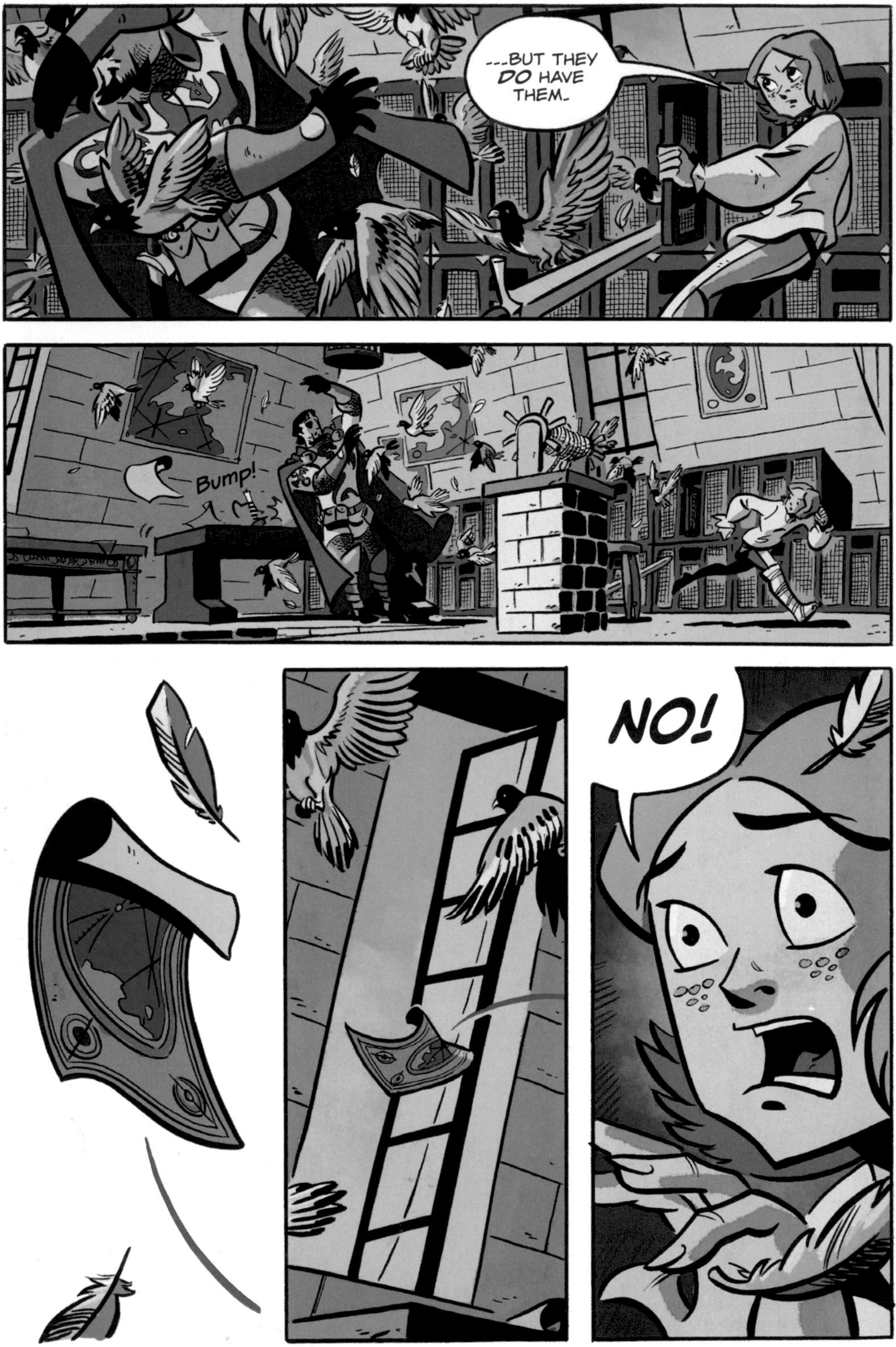
---BUT THEY DO HAVE THEM.
Bump!
NO!

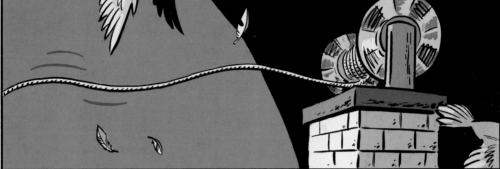

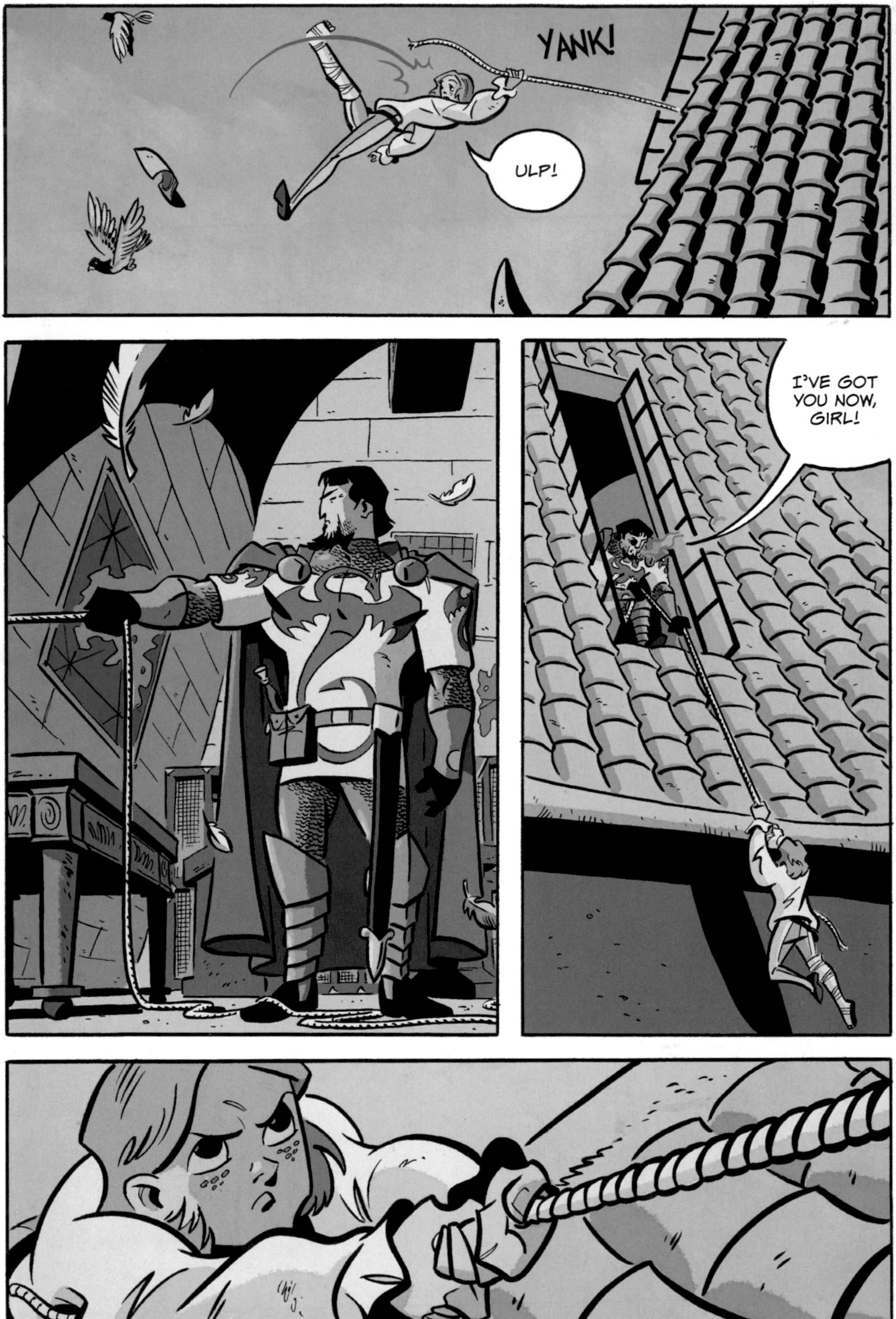
YANK!
ULP!
I'VE GOT YOU NOW, GIRL!

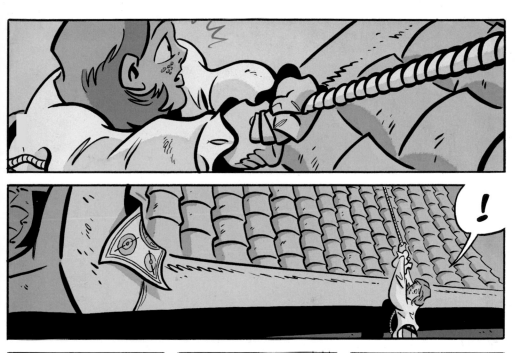

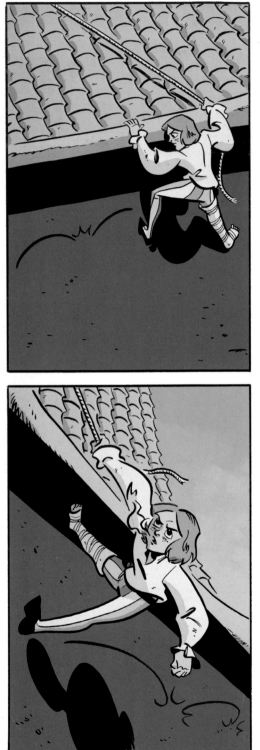

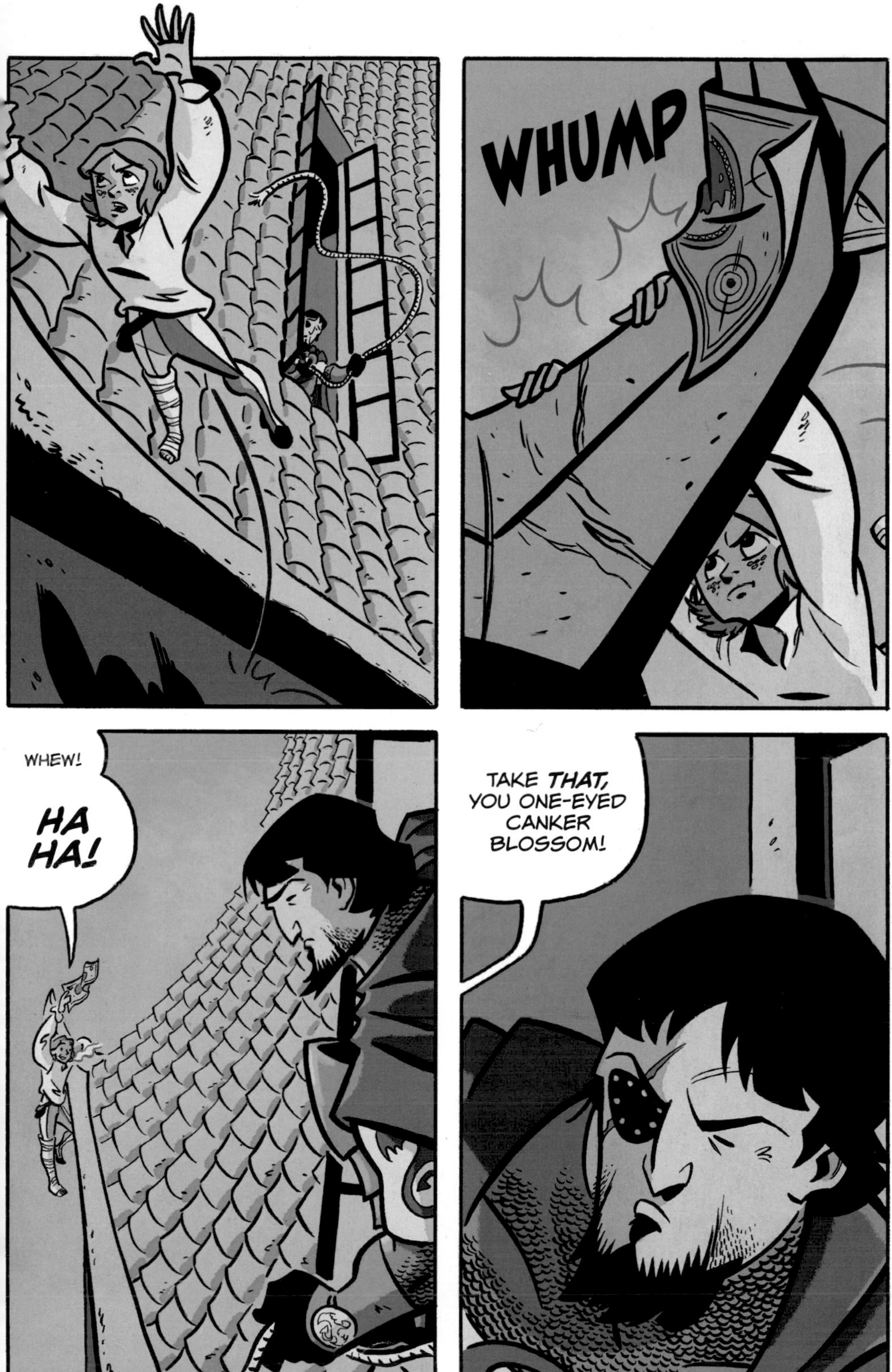
WHUMP
WHEW!
HA HA!
TAKE THAT, YOU ONE-EYED CANKER BLOSSOM!

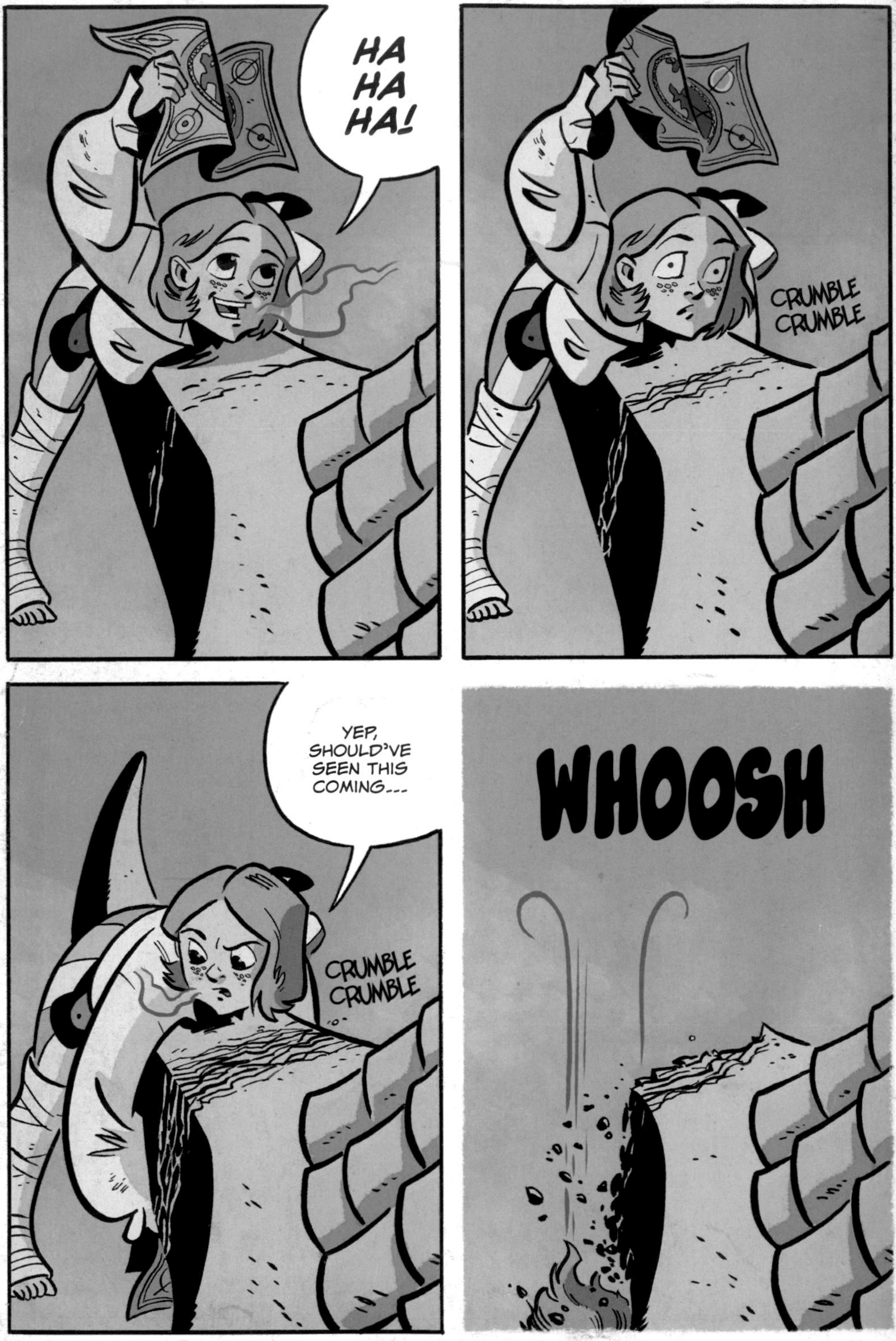
HA HA HA!
CRUMBLE CRUMBLE
YEP, SHOULD'VE SEEN THIS COMING...
CRUMBLE CRUMBLE
WHOOSH

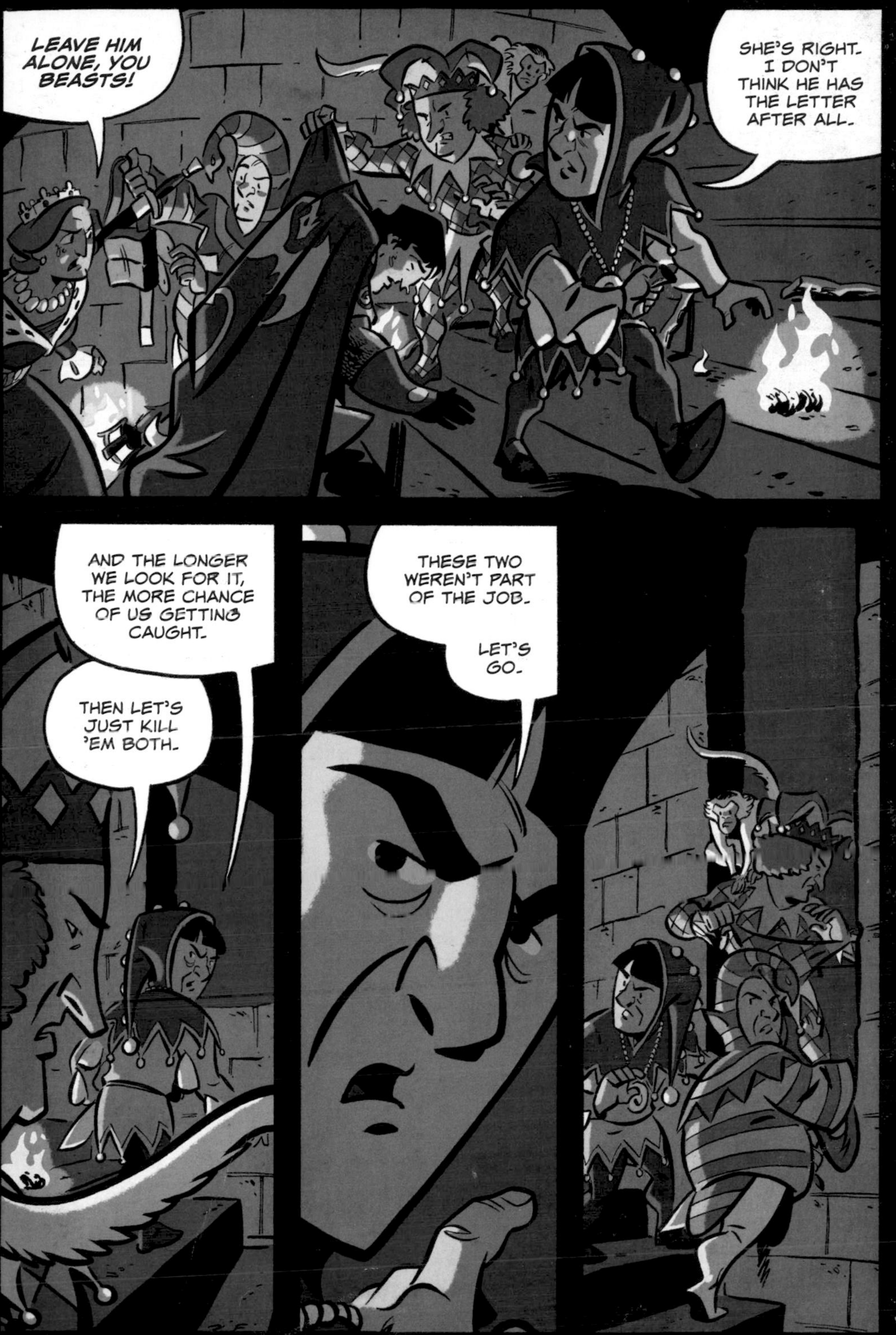
LEAVE HIM ALONE, YOU BEASTS!
SHE'S RIGHT. I DON'T THINK HE HAS THE LETTER AFTER ALL.
AND THE LONGER WE LOOK FOR IT, THE MORE CHANCE OF US GETTING CAUGHT.
THEN LET'S JUST KILL 'EM BOTH.
THESE TWO WEREN'T PART OF THE JOB.
LET'S GO.

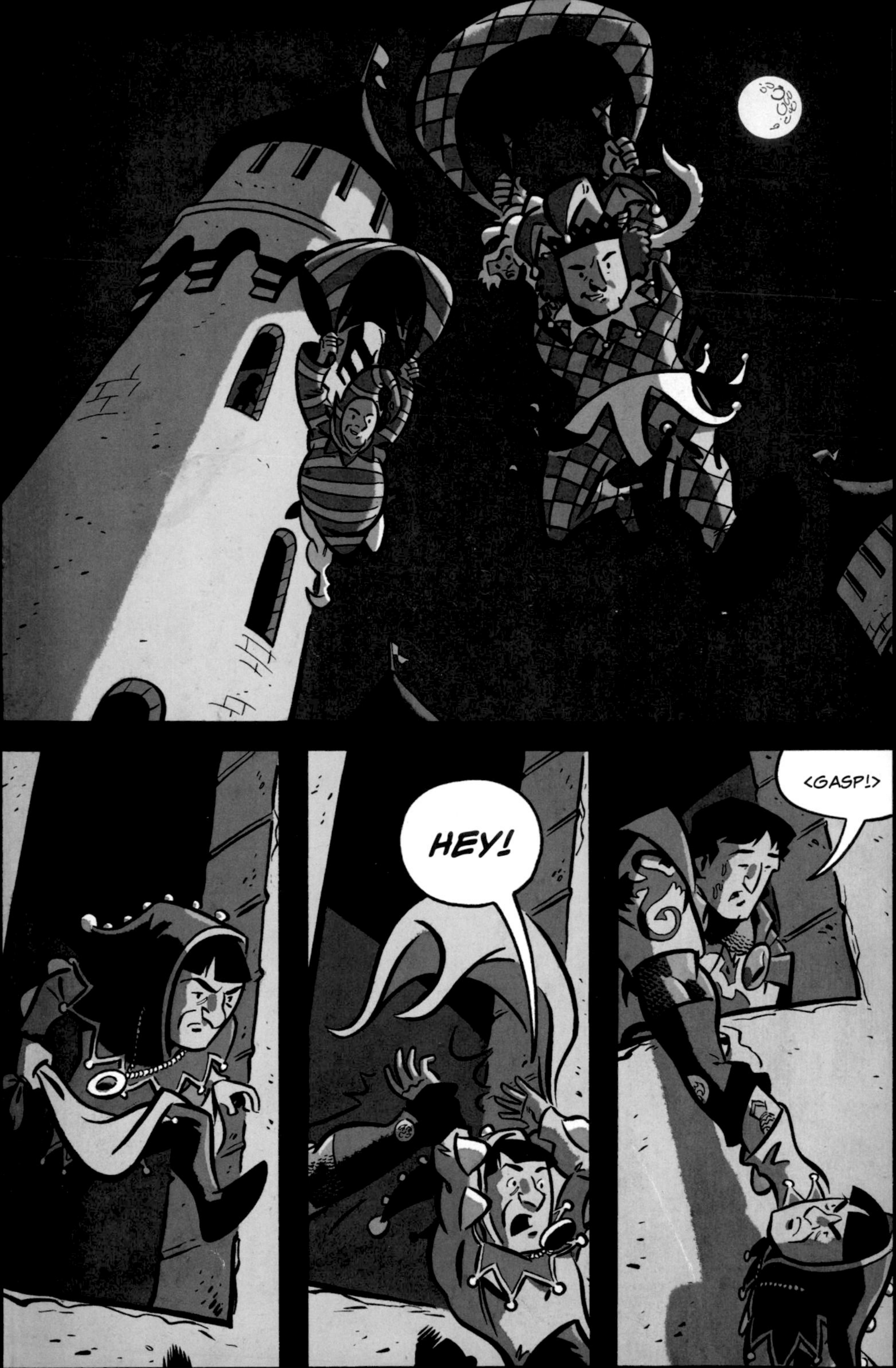
HEY!
<GASP!>

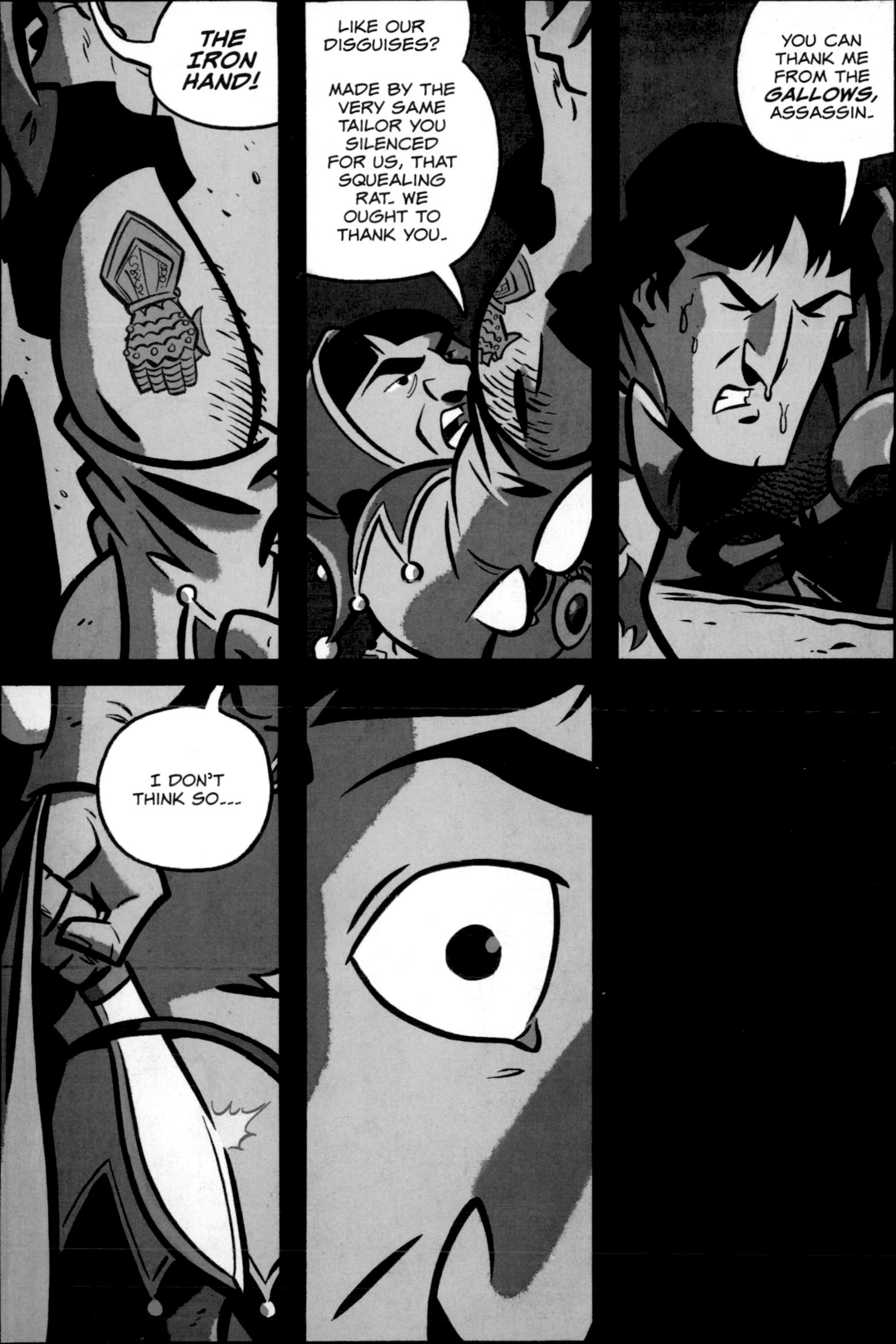
THE IRON HAND!
LIKE OUR DISGUISES?
MADE BY THE VERY SAME TAILOR YOU SILENCED FOR US, THAT SQUEALING RAT. WE OUGHT TO THANK YOU.
YOU CAN THANK ME FROM THE GALLOWS, ASSASSIN.
I DON'T THINK SO...

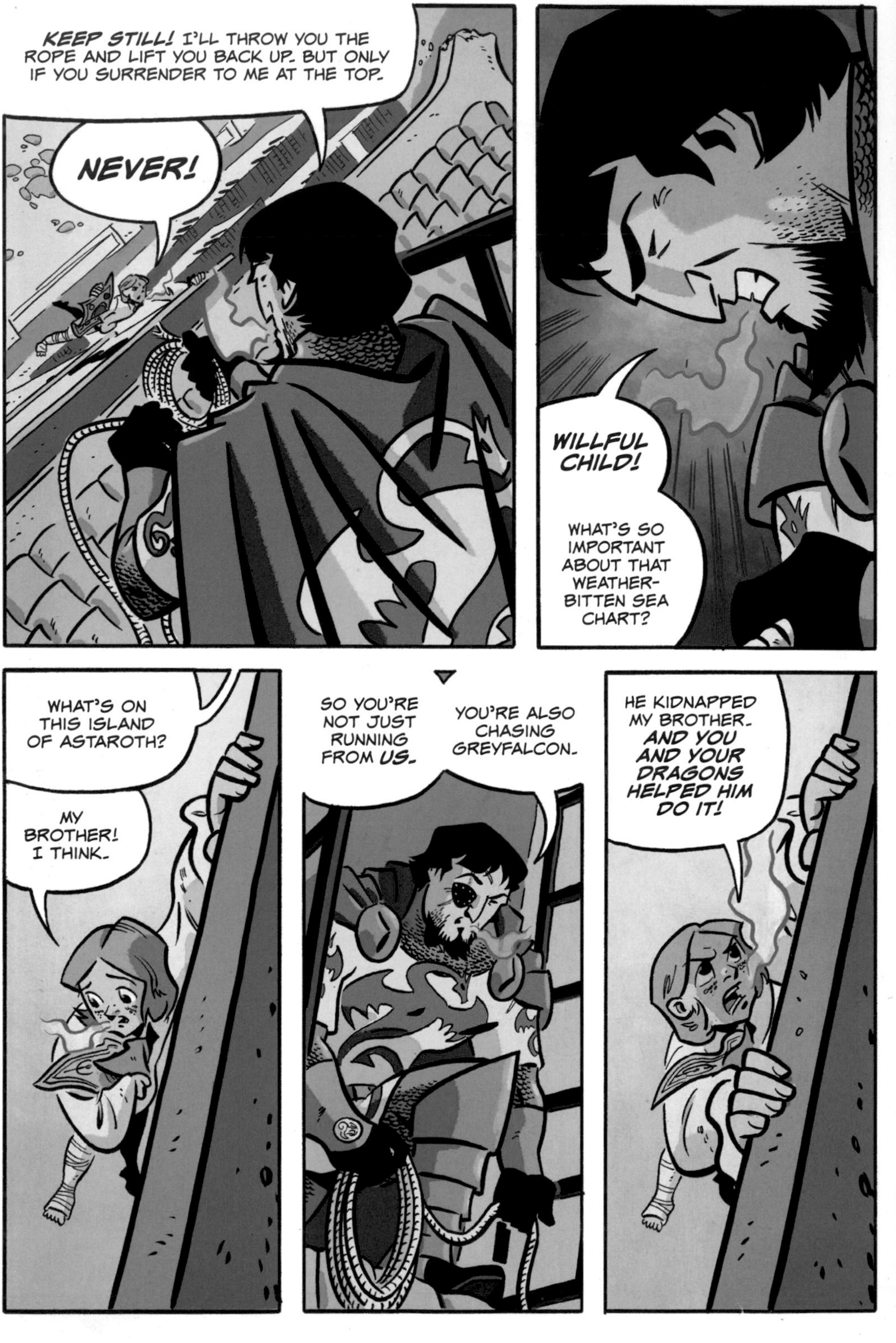
KEEP STILL! I'LL THROW YOU THE ROPE AND LIFT YOU BACK UP. BUT ONLY IF YOU SURRENDER TO ME AT THE TOP.
NEVER!
WILLFUL CHILD!
WHAT'S SO IMPORTANT ABOUT THAT WEATHER-BITTEN SEA CHART?
WHAT'S ON THIS ISLAND OF ASTAROTH?
MY BROTHER! I THINK.
SO YOU'RE NOT JUST RUNNING FROM US.
YOU'RE ALSO CHASING GREYFALCON.
HE KIDNAPPED MY BROTHER. AND YOU AND YOUR DRAGONS HELPED HIM DO IT!

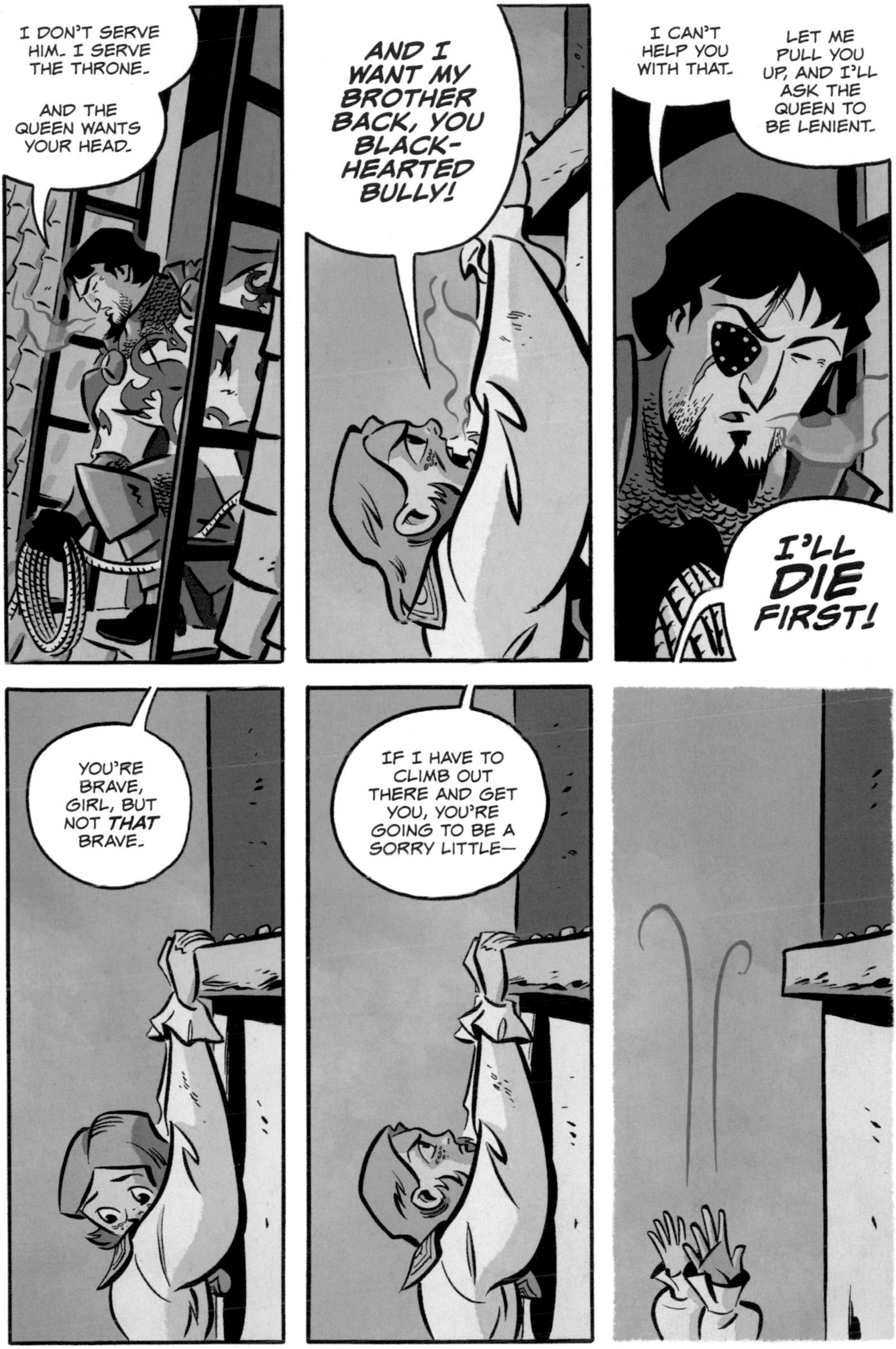
I DON'T SERVE HIM. I SERVE THE THRONE.
AND THE QUEEN WANTS YOUR HEAD.
AND I WANT MY BROTHER BACK, YOU BLACK-HEARTED BULLY!
I CAN'T HELP YOU WITH THAT.
LET ME PULL YOU UP, AND I'LL ASK THE QUEEN TO BE LENIENT.
I'LL DIE FIRST!
YOU'RE BRAVE, GIRL, BUT NOT THAT BRAVE.
IF I HAVE TO CLIMB OUT THERE AND GET YOU, YOU'RE GOING TO BE A SORRY LITTLE—

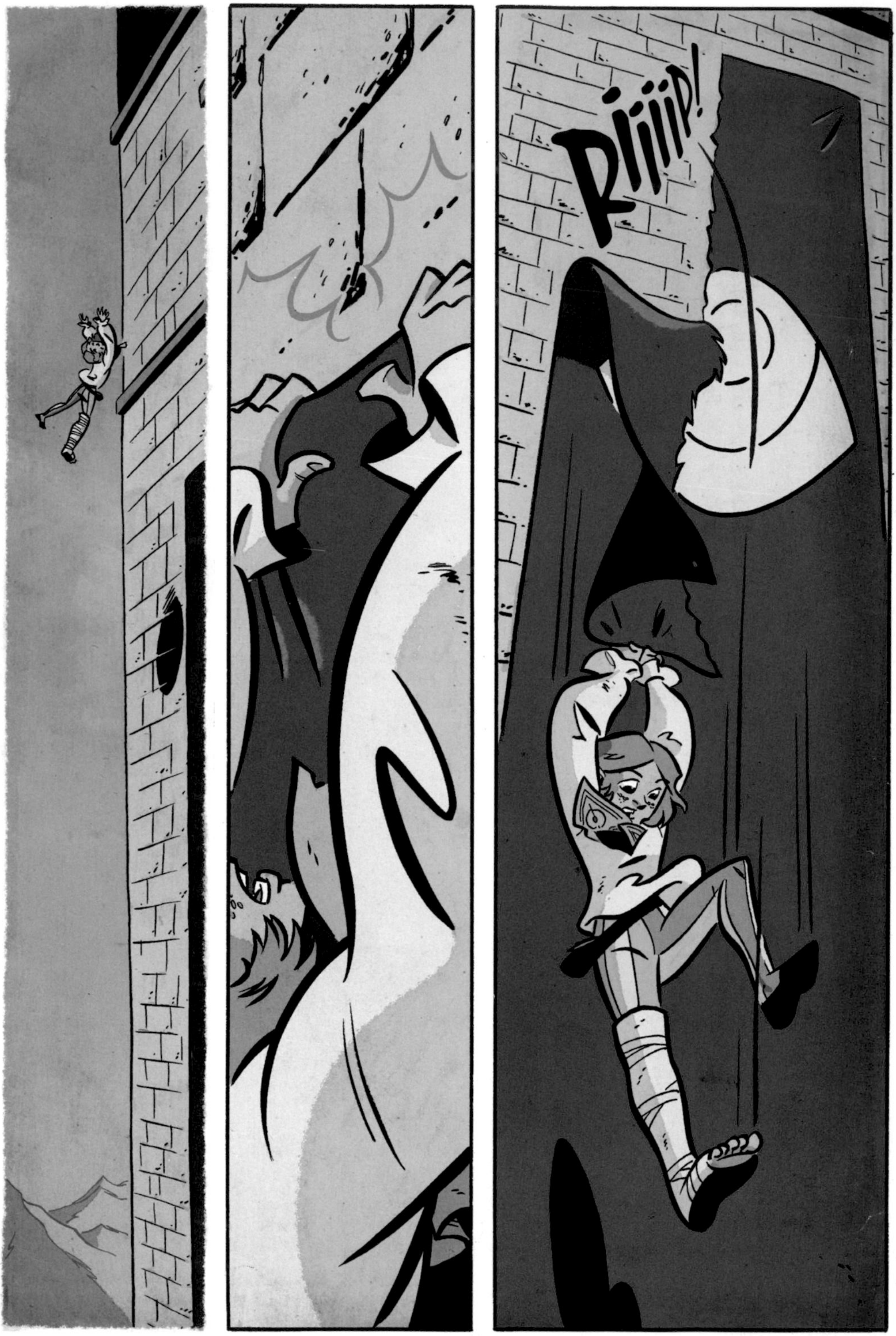
RIIIIP!

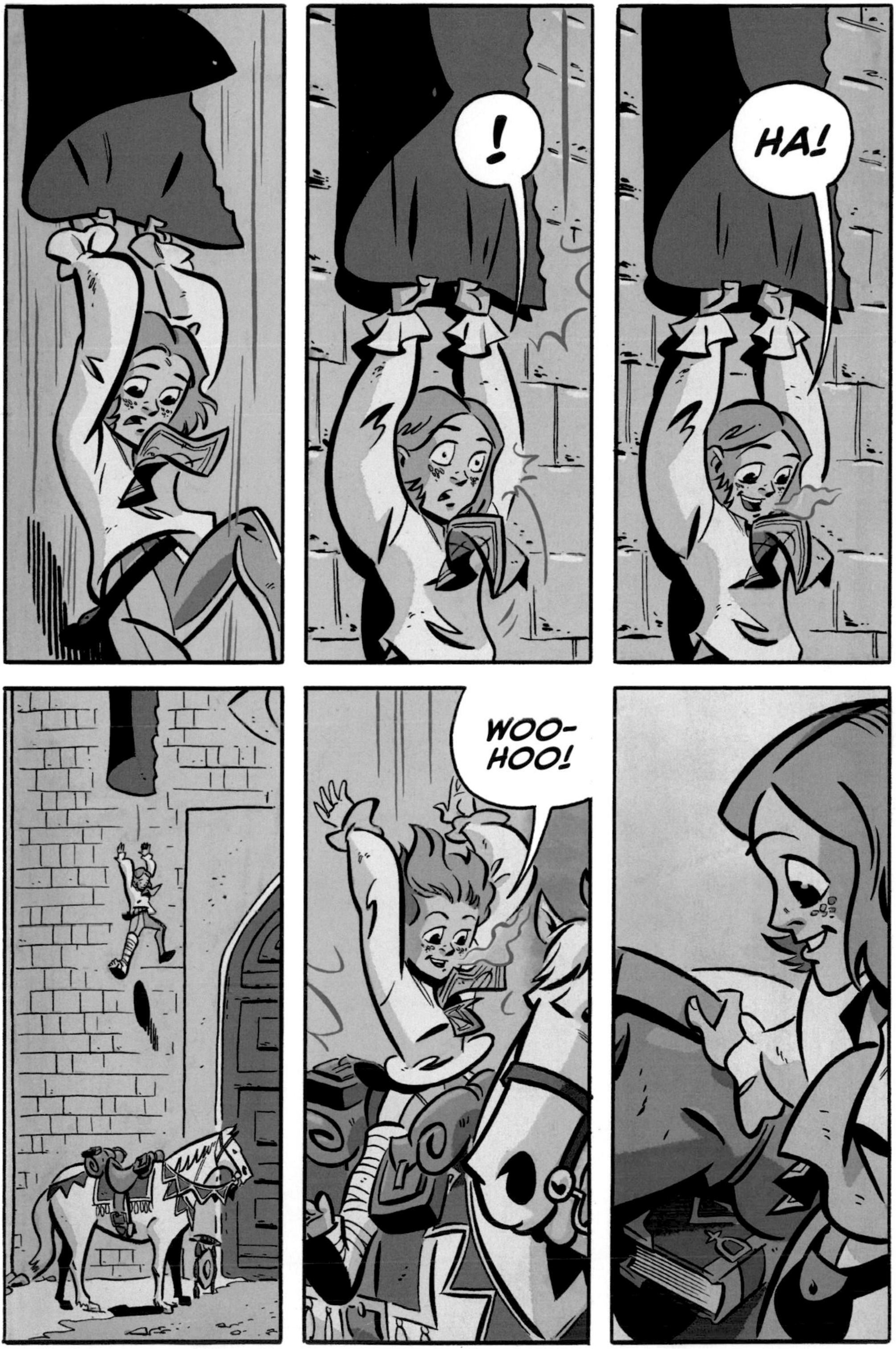
!
HA!
WOO-HOO!

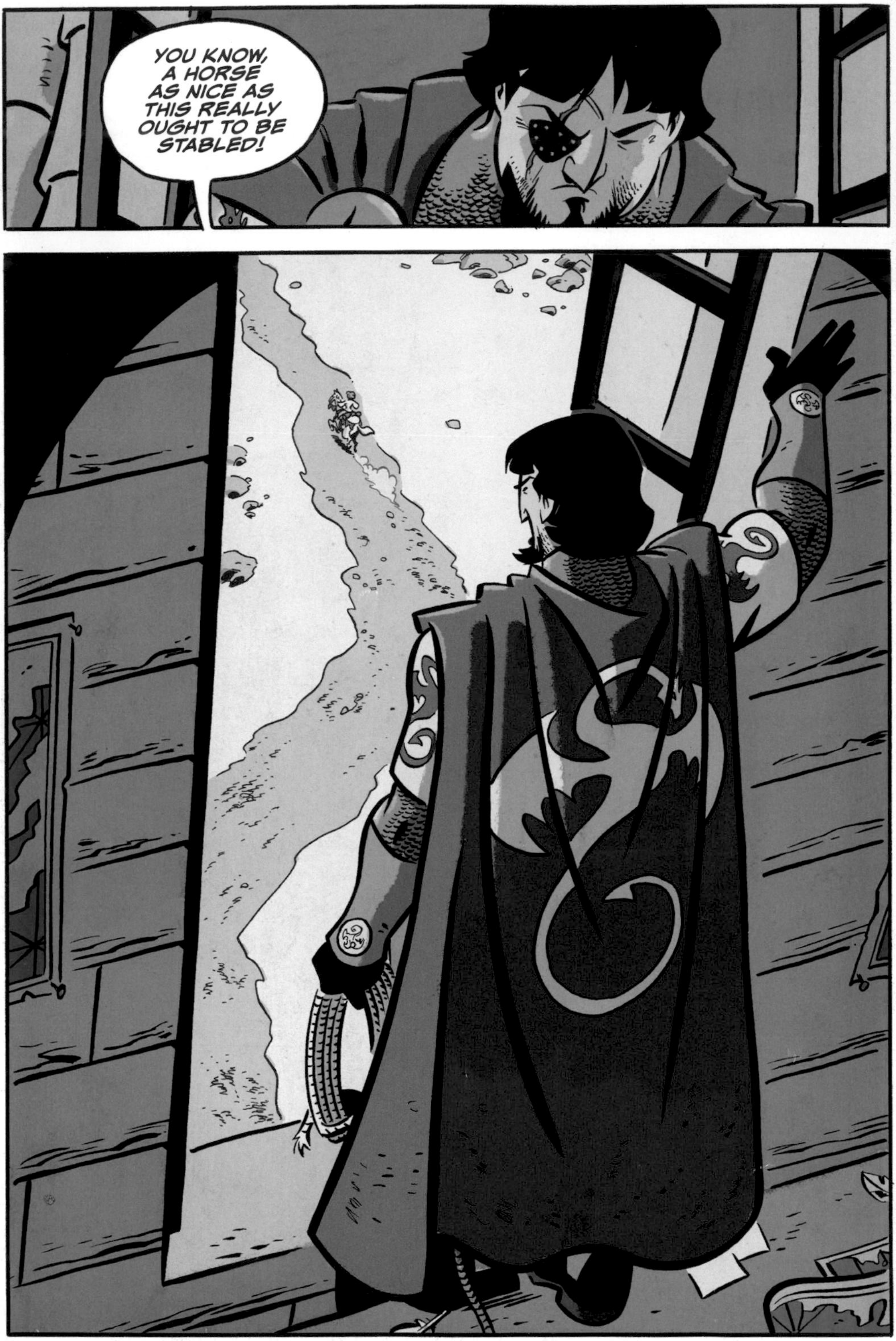
YOU KNOW, A HORSE AS NICE AS THIS REALLY OUGHT TO BE STABLED!

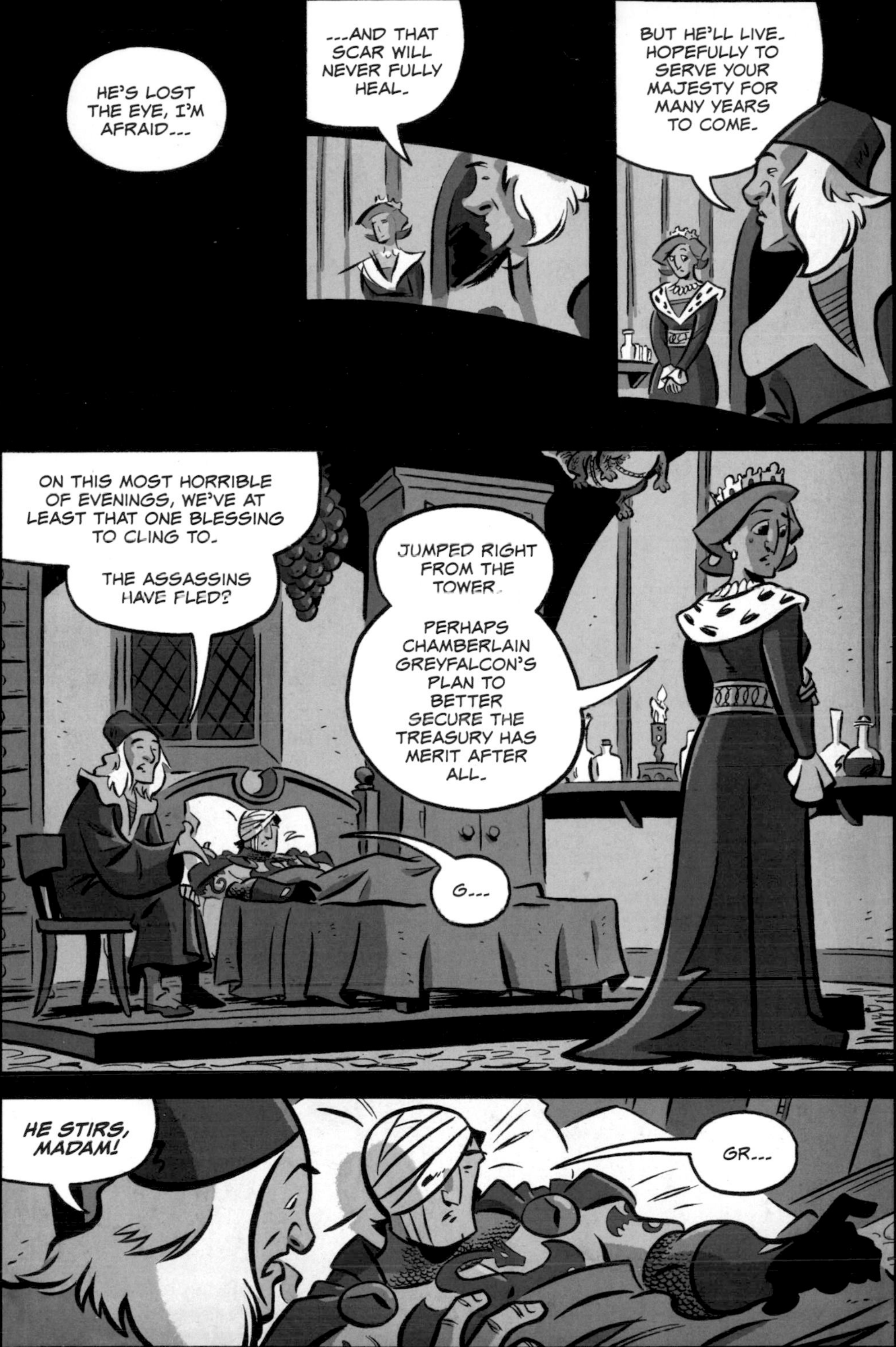
HE'S LOST THE EYE, I'M AFRAID...
...AND THAT SCAR WILL NEVER FULLY HEAL.
BUT HE'LL LIVE. HOPEFULLY TO SERVE YOUR MAJESTY FOR MANY YEARS TO COME.
ON THIS MOST HORRIBLE OF EVENINGS, WE'VE AT LEAST THAT ONE BLESSING TO CLING TO.
THE ASSASSINS HAVE FLED?
JUMPED RIGHT FROM THE TOWER.
PERHAPS CHAMBERLAIN GREYFALCON'S PLAN TO BETTER SECURE THE TREASURY HAS MERIT AFTER ALL.
G...
HE STIRS, MADAM!
GR...

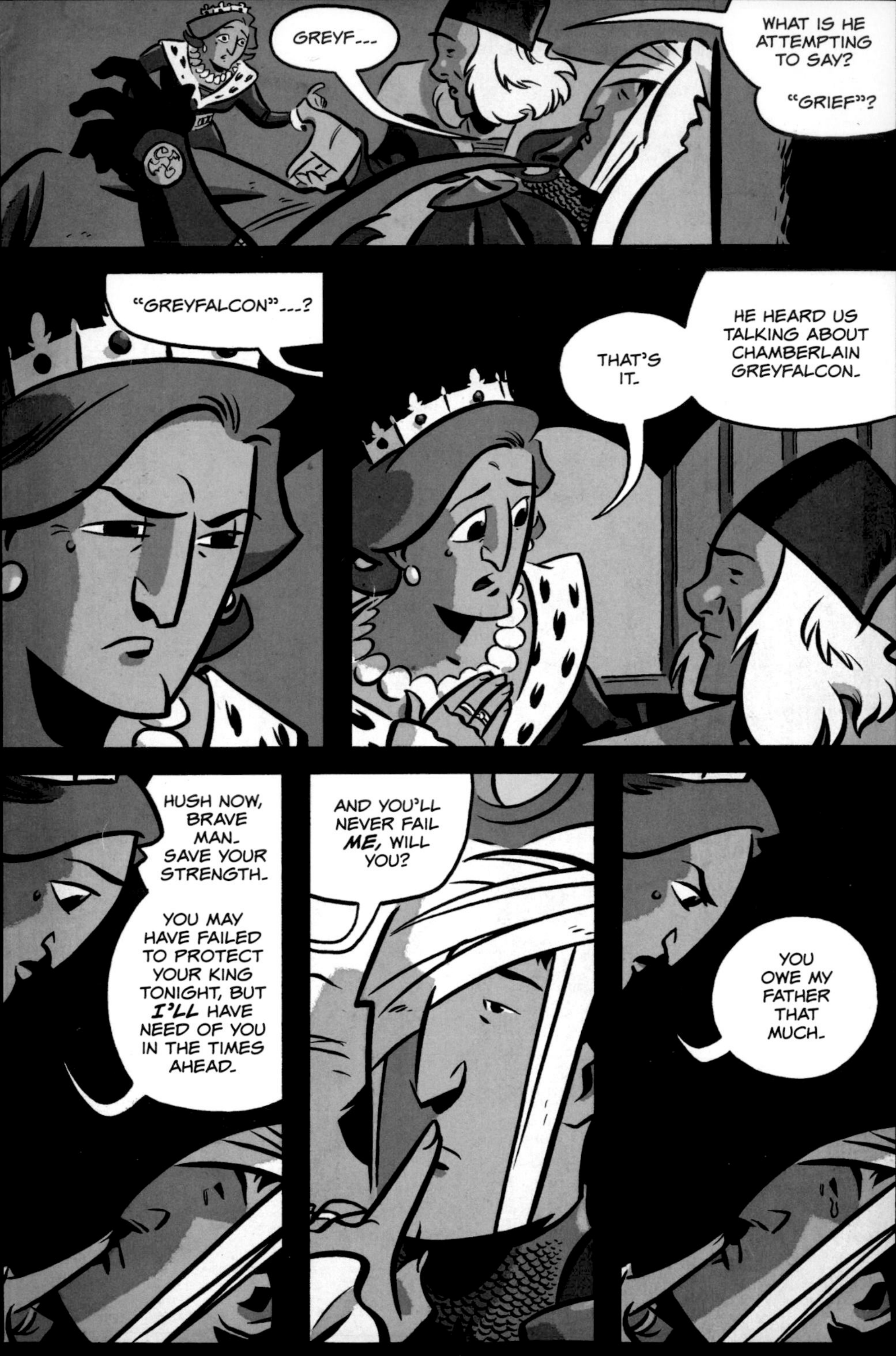
GREYF...
WHAT IS HE ATTEMPTING TO SAY?
"GRIEF"?
"GREYFALCON"...?
HE HEARD US TALKING ABOUT CHAMBERLAIN GREYFALCON.
THAT'S IT.
HUSH NOW, BRAVE MAN. SAVE YOUR STRENGTH.
YOU MAY HAVE FAILED TO PROTECT YOUR KING TONIGHT, BUT *I'LL* HAVE NEED OF YOU IN THE TIMES AHEAD.
AND YOU'LL NEVER FAIL *ME,* WILL YOU?
YOU OWE MY FATHER THAT MUCH.

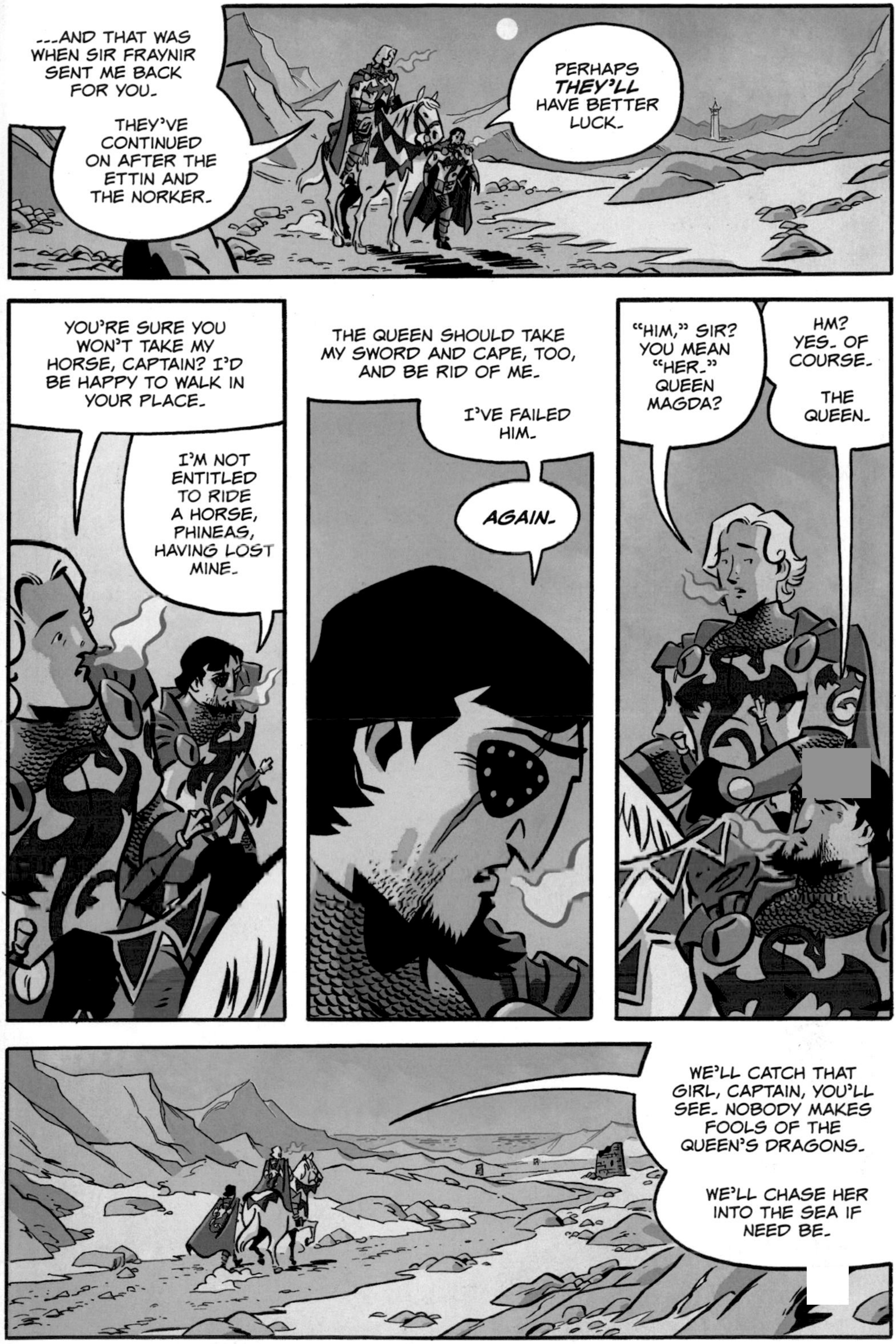
...AND THAT WAS WHEN SIR FRAYNIR SENT ME BACK FOR YOU.
THEY'VE CONTINUED ON AFTER THE ETTIN AND THE NORKER.
PERHAPS *THEY'LL* HAVE BETTER LUCK.
YOU'RE SURE YOU WON'T TAKE MY HORSE, CAPTAIN? I'D BE HAPPY TO WALK IN YOUR PLACE.
I'M NOT ENTITLED TO RIDE A HORSE, PHINEAS, HAVING LOST MINE.
THE QUEEN SHOULD TAKE MY SWORD AND CAPE, TOO, AND BE RID OF ME.
I'VE FAILED HIM.
AGAIN.
"HIM," SIR? YOU MEAN "HER." QUEEN MAGDA?
HM? YES. OF COURSE.
THE QUEEN.
WE'LL CATCH THAT GIRL, CAPTAIN, YOU'LL SEE. NOBODY MAKES FOOLS OF THE QUEEN'S DRAGONS.
WE'LL CHASE HER INTO THE SEA IF NEED BE.

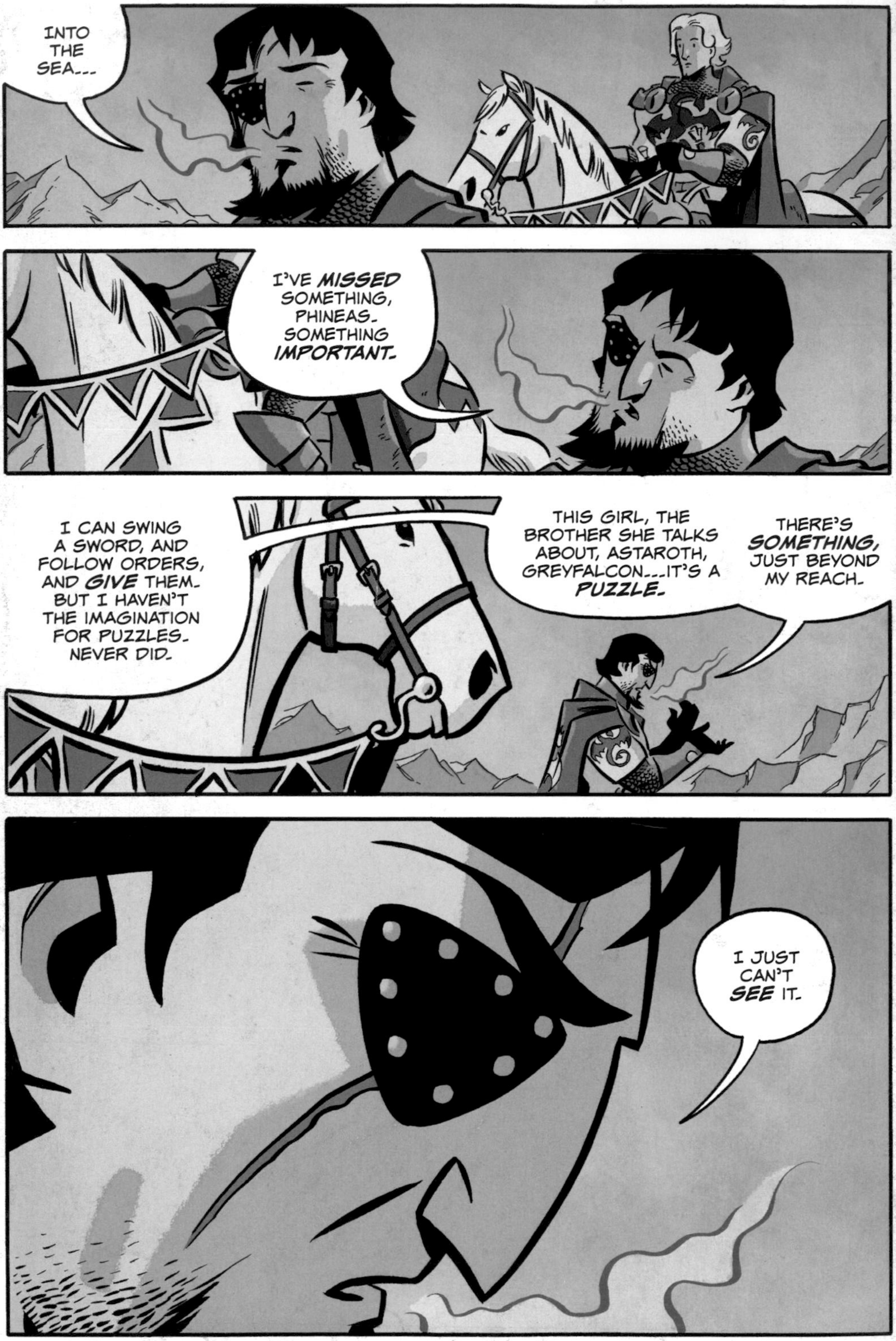
INTO THE SEA...
I'VE MISSED SOMETHING, PHINEAS. SOMETHING IMPORTANT.
I CAN SWING A SWORD, AND FOLLOW ORDERS, AND GIVE THEM. BUT I HAVEN'T THE IMAGINATION FOR PUZZLES. NEVER DID.
THIS GIRL, THE BROTHER SHE TALKS ABOUT, ASTAROTH, GREYFALCON...IT'S A PUZZLE.
THERE'S SOMETHING, JUST BEYOND MY REACH.
I JUST CAN'T SEE IT.

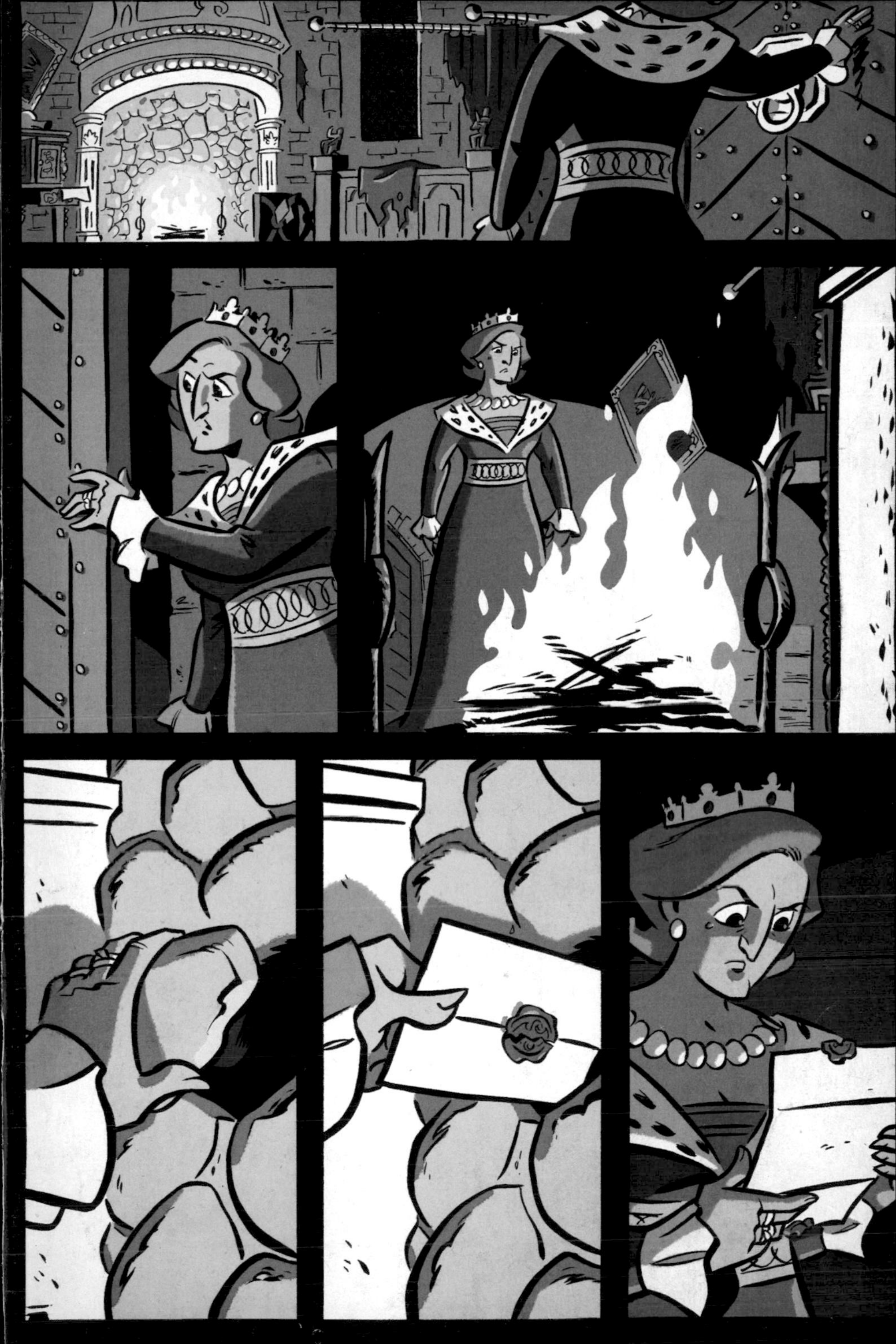

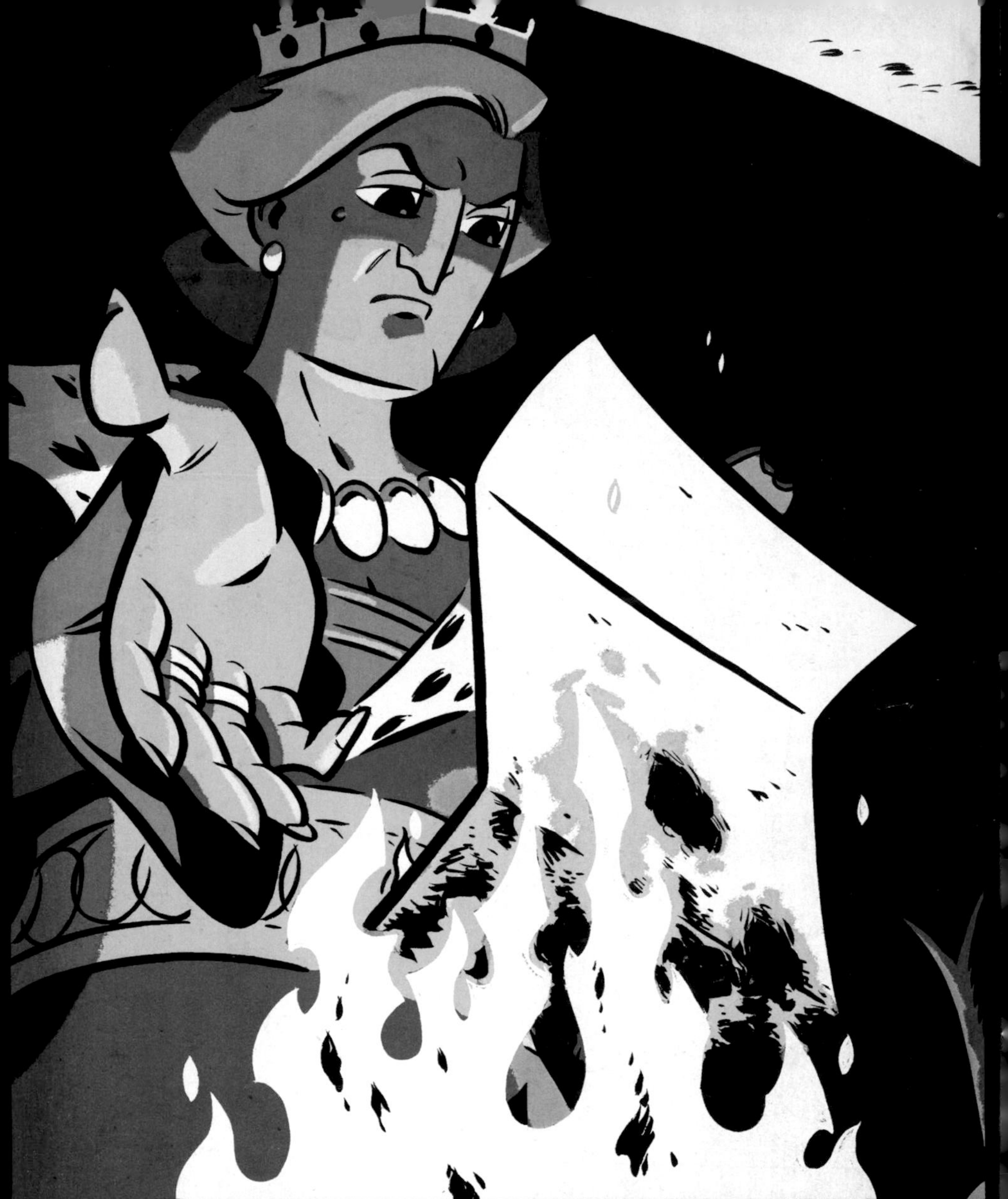

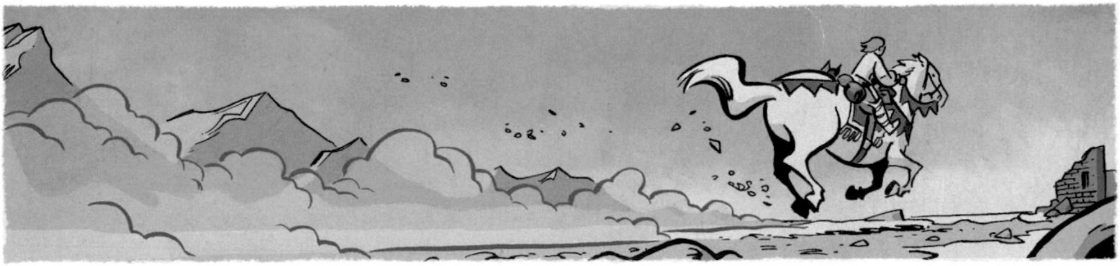